Hot & Cold Running Cities

HOT & COLD RUNNING CITIES

An Anthology of Science Fiction

compiled by Georgess McHargue

HOLT, RINEHART and WINSTON

New York • Chicago • San Francisco

Published simultaneously in Canada by Holt, Rinehart and Winston of Canada Limited.

Library of Congress Cataloging in Publication Data

McHargue, Georgess, comp.
  Hot and cold running cities.
    CONTENTS: van Vogt, A. E. Enchanted village.—Roberts, K. The deeps.—Heinlein, R. The menace from earth. [etc.]
    1. Science fiction. 2. City and town life—Juvenile fiction. [1. Science fiction. 2. City and town life—Fiction] I. Title.
PZ5.M23Ho [Fic] 74–8513 ISBN 0–03–012416–6

"Enchanted Village" by A. E. van Vogt (SFWA) copyright, 1950, by Clark Publishing Company. Reprinted by arrangement with the author's agent, Forrest J. Ackerman.

"The Deeps" copyright © 1966 by Keith Roberts. Reprinted by permission of Julian Bach Literary Agency, Inc.

"The Menace from Earth" by Robert R. Heinlein copyright © 1957 by Fantasy House, Inc. Reprinted by permission of the author's agent, Lurton Blassingame.

"Metropolitan Nightmare" from *The Selected Works of Stephen Vincent Benét* published by Holt, Rinehart and Winston, Inc. Copyright, 1927, 1928, by Stephen Vincent Benét. Copyright renewed, 1955, by Rosemary Carr Benét. Reprinted by permission of Brandt & Brandt.

"The Luckiest Man in Denv" by C. M. Kornbluth copyright © 1959 by Ballantine Books, Inc. Reprinted from *The Marching Morons* by permission of Ballantine Books, Inc., a Division of Random House, Inc.

"The City That Loves You" by Raymond Banks copyright © 1969 by Universal Publishing and Distributing Corporation, first appeared in *Galaxy* magazine of March, 1969, issue 3, volume 28. Reprinted by permission of the author.

"The Place Where Chicago Was" by James Harmon copyright © 1962 by Galaxy Publishing Corp. Reprinted by permission of the author.

"Natural State" by Damon Knight copyright, 1951, by World Editions, Inc. Reprinted by permission of the author and the author's agent, Robert P. Mills, Ltd.

"Plenitude" by Will Worthington copyright © 1959 by Will Worthington. Reprinted by permission of the author and the author's agent, Robert P. Mills, Ltd.

Designer: Mary M. Ahern
Printed in the United States of America: 065/074
First Edition

Contents

Introduction

Any competent visitor from outer space who desired to make a survey of Earth (or Sol III) would soon notice that the population density of its dominant species is highly variable. Or, in the language of human beings, rather than that of robot bureaucrats, there are many more people in some parts of the planet than in others.

Recently, the fact that increasing numbers of us human creatures live in population clots called cities has caused us so much excitement that we have invented a whole branch of learning to deal with it. We have named this field of study urbanology and, with its help, we are now able to quote endless reams of statistics showing what percentage of us now live in cities, will live in cities by the year 2,000, live more than three miles from an urban center, eat popcorn with chocolate sauce on the subway, and so on. Human beings as a species are fond of that sort of statistics—so fond that they can sometimes convince themselves that statistics, or the art of counting things, is a substitute for thinking, the art of understanding things.

Our imaginary Otherworlder might also note that the species has another characteristic that *seems* to be the opposite of the first one. Human beings are often emotional, unpredictable, and downright pig-headed in their reaction to apparently simple facts. Ever since the appearance of the first large towns (that is, for about eight thousand years), city dwellers have looked down on the supposed simple-mindedness of "country bumpkins," while country dwellers have distrusted "city slickers." The fact that many city dwellers themselves believe city life is crowded, crime-ridden, polluted, and dehumanizing does not bring about the redesign or abandonment of the cities. Neither does the common complaint of country dwellers—that their lives are stodgy and colorless—make them willing to pay to improve the conditions of the cities they so love to visit and criticize, or to try to spread the better features of city life more evenly across the globe. Instead, the prevailing conditions serve only to bolster the countryman's belief that his life is morally superior and the cityman's belief that all culture stops short at the city limits.

The lines of this debate have certainly not changed since the seventeenth century, when La Fontaine wrote his fable "The Town Mouse and the Country Mouse." That tale might almost have appeared in this anthology, since it would show our extraterrestrial visitor how fiction (although not quite science fiction, in that case) can say more about human beings and their cities than a whole computer bank of urbanological statistics.

In this collection of stories, the space spy would find plenty of evidence that that old fear and distrust are growing even stronger as the cities develop urban sprawl, traffic paralysis, and technological twitch. Equally, however, he would find voices for the other side of the argument— writers who see the cities of the future as great opportunities, challenges to man's adaptability, and the birthplaces of everything from the ultimate free society to new and delightful lunar sports.

Meanwhile, our technology is sweeping us along toward the time when Roberts's undersea community, Heinlein's Luna City, or Banks's "City That Loves You" may become actual possibilities. Then, the authors seem to imply, we would do well to have confounded our space visitor by doing a little rational thinking.

Otherwise, Benet's New York or Harmon's Chicago is gonna get us. And then, who will inherit the earth?

—G. McH., Shell Beach, California

Hot & Cold Running Cities

For years, scientists have studied the environment's influence on the genetic development of the human species and on the cultural development of the individual. But no earthly environment ever influenced a human being in quite as bizarre a way as van Vogt's Martian village.

Enchanted Village

by A. E. van Vogt

Explorers of a new frontier, they had been called before they left for Mars.

For a while after the ship crashed into a Martian desert, killing all on board except—miraculously—this one man, Bill Jenner spat the words occasionally into the constant, sand-laden wind. He despised himself for the pride he had felt when he first heard them.

His fury faded with each mile that he walked, and his black grief for his friends became a gray ache. Slowly he realized that he had made a ruinous misjudgment.

He had underestimated the speed at which the rocketship had been traveling. He'd guessed that he would have to walk three hundred miles to reach the shallow, polar sea he and the others had observed as they glided in from outer space. Actually, the ship must have flashed an immensely greater distance before it hurtled down out of control.

The days stretched behind him, seemingly as numberless as the hot, red, alien sand that scorched through his tattered clothes. This huge scarecrow of a man kept moving across the endless, arid waste—he would not give up.

By the time he came to the mountain, his food had

1

long been gone. Of his four water bags, only one remained; and that was so close to being empty that he merely wet his cracked lips and swollen tongue whenever his thirst became unbearable.

Jenner climbed high before he realized that it was not just another dune that had barred his way. He paused, and as he gazed up at the mountain that towered above him, he cringed a little. For an instant, he felt the hopelessness of this mad race he was making to nowhere—but he reached the top. He saw that below him was a depression surrounded by hills as high as or higher than the one on which he stood. Nestled in the valley they made was a village.

He could see trees and the marble floor of a courtyard. A score of buildings were clustered around what seemed to be a central square. They were mostly low-constructed, but there were four towers pointing gracefully into the sky. They shone in the sunlight with a marble luster.

Faintly, there came to Jenner's ears a thin, high-pitched whistling sound. It rose, fell, faded completely, then came up again clearly and unpleasantly. Even as Jenner ran toward it, the noise grated on his ears, eerie and unnatural.

He kept slipping on smooth rock, and bruised himself when he fell. He rolled halfway down into the valley. The buildings remained new and bright, when seen from nearby. Their walls flashed with reflections. On every side was vegetation—reddish green shrubbery—yellow-green trees laden with purple and red fruit.

With ravenous intent, Jenner headed for the nearest fruit tree. Close up, the tree looked dry and brittle. The large red fruit he tore from the lowest branch, however, was plump and juicy.

As he lifted it to his mouth, he remembered that he had been warned during his training period to taste nothing on Mars until it had been chemically examined. But that was meaningless advice to a man whose only chemical equipment was in his own body.

Nevertheless, the possibility of danger made him cautious. He took his first bite gingerly. It was bitter to his tongue, and he spat it out hastily. Some of the juice which remained in his mouth seared his gums. He felt the fire of it, and he reeled from nausea. His muscles began to jerk, and he lay down on the marble to keep himself from falling. After what seemed like hours to Jenner, the awful trembling finally went out of his body, and he could see again. He looked up despisingly at the tree.

The pain finally left him, and slowly he relaxed. A soft breeze rustled the dry leaves. Nearby trees took up that gentle clamor, and it struck Jenner that the wind here in the valley was only a whisper of what it had been on the flat desert beyond the mountains.

There was no other sound now. Jenner abruptly remembered the high-pitched, ever-changing whistle he had heard. He lay very still, listening intently, but there was only the rustling of the leaves. The noisy shrilling had stopped. He wondered if it had been an alarm, to warn the villagers of his approach.

Anxiously, he climbed to his feet and fumbled for his gun. A sense of disaster shocked through him. It wasn't there. His mind was a blank, and then he vaguely recalled that he had first missed the weapon more than a week before. He looked around him uneasily, but there was not a sign of creature life. He braced himself. He couldn't leave, as there was nowhere to go. If necessary, he would fight to the death to remain in the village.

Carefully Jenner took a sip from his water bag, moistening his cracked lips and his swollen tongue. Then he replaced the cap, and started through a double line of trees toward the nearest building. He made a wide circle to observe it from several vantage points. On one side a low, broad archway opened into the interior. Through it, he could dimly make out the polished gleam of a marble floor.

Jenner explored the buildings from the outside, always keeping a respectful distance between him and any of the entrances. He saw no sign of animal life. He reached the far side of the marble platform on which the village was built, and turned back decisively. It was time to explore interiors.

He chose one of the four-tower buildings. As he came within a dozen feet of it, he saw that he would have to stoop to get inside.

Momentarily, the implications of that stopped him. These buildings had been constructed for a life form that must be very different from human beings.

He went forward again, bent down, and entered reluctantly, every muscle tensed.

He found himself in a room without furniture. However, there were several low, marble fences projecting from one marble wall. They formed what looked like a group of four wide, low stalls. Each stall had an open trough carved out of the floor.

The second chamber was fitted with four inclined planes of marble, each of which slanted up to a dais. Altogether, there were four rooms on the lower floor. From one of them, a circular ramp mounted up, apparently to a tower room.

Jenner didn't investigate the upstairs. The earlier fear that he would find alien life was yielding to the deadly conviction that he wouldn't. No life meant no food, nor any chance of getting any. In frantic haste, he hurried from building to building, peering into the silent rooms, pausing now and then to shout hoarsely.

Finally, there was no doubt. He was alone in a deserted village on a lifeless planet, without food, without water—except for the pitiful supply in his bag—and without hope.

He was in the fourth and smallest room of one of the tower buildings when he realized that he had come to the end of his search. The room had a single "stall" jutting out from one wall. Wearily, Jenner lay down in it. He must have fallen asleep instantly.

When he awoke, he became aware of two things, one right after the other. The first realization occurred before he opened his eyes—the whistling sound was back, high and shrill, it wavered at the threshold of audibility.

The other was that a fine spray of liquid was being directed down at him from the ceiling. It had an odor, of which Technician Jenner took a single whiff. Quickly he scrambled out of the room, coughing, tears in his eyes, his face already burning from chemical reaction.

He snatched his handkerchief and hastily wiped the exposed parts of his body and face.

He reached the outside, and there paused, striving to understand what had happened.

The village seemed unchanged.

Leaves trembled in a gentle breeze. The sun was poised on a mountain peak. Jenner guessed from its position that it was morning again, and that he had slept at least a dozen hours. The glaring white light suffused the valley. Half-hidden by trees and shrubbery, the buildings flashed and shimmered.

He seemed to be in an oasis in a vast desert. It was an oasis all right, Jenner reflected grimly, but not for a human being. For him, with its poisonous fruit, it was more like a tantalizing mirage.

He went back inside the building, and cautiously peered into the room where he had slept. The spray of gas had stopped, not a bit of odor lingered, and the air was fresh and clean.

He edged over the threshold, half-inclined to make a

test. He had a picture in his mind of a long dead Martian creature lazing on the floor in the "stall" while a soothing chemical sprayed down on its body. The fact that the chemical was deadly to human beings merely emphasized how alien to man was the life that had spawned on Mars. But there seemed little doubt of the reason for the gas. The creature was accustomed to taking a morning shower.

Inside the "bathroom," Jenner eased himself, feet first. into the stall. As his hips became level with the stall entrance, the solid ceiling sprayed a jet of yellowish gas straight down upon his legs. Hastily, Jenner pulled himself clear of the stall. The gas stopped as suddenly as it had started.

He tried it again, to make sure it was merely an automatic process. It turned on, then it shut off.

Jenner's thirst-puffed lips parted with excitement. He thought, "If there can be one automatic process, there may be others."

Breathing heavily, he raced into the other room. Carefully he shoved his legs into one of the two stalls. The moment his hips were in, a steaming gruel filled the trough beside the wall.

He stared at the greasy-looking stuff with a horrified fascination—food and drink. He remembered the poison fruit, and felt repelled, but he forced himself to bend down, and put his finger into the hot, wet substance. He brought it up, dripping, to his mouth.

It tasted flat and pulpy, like boiled wood fiber. It trickled viscously into his throat. His eyes began to water, and his lips drew back convulsively. He realized he was going to be sick, and ran for the outer door—but didn't quite make it.

When he finally got outside, he felt limp and unutterably listless. In that depressed state of mind, he grew aware again of the shrill sound.

He felt amazed that he could have ignored its rasping

even for a few minutes. Sharply, he glanced about, trying to determine its source, but it seemed to have none. Whenever he approached a point where it appeared to be loudest, then it would fade, or shift, perhaps to the far side of the village.

He tried to imagine what an alien culture would want with a mind-shattering noise—although, of course, it would not necessarily have been unpleasant to them.

He stopped and snapped his fingers as a wild but nevertheless plausible notion entered his mind. Could this be music?

He toyed with the idea, trying to visualize the village as it had been long ago. Here, a music-loving race had possibly gone about its daily tasks to the accompaniment of what was to them beautiful strains of melody.

The hideous whistling went on and on, waxing and waning. Jenner tried to put buildings between himself and the sound. He sought refuge in various rooms, hoping that at least one would be soundproof. None were. The whistle followed him wherever he went.

He retreated into the desert, and had to climb halfway up one of the slopes before the noise was low enough not to disturb him. Finally, breathless but immeasurably relieved, he sank down on the sand, and thought blankly: What now?

The scene that spread before him had in it qualities of both heaven and hell. It was all too familiar now—the red sands, the stony dunes, the small, alien village promising so much and fulfilling so little.

Jenner looked down at it with his feverish eyes, and ran his parched tongue over his cracked, dry lips. He knew that he was a dead man unless he could alter the automatic food-making machines that must be hidden somewhere in the walls under the floors of the buildings.

In ancient days, a remnant of Martian civilization had survived in this village. The inhabitants had died off but the village lived on, keeping itself clean of sand, able to provide refuge for any Martian who might come along. But there were no Martians. There was only Bill Jenner, pilot of the first rocketship ever to land on Mars.

He had to make the village turn out food and drink that he could take. Without tools, except his hands; with scarcely any knowledge of chemistry, he must force it to change its habits.

Tensely, he hefted his water bag. He took another sip, and fought the same grim fight to prevent himself from guzzling it down to the last drop. And, when he had won the battle once more, he stood up and started down the slope.

He could last, he estimated, not more than three days. In that time, he must conquer the village.

He was already among the trees when it suddenly struck him that the "music" had stopped. Relieved, he bent over a small shrub, took a good firm hold of it—and pulled.

It came up easily, and there was a slab of marble attached to it. Jenner stared at it, noting with surprise that he had been mistaken in thinking the stalk came up through a hole in the marble. It was merely stuck to the surface. Then he noticed something else—the shrub had no roots. Almost instinctively, Jenner looked down at the spot from where he had torn the slab of marble, along with the plant. There was sand there.

He dropped the shrub, slipped to his knees, and plunged his fingers into the sand. Loose sand trickled through them. He reached deep, using all his strength to force his arm and hand down—sand—nothing but sand.

He stood up, and frantically tore up another shrub. It also came out easily, bringing with it a slab of marble. It had no roots, and where it had been was sand.

With a kind of mindless disbelief, Jenner rushed over

to a fruit tree, and shoved at it. There was a momentary resistance, and then the marble on which it stood split, and lifted slowly into the air. The tree fell over with a swish and a crackle of its dry branches, and leaves broke and crumbled in a thousand pieces. Underneath it was sand. Sand everywhere. A city built on sand. Mars, planet of sand. That was not completely true, of course. Seasonal vegetation had been observed near the polar ice caps. All but the hardiest of it had died with the coming of summer. It had been intended that the rocketship land near one of those shallow, tideless seas.

By coming down out of control, the ship had wrecked more than itself. It had wrecked the chances for life of the only survivor of the voyage.

Jenner came slowly out of his daze. He had a thought then. He picked up one of the shrubs he had already torn loose, braced his foot against the marble to which it was attached, and tugged, gently at first, then with increasing strength.

It came loose finally, but there was no doubt that the two were a part of a whole. The shrub was growing out of the marble.

Marble? Jenner knelt beside one of the holes from where he had torn a slab, and bent over an adjoining section. It was quite porous—calciferous rock, most likely, but not true marble at all. As he reached toward it, intending to break off a piece, it changed color. Astounded, Jenner drew back. Around the break, the stone was turning a bright orange-yellow. He studied it uncertainly, then, tentatively, he touched it.

It was as if he had dipped his fingers into searing acid. There was a sharp, biting, burning pain. With a gasp, Jenner jerked his hand clear.

The continuing anguish made him feel faint. He swayed and moaned, clutching the bruised members to his body. When the agony finally faded, and he could look at the injury, he saw that the skin had peeled, and that already blood blisters had formed. Grimly, Jenner looked down at the break in the stone. The edges remained bright orange-yellow.

The village was alert, ready to defend itself from further attacks.

Suddenly weary, he crawled into the shade of a tree. There was only one possible conclusion to draw from what had happened, and it almost defied common sense. This lonely village was alive.

As he lay there, Jenner tried to imagine a great mass of living substance growing into the shape of buildings, adjusting itself to suit another life form, accepting the role of servant in the widest meaning of the term.

If it would serve one race, why not another? If it could adjust to Martians, why not to human beings?

There would be difficulties, of course. He guessed wearily that essential elements would not be available. The oxygen for water could come from the air . . . thousands of compounds could be made from sand . . . though it meant death if he failed to find a solution, he fell asleep even as he started to think about what they might be.

When he awoke, it was quite dark.

Jenner climbed heavily to his feet. There was a drag to his muscles that alarmed him. He wet his mouth from his water bag, and staggered toward the entrance of the nearest building. Except for the scraping of his shoes on the "marble," the silence was intense.

He stopped short—listened and looked. The wind had died away. He couldn't see the mountains that rimmed the valley, but the buildings were still dimly visible, black shadows in a shadow world.

For the first time, it seemed to him that, in spite of his new hope, it might be better if he died. Even if he survived, what had he to look forward to? He recalled only too well how hard it had been to rouse interest in the trip, and to raise the large amount of money required. He remembered the colossal problems that had had to be solved in building the ship, and some of the men who had solved them were buried somewhere in the Martian desert.

It might be twenty years before another ship from Earth would try to reach the only other planet in the solar system that had shown signs of being able to support life. During those uncountable days and nights, those years, he would be here alone. That was the most he could hope for—if he lived. As he fumbled his way to a dais in one of the rooms, Jenner considered another problem.

How did one let a living village know that it must alter its processes? In a way, it must already have grasped that it had a new tenant. How could he make it realize he needed food in a different chemical combination from that which it had served in the past; that he liked music, but on a different scale system; and that he could use a shower each morning—of water, not of poison gas?

He dozed fitfully, like a man who is sick rather than sleepy. Twice he wakened, his lips on fire, his eyes burning, his body bathed in perspiration. Several times he was startled into consciousness by the sound of his own harsh voice crying out in anger and fear at the night.

He guessed then that he was dying.

He spent the long hours of darkness tossing, turning, twisting, befuddled by waves of heat. As the light of morning came, he was vaguely surprised to realize that he was still alive. Restlessly, he climbed off the dais, and went to the door.

A bitingly cold wind blew, but it felt good to his hot face. He wondered if there was enough *pneumococcus* in his blood for him to catch pneumonia. He decided not.

In a few moments he was shivering. He retreated back into the house and, for the first time noticed that, despite the doorless doorway, the wind did not come into the building at all. The rooms were cold, but not draughty.

That started an association: Where had his terrible body heat come from? He teetered over to the dais where he had spent the night. Within seconds, he was sweltering in a temperature of about a hundred and thirty.

He climbed off the dais, shaken by his own stupidity. He estimated that he had sweated at least two quarts of moisture out of his dried-up body on that furnace of a bed.

This village was not for human beings. Here, even the beds were heated for creatures who needed temperatures far beyond the heat comfortable for men.

Jenner spent most of the day in the shade of a large tree. He felt exhausted, and only occasionally did he even remember that he had a problem. When the whistling started, it bothered him at first, but he was too tired to move away from it. There were long periods when he hardly heard it, so dulled were his senses.

Late in the afternoon, he remembered the shrubs and the tree he had torn up the day before, and wondered what had happened to them. He wet his swollen tongue with the last few drops of water in his bag, climbed lackadaisically to his feet, and went to look for the dried-up remains.

There weren't any. He couldn't even find the holes where he had torn them out. The living village had absorbed the dead tissue into itself, and repaired the breaks in its "body."

That galvanized Jenner. He began to think again . . . about mutations, genetic readjustment, life forms adapting to new environments. There'd been lectures on that before the ship left Earth, rather generalized talks designed to acquaint the explorers with the problems men might face on an alien planet. The important principle was quite simple: adjust or die.

The village had to adjust to him. He doubted if he could seriously damage it, but he could try. His own need to survive must be placed on as sharp and hostile a basis as that.

Frantically, Jenner began to search his pockets. Before leaving the rocket, he had loaded himself with odds and ends of small equipment. A jackknife, a folding metal cup, a printed radio, a tiny superbattery that could be charged by spinning an attached wheel—and for which he had brought along, among other things, a powerful electric fire-lighter.

Jenner plugged the lighter into the battery, and deliberately scraped the red-hot end along the surface of the "marble." The reaction was swift. The substance turned an angry purple this time. When an entire section of the floor had changed color, Jenner headed for the nearest stall trough, entering far enough to activate it.

There was a noticeable delay. When the food finally flowed into the trough, it was clear that the living village had realized the reason for what he had done. The food was a pale, creamy color, where earlier it had been a murky gray.

Jenner put his finger into it, but withdrew it with a yell, and wiped his finger. It continued to sting for several moments. The vital question was: Had it deliberately offered him food that would damage him, or was it trying to appease him without knowing what he could eat?

He decided to give it another chance, and entered the adjoining stall. The gritty stuff that flooded up this time was yellower. It didn't burn his finger, but Jenner took one taste, and spat it out. He had the feeling that he had been offered a soup made of a greasy mixture of clay and gasoline.

He was thirsty now with a need heightened by the unpleasant taste in his mouth. Desperately, he rushed outside and tore open the water bag, seeking the wetness inside. In his fumbling eagerness, he spilled a few precious drops onto the courtyard. Down he went on his face, and licked them up.

Half a minute later, he was still licking, and there was still water.

The fact penetrated suddenly. He raised himself, and gazed wonderingly at the droplets of water that sparkled on the smooth stone. As he watched, another one squeezed up from the apparently solid surface, and shimmered in the light of the sinking sun.

He bent, and with the tip of his tongue sponged up each visible drop. For a long time, he lay with his mouth pressed to the "marble," sucking up the tiny bits of water that the village doled out to him.

The glowing white sun disappeared behind a hill. Night fell, like the dropping of a black screen. The air turned cold, then icy. He shivered as the wind keened through his ragged clothes. But what finally stopped him was the collapse of the surface from which he had been drinking.

Jenner lifted himself in surprise and, in the darkness, gingerly felt over the stone. It had genuinely crumbled. Evidently the substance had yielded up its available water and had disintegrated in the process. Jenner estimated that he had drunk altogether an ounce of water.

It was a convincing demonstration of the willingness of the village to please him, but there was another, less satisfying implication. If the village had to destroy a part of itself every time it gave him a drink, then clearly the supply was not unlimited.

Jenner hurried inside the nearest building, climbed onto a dais—and climbed off again hastily, as the heat blazed up at him. He waited, to give the Intelligence a chance to realize he wanted to change, then he lay down once more. The heat was as great as ever.

He gave that up because he was too sleepy to think of a method that might let the village know he needed a different bedroom temperature. He slept on the floor with an uneasy conviction that it could *not* sustain him for long. He woke up many times during the night, and thought: Not enough water. No matter how hard it tries. . . . Then he would sleep again, only to wake once more, tense and unhappy.

Nevertheless, morning found him briefly alert, and all his steely determination was back—that iron willpower that had brought him at least five hundred miles across an unknown desert.

He headed for the nearest trough. This time, after he had activated it, there was a pause of more than a minute, and then about a thimbleful of water made a wet splotch at the bottom.

Jenner licked it dry, then waited hopefully for more. When none came, he reflected gloomily that somewhere in the village, an entire group of cells had broken down and released their water for him.

Then and there he decided that it was up to the human being, who could move around, to find a new source of water for the village, which could not move.

In the interim, of course, the village would have to keep him alive, until he had investigated the possibilities. That meant, above everything else, he must have some food to sustain him while he looked around.

He began to search his pockets. Toward the end of his food ·supply, he had carried scraps and pieces wrapped in small bits of cloth. Crumbs had broken off into his pocket and he had searched often during those long days in the desert. Now, by actually ripping the seams, he discovered tiny particles of meat and bread, little bits of grease, and other unidentifiable substances.

Carefully, he leaned over the adjoining stall and placed the scrappings in the trough there. The village would not be able to offer him more than a reasonable facsimile. If the spilling of a few drops on the courtyard could make it aware of his need for water, then a similar offering might give it the clue it needed as to the chemical nature of the food he could eat.

Jenner waited, then entered the second stall and activated it. About a pint of thick, creamy substance trickled into the bottom of the trough. The smallness of the quantity seemed evidence that perhaps it contained water.

He tasted it. It had a sharp, musty flavor and a stale odor. It was almost as dry as flour—but his stomach did not reject it.

Jenner ate slowly, acutely aware that at such moments as this the village had him at its mercy. He could never be sure that one of the food ingredients was not a slow-acting poison.

When he had finished the meal, he went to a food trough in another building. He refused to eat the food that came up, but activated still another trough. This time he received a few drops of water.

He had come purposefully to one of the tower buildings. Now, he had started up the ramp that led to the upper floor. He paused only briefly in the room he came to, as he had already discovered that they seemed to be additional bedrooms. The familiar dais was there in a group of three.

What interested him was that the circular ramp continued to wind on upward. First to another, smaller room that seemed to have no particular reason for being. Then it wound on up to the top of the tower, some seventy feet above the ground. It was high enough for him to see beyond the rim of all the surrounding hilltops. He had thought it might be, but he had been too weak to make the climb before. Now, he looked out to every horizon. Almost immediately, the hope that had brought him up faded.

The view was immeasurably desolate. As far as he could see was an arid wasteland, and every horizon was hidden in a mist of wind-blown sand.

Jenner gazed with a sense of despair. If there was a Martian sea out there, somewhere, it was beyond his reach.

Abruptly, he clenched his hands in anger against his fate, which seemed inevitable now. At the very worst, he had hoped he would find himself in a mountainous region. Seas and mountains were generally the two main sources of water. He should have known, of course, that there were very few mountains on Mars. It would have been a wild coincidence if he had actually run into a mountain range.

His fury faded, because he lacked the strength to sustain any emotion. Numbly, he went down the ramp.

His vague plan to help the village ended as swiftly and finally as that.

The days drifted by, but as to how many he had no idea. Each time he went to eat, a smaller amount of water was doled out to him. Jenner kept telling himself that each meal would have to be his last. It was unreasonable for him to expect the village to destroy itself when his fate was certain now.

What was worse, it became increasingly clear that the food was not good for him. He had misled the village as to his needs by giving it stale, perhaps even tainted samples, and prolonged the agony for himself. At times, after he had eaten, Jenner felt dizzy for hours. All too frequently, his head ached, and his body shivered with fever.

The village was doing what it could. The rest was up to him, and he couldn't even adjust to an approximation of Earth food.

For two days, he was too sick to drag himself to one of the troughs. Hour after hour, he lay on the floor. Some time during the second night, the pain in his body grew so terrible that he finally made up his mind.

"If I can get to a dais," he told himself, "the heat alone will kill me; and, in absorbing my body, the village will get back some of its lost water."

He spent at least an hour crawling laboriously up the ramp of the nearest dais and, when he finally made it, he lay as one already dead. His last waking thought was: Beloved friends, I'm coming.

The hallucination was so complete that, momentarily, he seemed to be back in the control room of the rocketship, and all around him were his former companions.

With a sigh of relief, Jenner sank into a dreamless sleep.

He woke to the sound of a violin. It was sad-sweet music that told of the rise and fall of a race long dead.

Jenner listened for a while, and then, with abrupt excitement, realized the truth. This was a substitute for the whistling—the village had adjusted its music to him!

Other sensory phenomena stole in upon him. The dais felt comfortably warm, not hot at all. He had a feeling of wonderful physical well-being.

Eagerly, he scrambled down the ramp to the nearest food stall. As he crawled forward, his nose close to the floor, the trough filled with a steamy mixture. The odor was so rich and pleasant that he plunged his face into it, and slopped it up greedily. It had the flavor of thick, meaty soup, and was warm and soothing to his lips and mouth. When he had eaten it all, he did not need a drink of water for the first time.

"I've won!" thought Jenner. "The village has found a way!"

After a while, he remembered something, and crawled to the bathroom. Cautiously, watching the ceiling, he eased himself backward into the shower stall. The yellowish spray came down, cool and delightful.

Ecstatically, Jenner wriggled his four-foot tail and lifted his long snout to let the thin streams of liquid wash away the food impurities that clung to his sharp teeth.

Then he waddled out to bask in the sun and listen to the timeless music.

The idea of undersea cities figures in the myths of many of the earth's peoples and may become a reality as the human race crowds itself off the land. In "The Deeps" Keith Roberts considers whether or not such a radical change of environment could be made without producing extreme psychological changes in the undersea dwellers themselves.

The Deeps

by Keith Roberts

It was bound to happen. For generations, the chain reaction of population explosion had been going on and on. While medical skill grew, while longevity increased nearly beyond belief, humankind everywhere bred and bred and bred. Houses, estates, factories to serve the vast new economies spread and sprawled, twitching out across good land and bad, climbing mountains, suffocating rivers. Town touched town, touched town; the pink octopus tentacles of houses grew and thickened as the machines graded and scraped and hammered. Green belts and parks vanished, fields were swallowed overnight. Here and there voices were raised; the voices of economists, scientists, philosophers, even, at last, theologians. But they were swamped in the great universal cry.

Give us room. . . . The shout went up night and day from a hundred million throats, the slogan blared from loudspeakers, blazed from hoardings as political parties jockeyed for power. Increasingly, room was what they promised. Room for more houses, more estates, room to rear new families that cried in their turn for room and still more room. . . .

All over the world countrysides vanished, eaten. Wars flared as nations bit at each other's borders, but still the Cities grew. The huge estates were searched, forced to yield their last acres, their secret gardens. And all for nothing, it seemed, because still the cry was heard for room. Skyscrapers soared, fifty stories, seventy, a hundred, and it was not enough. The Cities bulged outward, noisy with music and the sound of human life. A hundred yards thick, they were, and blaring with light, complex with stack on twinkling stack of avenues. Raucous, Technicolored, sleepless. Everywhere, they reached the sea.

And they could not stop. The pressure, the need for room, pushed them out again. The houses sank like silver bells into blueness and quiet, and at last there was room enough.

Mary Franklin sat in the living area of her bungalow, knitting quiet for once in her lap, and tried to watch the telscreen at the other side of the room. Across her line of sight Jen passed scuttling, bare feet scuffing the carpet, the straps of her lung flapping around her shoulders. Across and back, then across again, frantic now, going to a party at the Belmonts on the other side of town, and late. Mary raised her eyes to heaven, represented temporarily by a curved steel shell. She concentrated on the screen where a demonstrator, in a vivid color, divulged to her audience the inner secrets of a variant of crawfish mayonnaise. Jen yelped something inaudible from the bedroom, thumped the wall. (Why? . . .) She padded across again and back. Mary raised her voice suddenly.

"Jen? . . ."

Thump. Mumble.

"Jen!"

"Mummy, I can't find my . . ." Indistinguishable.

"Jen, you're not to be late. No more than nine, understand?"

"Yes . . ."

"And for *land's* sake child, *put something on* . . ."

"Yes, Mummy . . ." That in a high voice, wearily. And almost instantly the roar of the sealock. Mary got up in quick rage, walked halfway to the radio gear, changed her mind, went back to her chair. Jen, she knew well enough, would conveniently have forgotten her phone leads.

She kicked the channel switch irritably in passing; the picture on the wall screen jumped and altered. The set began to disgorge a Western; Mary lay back, eyes nearly shut, half her mind on the ancient film and half on the blueness overhead—the endless blue.

Jen, defiantly bare, hung twenty feet above the hemispherical roof of her home. Bubbles from her breathing rose in a series of shimmering, dimly seen sickles to the Surface overhead. As always, the sea had made her forget her compulsion to hurry; she began to paddle slowly, feet in their long fins catching and driving back wedges of water. As she moved she looked below her, at the lines of domes with their neat, almost suburban gardens of waving weed. She saw the misty squares of their windows, the brighter green-blue globes of the street lighting swung from thin wires above the ocean bed. Warnings were hung on long, wire streamers for swimmers; there were well-marked lanes, corresponding to the streets of the city complexes, Jen barely remembered, but many people ignored them. And most of the children. Technically she was out of bounds now, gliding along like this only a few feet from Surface.

Visibility was good tonight; onshore winds could kick up a smother that lasted for days, but there had been nearly a week of calm. Jen could make out through the almost haze-free water the faint shimmer where the engineers, her father among them, were working on the new extension to the theater and civic center. When it was finished, the installation would be the pride of Settlement Eighty, the town its inhabitants called Oceanville. There were a dozen other Oceanvilles scattered up and down this one stretch of coast, hundreds possibly in all the seas of the world. She shivered slightly although the water was not cold.

Beyond the lights, beyond where the divers floated around the tall, steel skeletons, were long sloping stretches where the town buildings petered out and the coral and sand of the inshore waters gave place to the silt of real ocean. There was a graveyard, tiny as yet, where a few bodies lay in their metal cans; beyond again, past gray dunes where the light faded imperceptibly to navy blue and black, were the Deeps. Above anything else Jen liked to go to the new buildings, sit on one of the girders, look down into the vagueness that was the proper sea, bottomless and immense. Just stare, and listen, and wait. She would go there tonight maybe, after the party.

She let herself relax, holding air in her lungs to increase buoyancy. Her body floated upward, legs and arms slack; Surface appeared above her, a faintly luminous upside-down plain. Points of light sparkled where the moontrack refracted into the depths. Jen wagged lazily with her flippers, once, twice; her body broke the Surface and she felt herself lifted by the slight action of the waves.

She looked round. The sea was flatly calm, dark at the horizon, glinting with bluish swirls of phosphorescence around her shoulders and neck. When she looked closely, she could see the organisms that made the light floating in it like grains of brightness. Way off was the orange-cloud reflection over the land, where the universal Cities bawled and yammered. Jen lay still, supported by the water. Once she would have pulled her mask aside, breathed in the wet salt of ordinary air. Now she felt no desire to do so. She turned slowly, treading water, took a last look at the moon, and dived. Her heels stirred up a momentary flash of light. Once below, she moved powerfully, stroking with her arms. She arrowed down to West Terrace where the Belmonts had their dome. The party would be in full swing already; she was missing good dancing time.

Hours later, Mary prodded one of her rare cigarettes from the wall dispenser. She frowned a little, drawing in smoke and letting it dribble from her nostrils. She lay back and watched the fumes being sucked toward the ceiling vent. The telscreen was off; the last badman had bitten the dust and she had grown tired of watching. The bungalow seemed very quiet; the buzz of the air-conditioning plant sounded unusually loud, as did the recurring clink-thump of the refrigerator solenoids from the kitchen.

She stood uncertainly, fingered her throat, took a step, paused. She went to the alcove by the kitchen, which housed the radio link and telephone. Beside the handset the dome-metering equipment chuckled faintly. Inside the gray housings, striped discs spun, needles wavered against their dials. Force of habit made her check the readings. All normal, of course. . . . She touched the phone, pulled at her lip with her teeth, made herself take her hand away. A quarter of an hour, that was nothing. When she was dancing, Jen forgot the time. They all did. She would be home in a few minutes, by nine-thirty at the latest. She knew exactly how long to outstay an order. . . . Mary went back to the living area, turned the telscreen on, clicked the channel switch to five. While the set was warming she walked through to David's cubicle, peered in. He was asleep, hair tousled on the pillow.

Nine-fifty.

Mary got up again, walked to the window in the curved wall. She drew the curtains back, looked across the

street at the neighboring houses visible through the faint re-
sidual haze. A little fear stirred somewhere at the back of
her mind, throbbed, stilled itself again. She wondered, fear
of what? Accidents maybe; they happened, even in the
best-run towns. Jack—but it wasn't that. She laughed at
herself quietly, trying to shrug away her fit of nerves.

These late-shifts of her husband's were a curse, but
there was no help for them; the new building was going
ahead fast and, as engineering controller for the sector,
Jack had to be almost constantly on the site. She told herself, physically her husband was not far away. She could
ring him if she had to. How far off was the new complex, a
hundred-and-fifty yards, two hundred? No distance, by
terrestrial standards. . . . But here, under the sea, just how
far was a hundred yards? Could be a lifetime, or an epoch.
She grimaced. That was what the fear was about, what the
. . . throb . . . tried to tell her, maybe. That under the sea,
patterns and values could change ineradicably.

She sat down, crossed her knees, laid her head against
the back of the chair. After a few moments she picked up
the abandoned knitting and stared at it. She was making a
sweater, though there was no point in the exercise. The
domes were air-conditioned and sea temperature only var-
ied a few degrees through the year; nobody needed sweat-
ers down here, and the yarn was expensive. It came from
Surface and all Surface things were dear. But it was something to do, it kept her hands busy. Above all, it was a link
with the past . . .

A quarter after ten.

The face of the clock was round and sea blue, the
hands plain white needles. They moved in one-minute
jerks; Mary imagined that she could see the tiny quiver
that preceded each jump. She stubbed out the cigarette.
The party would be long-finished now, the dancers dis-
persed . . .

Dancers? She shook her head. She could remember the

dancing in the Cities, the pulsing rhythms, frenetic jerking. That pattern, like everything else, had changed. She remembered the first time she had heard what they called sea-jazz, the shock it had given her. Jen had a player in her bedroom, it wailed and bumped half the night, but the rhythms, the melodies, were like nothing she had ever heard landside. The music howled and dragged, the beats developed timings that defied notation, had in them something of the slow surge of the tides. It was music for swimming to.

The Belmonts had a dance floor but it was outside, in the sea. Airposts surrounded it, and speaker casings; around them the kids would swirl like pale flakes among the hordes of fish that always seemed to be attracted. "But Mummy," Jen would say if she protested, "you just don't *gel*, you're not *wavy* . . ." It was all part of the new phraseology; the boy down the block, Kev Hartford was not it, he *gelled* for Jen, he was a *wave;* but the lad from the airplant, Cy Scheinger, who had visited once or twice, was out of favor. He was *neapy*, a *scorp*. (Scorpion fish?) The sea, and thoughts of the sea, pervaded their whole lives now, even to the language they spoke. Which was natural, and as it should be . . .

Why did we call her Jennifer? Why, of all the names we could have used? The Jennifer was a sea-thing, and cursed . . .

It was no use. Mary killed the sound from the screen, walked back to the phone, lifted the handset, and dialed. She listened to the clicking of the exchange relays, the faint purr-purr at the other end of the line. An age, and the receiver was lifted.

"Ye-es?" The slight coo in the voice, unmistakable even through the surging distortion of the sea. The Belmonts were just a little conscious of their status; Alan Belmont was fisheries manager for the area. Mary licked her lips. "Hello? Hello, Anne, this is Mary. Mary Franklin . . .

What? Yes, fine thank you . . . Anne . . . is Jen still at your place by any chance? I told her nine, she's late, I wondered if . . ."

Anne Belmont sounded vaguely surprised. "My dear, I shooed them off positively hours ago. Well, an hour . . . Hold the line . . ."

Unidentifiable human sounds. Someone calling faintly. The wash . . . crash . . . of the sea.

"Hello?"

"Yes . . ."

"Just before nine," said the phone. "We sent them all off, there's no one here now. . . . You say she's not back?"

"No," said Mary, "no, she's not." Her knuckles had whitened on the handset.

The phone clucked. "My dear, they're all the same; ours are hopeless, time means *nothing*, absolutely *nothing* . . . But I'm quite *sure* you needn't worry, she'll be along any moment. Perhaps she's with that *Cy* boy, whatever his name is . . . yes . . ."

Ice, along the spine, moving out like fingers that gripped and clutched. "Thank you," said Mary. "No, no, of course not. Yes, I'll let you know. . . . Yes, good-bye, Anne . . ." She laid the handset on its cradle, stood looking at it, not knowing what to do. The sea pushed at the dome gently, slurringly.

A quarter after ten.

Mary stood very still in the middle of the living area, lips pursed. She had called the airworks—Cy was off duty, could not be traced—and two or three neighbors and friends. No Jen. She could not ring Jack at the construction office, not again. Down here you helped your husband, pulled your weight. You didn't run panicking at every little thing. . . . The trembling had started, in her legs; she rubbed her thighs unconsciously through her dress. She touched the hair pinned into a chignon at the nape of her neck. In front of her, on the sill of the window, a plaster foal pranced, hooves outlined against greenness. The greenness was the sea.

Decision. She pulled at her hair, shook it free around her shoulders. She unsnapped the clasp at her neck, wriggled her dress up over her head. Beneath it she wore the conventional blue leotard of a married woman. She plucked automatically at the high line of the legs, kicked her sandals off, crossed to the equipment locker. She came back with her sea gear, lung, mask, and flippers. She dressed quickly, fastening the broad straps around her waist and between her legs, the lighter shoulder harness that held the meter panel across her chest. Habit again made her check the dials, valve air, slap the red cancelator-tab on her shoulder. That was another safety factor; if for any reason air stopped flowing from the pack and that tab was not touched, a built-in radio beacon would arrow town guards down to the wearer.

She looked in at David again, satisfied herself he was still sleeping. She walked to the sealock, stopped on the way to see herself in the half-length mirror. She was heavier now, her hips had broadened and there were maybe faint worry lines around her mouth. But her hair was brown and soft; landside she would still be a desirable woman.

She looked around the dome slowly, seeming to see familiar things in a new light that was bright and strange. The bungalow was double-skinned, the inner ceiling finished in octagonal plates of white and pale blue plastic. The half-round shape, dictated by considerations of pressure, had the secondary advantage of enclosing the greatest possible volume of space; deep-pile carpets covered the floors, the furniture was low and streamlined, easy to live with. The telscreen was tucked neatly into an alcove; to each side of it were wall tanks with fish and anemones.

Through a half-open door she could see the kitchen. It was miniaturized but well equipped, with plenty of stainless steel like the galley of a ship.

The whole bungalow was as safe as it was functional. In the unlikely event of a fracture in the pressure shell, the second skin would hold the sea while instantaneous warnings were flashed to a central exchange, insuring help within minutes. Not that anything could or would go wrong, of course, the whole system was too carefully worked out for that. People had been living undersea for years now, and fatalities were far fewer than on the overcrowded land.

Mary grimaced, stepped through into the lock, and closed the inner hatch. The ceiling lamp came on; she pressed the filler control, heard the hiss as air was expelled through the outlet valves.

She squatted in rising water to work the straps of the flippers over her heels, then straightened up. The coolness touched her hips; she brushed her hair back, spat in the mask and rinsed it, pressed the transparent visor onto her face. The plastic was self-adhesive, molded to her skull contour; it fitted from forehead to chin. She palmed the earphones into place, reached under her arm for her mike leads, flicked the tags onto the magnetic contacts in her throat. The compartment filled, water rising greenly over her head. As the pressure equalized, the outer segment of wall slid aside automatically, letting in the hazy glow of the street lighting. Mary kicked away and floated up from the dome, sensing the old lift as the sea shucked off her weight. Her hair swirled across her eyes gracefully, like fronds of black fern.

She swam slowly across the town. To each side, lines of round-topped buildings marched out of the haze. Some of the houses were still new and bright with their coated, steel skins, others had grown a rich, waving cover of algae. On the main street the shop windows were brightly lit; the plate-glass ports displayed seafoods set on white dishes, garnished with fronds of weed; there were Aqualungs and radiophones, Surface-ware of all sorts, clothes and books, records, dolls, toys. Here the ocean floor had been cleared to the rock that underlay the sand; overhead were slim arches to which were moored the sledges of out-of-towners, the fish herders and oceanographers whose work took them to lonely domes scattered over the bed of the sea. There were lights on the gantries; each globe hung, glaring in greenness, surrounded by a flickering cloud of tiny fish, like moths around a terrestrial lamp. Over everything was an air of peace; the dreamy peace of dusk on an ancient, unspoiled Earth.

There were few human swimmers about, but here and there, careening over the roofs of buildings, Mary caught sight of glistening shapes. Dolphins—they had been quick to discover the sea-floor communities and take advantage of them. Many families, in fact, kept one or more of them as semipermanent pets, became very attached to them. Other creatures occasionally troubled the townships—sharks, rays, the odd squid. But the repellents carried by the swimmers in their harness had been developed to a stage where there was little to fear. The town guards could be relied on to harpoon or shoo off any of the big fellows who hung around too close or too long, though in the main there was little to attract predators.

Disposal of garbage was rigidly controlled; locking offal into the sea was about the worst crime in the book; it could result in being sent landside. The "monsters of the deep," in so far as they existed, tended to avoid the colonies. They disliked the brightness and noise, the bustle, the thud of many vibrations crisscrossing in the water. As Jack never tired of pointing out, life down here was as safe or safer than on land.

Mary doubled back, passing the king-size domes that held the town distillation plant. The per capita consumption of fresh water was fifty percent higher for Sea People than for Terrestrials. Frequent bathing was neccessary to remove ingrained salt from the skin; supplying salt-free water was one of the biggest problems of the ocean-floor settlements. Beyond the distillery was the airworks. The electrolyzers reached halfway to Surface, each mass of tubes contained in an insulating shell of helium. The current for the oxygen separation came from strategically sited tidal-generating stations up and down the coast. Many domes were already on tap from the plant; eventually they would all avail themselves of the new municipal service, though they would retain their own gear as a fail-safe in case of emergency.

Mary swam around the huge stacks, peering into locked shadows, calling softly through her mask. "Jen . . . Jen . . ." The harness pack radiated the word into the water, farther than a human voice could reach in air, but there was no answer. She clung to a steel stay twenty feet above the seabed. Bubbles curled up from her in a shimmering stream as she tried to quiet her breathing. A group of children went by, out late and swimming fast; she heard their chattering, realized with a cold shock how similar it was to the noises of a fish herd in the hydrophones. She shivered. Thoughts like that had been plaguing her for months now, maybe years. She called urgently, but the child-shoal swerved aside, accelerating and vanishing in the gloom. There was quiet; beside her the great cans vibrated, the sensation more felt than heard. The stay seemed to buzz in her fingers.

She let go quickly, because electrolyzer stacks cannot make any sound. She concentrated. That deep, thudding boom. . . . Was it her heart, or just fear, or was there something . . . something else? . . . No, it was gone— slipped over the edge of perception, into silence. She started to swim again, thoughts churning confusedly. She remembered a conversation she had had with her husband weeks back. They had been lying abed after his shift was done; the house had been silent, or as silent as it could get. Just the airplant, buzzing in the dark . . .

She had spoken to blackness. "Jack," she had said, wondering at herself, "the Deeps. Have you heard what they've been saying about them—that they talk?"

"I've heard a lot of rubbish."

She said, "They talk. That's what the kids say. Jen . . . she says she's heard it, a . . . thing, I don't know what. A calling. Jack, be serious, listen to me . . ."

"I am serious," he said. "Completely. Mary, there's nothing in the Deeps except one hell of a lot of water, at one hell of a pressure. Oh, there could be a slip somewhere, volcanic activity maybe, a long way down, that would send up pressure waves, you might be able to feel them, but that's all. I'm an engineer, I've been working with the sea more years than I want to think about, now take my word, I *know*. This . . . thing, it's a fad with the kids. You get little gangs of them floating out there waiting for revelations, I've seen 'em. I don't know where it started but it's just a craze, it'll die off when something new comes along . . ."

She was quiet, thinking of all the towns stretching through the warm seas of the world, all along the Continental Shelves. The domes were snug and secure, automated; nothing could go wrong. But what if . . . what if there was an enemy, something more insidious than pressure? Something in people, in me, she told herself, or in Jen. Something working outward from the roots of the brain. . . . She said abruptly, "Jack, how can you be so damn sure you're always right?"

The bed creaked as he moved. "You going Continental on me, Mary?"

She did not answer. His hand reached the contacts on her throat, stroked. "You know what I told you. What we agreed when they put these in. Once down, always down." He paused. Then, softly, "What's for us on land?"

She lay remembering the lowness of the roofed City streets, the flaring miles of fluorescent strip, the crushing sense of overcontact. Hive phobia of a crowded planet.

He could play her mind, he always could. "Listen," he said. "You can still hear it deep down. The roaring. Escalators, pedivators. Traffic. Dance halls. Wall screens all yelling, fighting one against another. Buy this. Buy that. Vote for freedom. Use our toothpaste. Don't copulate. . . . Just remember it, Mary. Markets. Movie houses. The whole heaped-up, tipped-up jumble we made for ourselves. Is that a thing to go back to? Take the kids to? Well, is it?"

No answer. He kept talking. The old vision. "Down here we've got peace. We've got security. Well, as much security as people can find anywhere. And more important, we've got a democracy. A real, practical, working democracy, maybe for the first time ever. Down here your neighbor's house is always open because that's the way it has to be. We can't afford to fight each other, the sea takes care of that. And the sea's forever.

"So we've got unity, and drive. Right now maybe you reckon there's a lot of us but I say we're still villages, settlements. We're dependent on Surface, we still buy down supplies. But it won't always be like that. I can see whole nations and tribes of us scattered over the oceans, everywhere in the world. Right down into the Deeps. We'll be independent. We'll draw everything we need straight out of the sea. Gold, tin, lead, copper, uranium, you name it, you'll find it's right here in the sea. Billions of tons of it, waiting to be used. In a small way we've started already. The land's old, burned out. Let the Continentals keep it . . ." He chuckled. "Tell you what, we'll pop up one day, in a thousand years, maybe, for a little trade. Find they've gone. All of them. Blown each other apart, starved, lit out for the planets, anywhere. We wouldn't know. If the whole world burned up, how should we tell? We shouldn't care . . ."

She was making patterns in blackness, drawing on the pillow with one finger. Biting her lip. He touched her hair; his hand found the pendant warmth of a breast, and she moved irritably, twisting away from him. "I was thinking," she said, "about the kids. All the kids we've got down here—"

"All the kids," he said tiredly. "Mary, all the kids have *changed*. Adapted to their surroundings. Now that's the most natural thing. We'd be having to worry if it wasn't happening. This environment, after all, it's alien. Outside racial experience. In a sense this life of ours is being lived on a new planet. We must expect new skills, new adaptations, and they'll show in the children quicker because the children have known nothing else. That's the way it has to be, that way's right. This has taken a long time coming out in you, Mary, can't you see what's happening?"

"I can," she said bitterly. "Can you?"

"Mary, listen here a minute . . ."

She felt obscurely that he was still hedging, that his mind would automatically reject anything that could not be measured and calibrated. She wanted to scream; the confidence, the know-how, suddenly it all seemed so much smugness. The sea was infinite, from it could come an infinity of fears. She said, "We all . . . they say we all came from the sea. Well, couldn't we . . . regress, you know, sort of slip back . . ."

He clicked on the bedside light. "Mary, do you have any clear idea what you're saying?"

She nodded vigorously, trying to make him understand. "I thought it all through, Jack. I mean about birds losing their wings, and seals—didn't seals go back into the sea, degenerate somehow? And now us, the children, they . . . swim like fish, more and more like fish . . ."

"But hell," he said, "Mary, do you know how *long* a thing like that takes? A biological degeneration? How many millions of. . . . Oh look, Mary, look here. A million years. That's how long we've been around, give or take a few thousand. And that's nothing, nothing at all. It isn't . . . that." He snapped his fingers. "You're thinking on the fine scale, the historical scale. All that time, that million years, wasn't enough for us to lose our little toes. Look, the Earth's a day old. Took twenty-four hours to evolve, go through all the cycles of life and get to us. You know what we are, what all our history is? The last tick of the clock. . . . That's how long evolution takes, it's a very big thing . . ."

But it was no use, she had heard it all before. "Maybe it won't be like that this time," she said. "We . . . evolved that quick, at the end. Maybe we'll go back now just as fast . . ."

"It hasn't anything to do with it," he said. "Nothing at all."

She said desperately, "We were so smart, Jack, getting out like this, living in the sea. Making a new world. But maybe . . . couldn't that somehow be what the sea really wanted, all along? What we were *meant* to do? Oh, I know this sounds crazy but, believe me, when I see the kids . . . Jen slipped the other day, in the kitchen. When she tried to get up, I think she tried to turn like she was swimming— she forgot she was in air. . . . And David, he swims just like a little shrimp. . . . When I see things like that I think. . . . Oh, I don't know what I think sometimes—maybe we're not . . . pioneers at all. This thing about the Deeps, they say they call, pull. . . . Maybe we're just sort of being sucked back, that's where we belong . . ."

He was angry, finally. "All right. So this craziness is all true. We've got a racial memory in our brains, in our nervous systems. We remember the beginnings of life all those years back, so many years we can't even count the thousands. Well, then, we're home already, Mary. Right where we are, this is where life started. In the shallows, swilling in the sunlight. Not in the Deeps. It moved down there, same time some of it spread onto land. There's nothing can call us from there. We don't belong there, never did."

She was quivering a little, looking at the pillow, seeing the texture of it. Every strand in the weave of the cloth. "I wanted to stay human," she said. "That was all. Just to stay human, and the kids . . ."

He touched her. "You're human. You're all right."

She wouldn't look at him. "I think," she said, "I think now . . . I'd take the Cities. Jack . . ."

He did not answer, and she knew the expression on his face without looking. Something inside her seemed to twist and become cold. He would do anything for her maybe, except that. He would not go landside, not now. The empires, the herds and tribes of the sea, they were in his brain, they called too. The dream was too strong, he could not let it go.

He pushed the clothes back and swung his legs off the bed. She heard the little swish as he picked up a robe. "Mary," he said, "why don't you get a little checkup. You're rundown, it's my fault, I should have realized. . . . Too much time on your own, you don't get about. Not anymore. Maybe you should have a trip landside. Go and see your folks. Tell you what—I'll get a couple of days' leave, we'll have a run up to Seventy-five, take the kids, how's that? They've got the new theater up there, whole pile of junk. Sound okay?"

She did not answer. "I'll have a talk with Jen," she said. "I'll do it tomorrow. This is silliness, it can be stopped . . ." He walked out, turned on a light, and started tinkering in the kitchen. He brought back coffee laced with rum. She pulled a bedjacket over her shoulders, sat drinking, hands gripped around the warmth of the cup. Feeling the trembling still deep in her body, hearing the buzz of the airplant, imagining the silly, silly meters checking and recording. Pressure, humidity, oxy-level, all the things that did not matter. While Jack sat and watched her, smoked and smiled and did not understand . . .

Mary swam the length of the town again, moving slowly, watching to right and left at the domes nested in shadows, their windows like square, bright eyes. The sea was darker now; in the real world above, the moon was setting. Surface was just visible as a grayish sheen; tall weed fronds were silhouetted against it, leaning majestically to the currentlike trees bowed by an endless wind. The tide was setting out, toward the Deeps.

After that talk with her husband, her restlessness had become worse. Quite suddenly it seemed the whole furnishing of the dome was oppressive, stultifying. The curtains had come down, the glinting blue fabric with its faint, interlapping tidal patterns had been put away. Mary had hung new yellow cloth, sun yellow, printed with designs of buds and flowering trees. She had banished the spiny amber-spotted shells and the urchin lamps, Jen's untidy collection of seabed fossils, even the cushion covers on which she herself had once worked swirling Minoan patterns of weed and octopuses. In their places were landside things, figurines of horses and kittens, panting china dogs. Creatures long-vanished now but that reminded her of Earth and the way humans lived once upon a time.

Every ornament, every yard of cloth, had had to be bought from Surface; the cost had been enormous but once started Mary had seemed unable to stop. Jack had raised his eyebrows but said nothing; Jen had protested more noisily.

Things had reached crisis-pitch the day Mary found, in the wall tank in Jen's room, a piece of old human skull, coral-crusted, put there as a home for crabs. She had slapped her daughter for that, a thing she had never done before, and emptied tank and contents through the lock. Jen had fled squalling, into the sea, and not to come home for hours. After that Mary spent a week scraping the whole top of the dome, polishing away the velvet coat of sea-growth till the plastic-covered panels gleamed like new; but it seemed the more she did, the more she tried to banish the presence of the sea from her home, the more the sea invaded. At night, lying quiet, she imagined she could feel the slow push of the wave force against the bungalow, tilting it this way and that, slow, slow, this way . . . then that . . .

She drove herself across to West Terrace, built slightly higher than the rest of town on a curving ridge of rock, nearly to the Belmonts' dome and back, calling all the way. Jen was not in town; or if she was, she refused to answer. Mary's face was wet now inside the mask and her lungs were laboring. Thoughts tumbled in her mind. Nitrogen narcosis, the thing they used to call rapture of the depths . . . no longer possible, the lungs delivered an oxy-helium mix. Oxygen intoxication, then; that could make you throw your mask off, breathe water and die. But it was nearly unheard of. Low down on Mary's back, and on Jen's, were other contacts. They led to cells deep in the body that metered the blood itself, testing it for oxy-content. The lungs were self-compensating. Pack failure? Crazy, the gulp-bottle on Jen's belt would give her twenty minutes' breathing. And the beacon, there was the beacon. But beacons could go out . . .

Mary doubled back, swerving under the rigging of the street lamps. Across to where she could see the divers working on the new building complex. The bodies hung round the curving ribs, tiny with distance, silver as fish under the glare of the lamps; below, the windows of the construction office just showed in the gloom. Soon she would call Jack, she would have to. . . . She felt the fear again, like a coldness round her heart. There was only one place she had not been. She began to swim purposefully away from the town and its lights, toward the Deeps.

Just beyond the domes the seabed fell away in a series of troughs, miles long and wide. Unseen, their contours could still appall the mind. This was the frontier, the last frontier, maybe, on the planet. She passed over the graveyard, trying not to see the frail crosses sticking up from the silt, name tags fluttering in the current like gray leaves. Out to where the last light faded, and beyond . . .

She was in a void—bottomless, pit-black. Above her a vagueness that was just one shade less dark than darkness itself. Not light; some trailing ghost maybe, that light had left behind it. Mary drove deeper, hopelessly, feeling pressure begin to squeeze her body like cold hands. She was panting, though there was no sound of it in her ears; her breathing alone could not activate the throat mike. She called again; her voice was a vibrating thread, nearly lost in the immensity.

And there was something, a blemish in the gulf. Tiny, nearly invisible, its shape so vague it mocked the retinas. Mary swam, hair flowing, there was a longness, a paleness, like a body caught and floating on some denser stratum of the sea. Deep down, far below . . .

"*Jen!*"

Mary kicked out, desperate now, her movements losing smoothness and coordination. Fighting the pressure was like butting at a wall; she imagined her whole body shrinking, condensing, becoming tiny as a fish.

"JEN!"

She'd reached the thing, she was stretching for it with her hands, when it moved. Eeled away, rolled. . . . She saw the bright cloud of breathing suddenly released, the fins threshing. Heard her daughter chuckling in her earphones.

Fear turned to anger. Mary arced in the water. "Jen, get back this *instant* . . ." She grabbed again and the girl eluded her, quick as a fish.

"Mummy, *listen* . . ." The voice bubbled through the sea. "It's loud tonight, *listen* . . ."

Mary opened her mouth to yell again, and stopped. The noise . . . *was there a noise?*

She listened, straining. Found herself not breathing. It was impossible; no outside sound could come through her blocked ears. Nonetheless, it came. There, and again. . . . A thudding, but not a thudding. Some pressure, like a concussion against the brain. Immeasurably slow and powerful and somehow *ancient*. . . . Pulsing with her heart, fading, swelling back to touch her body. Earthquake or volcano, she had no idea. Nor did she care. Somehow it was sufficient that the sensation, the not-sound, was there. This was something immemorial, eternal. The true, dark, jet-blue voice of the sea . . .

Woman and girl hung a little apart, bodies vaguely glowing motes against a hugeness of water. Mary felt that she could lie all night, not speaking, just soaking in the strangeness that seemed to fill her by rich stages from feet to head. Hearing rhythms that were not rhythms, that blended and crossed, melding each into each like the sounds of the sea-jazz. Soothing, calming, somehow *warm* . . .

She could hear Jen calling but the voice was unimportant, remote. It was only when the girl swam to her, grabbed her shoulders and pointed at the gauges between her breasts that she withdrew from the half-trance. The thing below still called and thudded; Mary turned reluctantly, found Jen's hand in her own. She let herself float. Jen kicking slowly and laughing again delightedly, chuckling into her earphones. Their hair, swirling, touched and mingled; Mary looked back and down and knew suddenly her inner battle was over.

The sound, the thing she had heard or felt, there was no fear in it. Just a promise, weird and huge. The Sea People would go on now, pushing their domes lower and lower into night, fighting pressure and cold until all the seas of all the world were truly full; and the future, whatever it might be, would care for itself. Maybe one day the technicians would make a miracle and then they would flood the domes and the sea would be theirs to breathe. She tried to imagine Jen with the bright feathers of gills floating from her neck. She tightened her grip on her daughter's hand and allowed herself to be towed, softly, through the darkness.

Like Mars or the sea, the moon would influence the outlook (not to mention the leisure activities) of its citizens. But Heinlein here reminds us of an important fact—human nature remains human nature, on earth or off.

The Menace from Earth
by Robert Heinlein

My name is Holly Jones and I'm fifteen. I'm very intelligent but it doesn't show, because I look like an underdone angel. Insipid.

I was born right here in Luna City, which seems to surprise Earthside types. Actually, I'm third generation; my grandparents pioneered in Site One, where the Memorial is. I live with my parents in Artemis Apartments, the new co-op in Pressure Five, eight hundred feet down near City Hall. But I'm not there much; I'm too busy.

Mornings I attend Tech High and afternoons I study or go flying with Jeff Hardesty—he's my partner—or, whenever a tourist ship is in, I guide groundhogs. This day the *Gripsholm* grounded at noon so I went straight from school to American Express.

The first gaggle of tourists was trickling in from Quarantine, but I didn't push forward as Mr. Dorcas, the manager, knows I'm the best. Guiding is just temporary (I'm really a spaceship designer), but if you're doing a job you ought to do it well.

Mr. Dorcas spotted me. "Holly! Here, please. Miss Brentwood, Holly Jones will be your guide."

" 'Holly,' " she repeated. "What a quaint name. Are you really a guide, dear?"

I'm tolerant of groundhogs—some of my best friends are from Earth. As daddy says, "Being born on Luna is luck, not judgment, and most people Earthside are stuck there." After all, Jesus and Gautama Buddha and Dr. Einstein were all groundhogs.

But they can be irritating. If high school kids weren't guides, who could they hire? "My license says so," I said briskly and looked her over the way she was looking me over.

Her face was sort of familiar and I thought, perhaps, I had seen her picture in those society things you see in Earthside magazines—one of the rich playgirls we get too many of. She was almost loathsomely lovely . . . nylon skin, soft, wavy, silver-blonde hair, basic specs about 35-24-34 and enough this and that to make me feel like a matchstick drawing, a low intimate voice, and everything necessary to make plainer females think about pacts with the Devil. But I did not feel apprehensive; she was a groundhog and groundhogs don't count.

"All City guides are girls," Mr. Dorcas explained. "Holly is very competent."

"Oh, I'm sure," she answered quickly and went into tourist routine number one: surprise that a guide was needed just to find her hotel, amazement at no taxicabs, same for no porters and raised eyebrows at the prospect of two girls walking alone through "an underground city."

Mr. Dorcas was patient, ending with, "Miss Brentwood, Luna City is the only metropolis in the solar system where a woman is really safe—no dark alleys, no deserted neighborhoods, no criminal element."

I didn't listen; I just held out my tariff card for Mr. Dorcas to stamp and picked up her bags. Guides shouldn't carry bags and most tourists are delighted to experience the fact that their thirty-pound allowance weighs only five pounds, but I wanted to get her moving.

We were in the tunnel outside and me with a foot on the slidebelt, when she stopped. "I forgot! I want a City map."

"None available."

"Really?"

"There's only one. That's why you need a guide."

"But why don't they supply them? Or would that throw you guides out of work?"

See? "You think guiding is makework? Miss Brentwood, labor is so scarce they'd hire monkeys if they could."

"Then why not print maps?"

"Because Luna City isn't flat like—" I almost said, "groundhog Cities," but I caught myself.

". . . like Earthside Cities," I went on. "All you saw from space was the meteor shield. Underneath it spreads out and goes down for miles in a dozen pressure zones."

"Yes, I know, but why not a map for each level?"

Groundhogs always say, "Yes, I know, but—"

"I can show you the one City map. It's a stereo tank twenty feet high and, even so, all you see clearly are big things like the Hall of the Mountain King and hydroponics farms and the Bats' Cave."

"'The Bats' Cave,'" she repeated. "That's where they fly, isn't it?"

"Yes, that's where we fly."

"Oh, I want to see it!"

"OK. It first . . . or the City map?"

She decided to go to her hotel first. The regular route to the Zurich is to slide up and west through Gray's Tunnel past the Martian Embassy, get off at the Mormon Temple, and take a pressure lock down to Diana Boulevard. But I know all the shortcuts; we got off at Macy-Gimbel Upper to go down their personnel hoist. I thought she would enjoy it.

But when I told her to grab a hand grip as it dropped past her, she peered down the shaft and edged back. "You're joking."

I was about to take her back the regular way when a neighbor of ours came down the hoist. I said, "Hello, Mrs. Greenberg," and she called back, "Hi, Holly. How are your folks?"

Susie Greenberg is more than plump. She was hanging by one hand with young David tucked in her other arm and holding the *Daily Lunatic*, reading as she dropped. Miss Brentwood stared, bit her lip, and said, "How do I do it?"

I said, "Oh, use both hands; I'll take the bags." I tied the handles together with my hanky and went first.

She was shaking when we got to the bottom. "Goodness, Holly, how do you stand it? Don't you get homesick?"

Tourist question number six. . . . I said, "I've been to Earth," and let it drop. Two years ago mother made me visit my aunt in Omaha and I was *miserable*—hot and cold and dirty and beset by creepy-crawlies. I weighed a ton and I ached, and my aunt was always chivvying me to go outdoors and exercise when all I wanted was to crawl into a tub and be quietly wretched. And I had hay fever. Probably you've never heard of hay fever—you don't die but you wish you could.

I was supposed to go to a girls' boarding school but I phoned daddy and told him I was desperate, and he let me come home. What groundhogs can't understand is that *they* live in savagery. But groundhogs are groundhogs and loonies are loonies and never the twain shall meet.

Like all the best hotels the Zurich is in Pressure One on the west side so that it can have a view of Earth. I helped Miss Brentwood register with the roboclerk and found her room; it had its own port. She went straight to it, began staring at Earth and going *ooh!* and *ahh!*

I glanced past her and saw that it was a few minutes past thirteen; sunset sliced straight down the tip of India—early enough to snag another client. "Will that be all, Miss Brentwood?"

Instead of answering she said in an awed voice, "Holly, isn't that the most beautiful sight you ever saw?"

"It's nice," I agreed. The view on that side is monotonous except for Earth hanging in the sky—but Earth is what tourists always look at even though they've just left it. Still, Earth is pretty. The changing weather is interesting if you don't have to be in it. Did you ever endure a summer in Omaha?

"It's gorgeous," she whispered.

"Sure," I agreed. "Do you want to go somewhere? Or will you sign my card?"

"What? Excuse me, I was daydreaming. No, not right now—yes, I do! Holly, I want to go out *there!* I must! Is there time? How much longer will it be light?"

"Huh? It's two days to sunset."

She looked startled. "How quaint. Holly, can you get us space suits? I've got to go outside."

I didn't wince—I'm used to tourist talk. I suppose a pressure suit looks like a space suit to them. I simply said, "We girls aren't licensed outside. But I can phone a friend."

Jeff Hardesty is my partner in spaceship designing, so I throw business his way. Jeff is eighteen and already in Goddard Institute, but I'm pushing hard to catch up so that we can set up offices for our firm: JONES & HARDESTY, SPACESHIP ENGINEERS. I'm very bright in mathematics, which is everything in space engineering, so I'll get my degree pretty fast. Meanwhile we design ships anyhow.

I didn't tell Miss Brentwood this, as tourists think that a girl my age can't possibly be a spaceship designer.

Jeff has arranged his classes to let him guide on Tuesdays and Thursdays; he waits at West City Lock and studies between clients. I reached him on the lockmaster's phone. Jeff grinned and said, "Hi, Scale Model."

"Hi, Penalty Weight. Free to take a client?"

"Well, I was supposed to guide a family party, but they're late."

"Cancel them. Miss Brentwood . . . step into pickup, please. This is Mr. Hardesty."

Jeff's eyes widened and I felt uneasy. But it did not occur to me that Jeff could be attracted by a *groundhog* . . . even though it is conceded that men are robot-slaves of their body chemistry in such matters. I knew she was exceptionally decorative, but it was unthinkable that Jeff could be captivated by any groundhog, no matter how well designed. They don't speak our language!

I am not romantic about Jeff; we are simply partners. But anything that affects Jones & Hardesty affects me.

When we joined him at West Lock he almost stepped on his tongue in a disgusting display of adolescent rut. I was ashamed of him and, for the first time, apprehensive. Why are males so childish?

Miss Brentwood didn't seem to mind his behavior. Jeff is a big hulk; suited up for outside he looks like a frost giant from *Das Rheingold*; she smiled up at him and thanked him for changing his schedule. He looked even sillier and told her it was a pleasure.

I keep my pressure suit at West Lock so that when I switch a client to Jeff he can invite me to come along for the walk. This time he hardly spoke to me after that platinum menace was in sight. But I helped her pick out a suit and took her into the dressing room and fitted it. Those rental suits take careful adjusting or they will pinch you in tender places once out in vacuum . . . besides there are things about them that one girl ought to explain to another.

When I came out with her, not wearing my own, Jeff

didn't even ask why I hadn't suited up—he took her arm and started toward the lock. I had to butt in to get her to sign my tariff card.

The days that followed were the longest in my life. I saw Jeff only once . . . on the slidebelt in Diana Boulevard, going the other way. She was with him.

Though I saw him but once, I knew what was going on. He was cutting classes, and three nights running he took her to the Earthview Room of the Duncan Hines. None of my business!—I hope she had more luck teaching him to dance than I had. Jeff is a free citizen and if he wanted to make an utter fool of himself neglecting school and losing sleep over an upholstered groundhog, that was his business.

But he should not have neglected the firm's business!

Jones & Hardesty had a tremendous backlog because we were designing starship *Prometheus*. This project we had been slaving over for a year, flying not more than twice a week in order to devote time to it—and that's a sacrifice.

Of course you can't build a starship today, because of the power plant. But daddy thinks that there will soon be a technological breakthrough and mass-conversion power plants will be built—which means starships. Daddy ought to know—he's Luna chief engineer for Space Lanes and Fermi lecturer at Goddard Institute. So Jeff and I are designing a self-supporting interstellar ship on that assumption: quarters, auxiliaries, surgery, labs—everything.

Daddy thinks it's just practice but mother knows better—mother is a mathematical chemist for General Synthetics of Luna, and is nearly as smart as I am. She realizes that Jones & Hardesty plans to be ready with a finished proposal while other designers are still floundering.

That was why I was furious with Jeff for wasting time over this creature. We had been working every possible chance. Jeff would show up after dinner, we would finish our homework, then get down to real work, the *Prometheus* . . . checking each other's computations, fighting bitterly over details, and having a wonderful time. But the very day I introduced him to Ariel Brentwood, he failed to appear. I had finished my lessons and was wondering whether to start or to wait for him—we were making a radical change in power-plant shielding—when his mother phoned me. "Jeff asked me to call you, dear. He's having dinner with a tourist client and can't come over."

Mrs. Hardesty was watching me so I looked puzzled and said, "Jeff thought I was expecting him? He has his dates mixed up." I don't think she believed me; she agreed too quickly.

All that week I was slowly convinced against my will that Jones & Hardesty was being liquidated. Jeff didn't break any more dates—how can you break a date that hasn't been made?—but we always went flying Thursday afternoons unless one of us was guiding. He didn't call. Oh, I know where he was; he took her ice-skating in Fingal's Cave.

I stayed home and worked on the *Prometheus*, recalculating masses and moment arms for hydroponics and stores on the basis of the shielding change. But I made mistakes and twice I had to look up logarithms instead of remembering them . . . I was so used to wrangling with Jeff over everything that I just couldn't function.

Presently I looked at the nameplate of the sheet I was revising. "Jones & Hardesty" it read, like all the rest. I said to myself, "Holly Jones, quit bluffing; this may be *the end*. You knew that someday Jeff would fall for somebody. Of course . . . but not a *groundhog*. But he *did*. What kind of an engineer are you if you can't face facts? She's beautiful and rich—she'll get her father to give him a job Earthside. You hear me? *Earthside!* So you look for another partner . . . or go into business on your own."

I erased JONES & HARDESTY and lettered JONES

& COMPANY and stared at it. Then I started to erase that, too—but it smeared; I had dripped a tear on it. That was ridiculous!

The following Tuesday both daddy and mother were home for lunch which was unusual as daddy lunches at the spaceport. Now daddy can't even see you unless you're a spaceship, but he picked that day to notice that I had dialed only a salad and hadn't finished it. "That plate is about eight hundred calories short," he said, peering at it. "You can't boost without fuel—aren't you well?"

"Quite well, thank you," I answered with dignity.

"Mmm . . . now that I think back, you've been moping for several days. Maybe you need a checkup." He looked at mother.

"I do not need a checkup either!" I had *not* been moping—doesn't a woman have a right not to chatter?

But I hate to have doctors poking at me so I added, "It happens I'm eating lightly because I'm going flying this afternoon. But if you insist, I'll order pot roast and potatoes and sleep instead!"

"Easy, punkin'," he answered gently. "I didn't mean to intrude. Get yourself a snack when you're through . . . and say hello to Jeff for me."

I simply answered, "Okay," and asked to be excused; I was humiliated by the assumption that I couldn't fly without Mr. Jefferson Hardesty, but did not wish to discuss it.

Daddy called after me, "Don't be late for dinner," and mother said, "Now, Jacob—" and to me, "Fly until you're tired, dear; you haven't been getting much exercise. I'll leave your dinner in the warmer. Anything you'd like?"

"No, whatever you dial for yourself." I just wasn't interested in food, which isn't like me. As I headed for Bats' Cave I wondered if I had caught something. But my cheeks didn't feel warm and my stomach wasn't upset even if I wasn't hungry.

Then I had a horrible thought. Could it be that I was jealous? *Me?*

It was unthinkable. I am not romantic; I am a career woman. Jeff had been my partner and pal, and under my guidance he could have become a great spaceship designer, but our relationship was straightforward . . . a mutual respect for each other's abilities, with never any of that lovey-dovey stuff. A career woman can't afford such things —why look at all the professional time mother had lost over having me!

No, I couldn't be jealous; I was simply worried sick because my partner had become involved with a groundhog. Jeff isn't bright about women and, besides, he's never been to Earth and has illusions about it. If she lured him Earthside, Jones & Hardesty was finished.

And somehow, "Jones & Company" wasn't a substitute: the *Prometheus* might never be built.

I was at Bats' Cave when I reached this dismal conclusion. I didn't feel like flying, but I went to the locker room and got my wings anyhow.

Most of the stuff written about Bats' Cave gives a wrong impression. It's the air-storage tank for the City, just like all the colonies have—the place where the scavenger pumps, deep down, deliver the air until it's needed. We just happen to be lucky enough to have one big enough to fly in. But it never was built, or anything like that; it's just a big volcanic bubble, two miles across, and if it had broken through, way back when, it would have been a crater.

Tourists sometimes pity us loonies because we have no chance to swim. Well, I tried it in Omaha and got water up my nose and scared myself silly. Water is for drinking, not playing in; I'll take flying. I've heard groundhogs say, oh yes, they had "flown" many times. But that's not *flying*. I did what they talk about, between White Sands and Omaha. I felt awful and got sick. Those things aren't safe.

I left my shoes and skirt in the locker room and slipped my tail surfaces on my feet, then zipped into my wings and got someone to tighten the shoulder straps. My wings aren't ready-made condors; they are Storer-Gulls, custom-made for my weight distribution and dimensions. I've cost daddy a pretty penny in wings, outgrowing them so often, but these latest I bought myself with guide fees.

They're lovely!—titanalloy struts as light and strong as bird bones, tension-compensated wrist-pinion and shoulder joints, natural action in the alula slots, and automatic flap action in stalling. The wing skeleton is dressed in styrene feather-foils with individual quilling of scapulars and primaries. They almost fly themselves.

I folded my wings and went into the lock. While it was cycling, I opened my left wing and thumbed the alula control—I had noticed a tendency to sideslip the last time I was airborne. But the alula opened properly and I decided I must have been overcontrolling, easy to do with Storer-Gulls; they're extremely maneuverable. Then the door showed green and I folded the wing and hurried out, glancing at the barometer. Seventeen pounds—two more than Earth sea level and nearly twice what we use in the City; even an ostrich could fly in that. I perked up and felt sorry for all groundhogs, tied down by six times proper weight, who never, never, *never* could fly.

Not even I could, on Earth. My wing-loading is less than a pound per square foot; as wings and all I weigh less than twenty pounds. Earthside that would be over a hundred pounds, and I could flap forever and never get off the ground.

I felt so good that I forgot about Jeff and his weakness. I spread my wings, ran a few steps, warped for lift, and grabbed air—lifted my feet and was airborne.

I sculled gently and let myself glide toward the air intake at the middle of the floor—the Baby's Ladder, we call it, because you can ride the up-draft clear to the roof, half a mile above, and never move a wing. When I felt it I leaned right, spoiling with right primaries, corrected, and settled in a counterclockwise soaring glide and let it carry me toward the roof.

A couple of hundred feet up, I looked around. The cave was almost empty, not more than two hundred in the air and half that number perched or on the ground—room enough for didoes. So as soon as I was up five hundred feet I leaned out of the updraft and began to beat. Gliding is no effort, but flying is as hard work as you care to make it. In gliding I support a mere ten pounds on each arm—shucks, on Earth you work harder than that lying in bed. The lift that keeps you in the air doesn't take any work; you get it free from the shape of your wings just as long as there is air pouring past them.

Even without an up-draft all a level glide takes is gentle sculling with your fingertips to maintain air speed; a feeble old lady could do it. The lift comes from differential air pressures but you don't have to understand it; you just scull a little and the air supports you, as if you were lying in an utterly perfect bed. Sculling keeps you moving forward just like sculling a rowboat . . . or so I'm told; I've never been in a rowboat. I had a chance to in Nebraska but I'm not that foolhardy.

But when you're really flying, you scull with forearms as well as hands and add power with your shoulder muscles. Instead of only the outer quills of your primaries changing pitch (as in gliding), now your primaries and secondaries clear back to the joint warp sharply on each downbeat and recovery; they no longer lift, they force you forward—while your weight is carried by your scapulars, up under your armpits.

So you fly faster, or climb, or both, through controlling the angle of attack with your feet—with the tail surfaces you wear on your feet, I mean.

Oh dear, this sounds complicated and isn't—you just

do it. You fly exactly as a bird flies. Baby birds can learn it and they aren't very bright. Anyhow, it's easy as breathing after you learn how . . . and more fun than you can imagine!

I climbed to the roof with powerful beats, increasing my angle of attack and slotting my alulae for lift without burble—climbing at an angle that would stall most fliers. I'm little but it's all muscle and I've been flying since I was six. Once up there I glided and looked around. Down at the floor near the south wall, tourists were trying glide wings —if you call those things "wings." Along the west wall the visitors' gallery was loaded with goggling tourists. I wondered if Jeff and his Circe character were there, and decided to go down and find out.

So I went into a steep dive and swooped toward the gallery, leveled off and flew very fast along it. I didn't spot Jeff and his groundhoggess but I wasn't watching where I was going and overtook another flier, almost colliding. I glimpsed him just in time to stall and drop under, and fell fifty feet before I got control. Neither of us was in danger as the gallery is two hundred feet up, but I looked silly and it was my own fault; I had violated a safety rule.

There aren't many rules but they are necessary; the first is that orange wings always have the right of way— they're beginners. This flier did not have orange wings but I was overtaking. The flier underneath—or being overtaken—or nearer the wall—or turning counterclockwise, in that order, has the right of way.

I felt foolish and wondered who had seen me, so I went all the way back up, made sure I had clear air, then stooped like a hawk toward the gallery, spilling wings, lifting tail, and letting myself fall like a rock.

I completed my stoop in front of the gallery, lowering and spreading my tail so hard that I could feel leg muscles knot, and grabbing air with both wings, alulae slotted. I pulled level in an extremely fast glide along the gallery. I could see their eyes pop and thought smugly, "There! That'll show 'em!"

When darn if somebody didn't stoop on *me!* The blast from a flier braking right over me almost knocked me out of control. I grabbed air and stopped a sideslip, used some shipyard words, and looked around to see who had blitzed me. I knew the black-and-gold wing pattern—Mary Muhlenburg, my best girl friend. She swung toward me, pivoting on a wing tip. "Hi, Holly! Scared you, didn't I?"

"You did not! You better be careful; the flightmaster'll ground you for a month."

"Slim chance! He's down for coffee."

I flew away, still annoyed, and started to climb. Mary called after me, but I ignored her, thinking, "Mary, my girl, I'm going to get over you and fly you right out of the air."

This was a foolish thought as Mary flies every day and has shoulders and pectoral muscles like Mrs. Hercules. By the time she caught up with me I had cooled off and we flew side by side, still climbing. "Perch?" she called out.

"Perch," I agreed. Mary has lovely gossip and I could use a breather. We turned toward our usual perch, a ceiling brace for flood lamps—it isn't supposed to be a perch but the flightmaster hardly ever comes up there.

Mary flew in ahead of me, braked, and stalled dead to a perfect landing. I skidded a little but Mary stuck out a wing and steadied me. It isn't easy to come into a perch, especially when you have to approach level. Two years ago a boy who had just graduated from orange wings tried it . . . knocked off his left alula and primaries on a strut—went fluttering and spinning down two thousand feet and crashed. He could have saved himself—you can come in safely with a badly damaged wing if you spill air with the other and accept the steeper glide, then stall as you land. But this poor kid didn't know how; he broke his neck, dead as Icarus. I haven't used that perch since.

We folded our wings and Mary sidled over. "Jeff is looking for you," she said with a sly grin.

My insides jumped but I answered coolly, "So? I didn't know he was here."

"Sure. Down there," she added, pointing with her left wing. "Spot him?"

Jeff wears striped red-and-silver, but she was pointing at the tourist glide slope, a mile away. "No."

"He's there all right." She looked at me sideways. "But I wouldn't look him up if I were you."

"Why not? Or for that matter, why should I?" Mary can be exasperating.

"Huh? You always run when he whistles. But he has that Earthside siren in tow again today; you might find it embarrassing."

"Mary, whatever are you talking about?"

"Huh? Don't kid me, Holly Jones; you know what I mean."

"I'm sure I don't," I answered with cold dignity.

"Humph! Then you're the only person in Luna City who doesn't. Everybody knows you're crazy about Jeff; everybody knows she's cut you out . . . and that you are simply simmering with jealousy."

Mary is my dearest friend but someday I'm going to skin her for a rug. "Mary, that's preposterously ridiculous! How can you even think such a thing?"

"Look, darling, you don't have to pretend. I'm for you." She patted my shoulders with her secondaries.

So I pushed her over backward. She fell a hundred feet, straightened out, circled and climbed, and came in beside me, still grinning. It gave me time to decide what to say.

"Mary Muhlenburg, in the first place I am not crazy about anyone, least of all Jeff Hardesty. He and I are simply friends. So it's utterly nonsensical to talk about me being 'jealous.' In the second place Miss Brentwood is a lady and doesn't go around 'cutting out' anyone, least of all me. In the third place she is simply a tourist Jeff is guiding —business, nothing more."

"Sure, sure," Mary agreed placidly. "I was wrong. Still—" She shrugged her wings and shut up.

" 'Still' what? Mary, don't be mealy-mouthed."

"Mmm . . . I was wondering how you knew I was talking about Ariel Brentwood—since there isn't anything to it."

"Why, you mentioned her name."

"I did not."

I thought frantically. "Uh, maybe not. But it's perfectly simple. Miss Brentwood is a client I turned over to Jeff myself, so I assumed that she must be the tourist you meant."

"So? I don't recall even saying she was a tourist. But since she is just a tourist you two are splitting, why aren't you doing the inside guiding while Jeff sticks to outside work? I thought you guides had an agreement?"

"Huh? If he has been guiding her inside the City, I'm not aware of it—"

"You're the only one who isn't."

". . . and I'm not interested; that's up to the grievance committee. But Jeff wouldn't take a fee for inside guiding in any case."

"Oh, sure!—not one he could *bank*. Well, Holly, seeing I was wrong, why don't you give him a hand with her? She wants to learn to glide."

Butting in on that pair was furthest from my mind. "If Mr. Hardesty wants my help, he will ask me. In the meantime I shall mind my own business . . . a practice I recommend to you!"

"Relax, shipmate," she answered, unruffled. "I was doing you a favor."

"Thank you, I don't need one."

"So I'll be on my way—got to practice for the gymkhana." She leaned forward and dropped off. But she didn't practice aerobatics; she dived straight for the tourist slope.

I watched her out of sight, then sneaked my left hand out the hand slit and got at my hanky—awkward when you are wearing wings but the floodlights had made my eyes water. I wiped them and blew my nose and put my hanky away and wiggled my hand back into place, then checked everything, thumbs, toes, and fingers, preparatory to dropping off.

But I didn't. I just sat there, wings drooping, and thought. I had to admit that Mary was partly right; Jeff's head was turned completely . . . over a *groundhog*. So sooner or later he would go Earthside, and Jones & Hardesty was finished.

Then I reminded myself that I had been planning to be a spaceship designer like daddy long before Jeff and I teamed up. I wasn't dependent on anyone; I could stand alone, like Joan of Arc, or Lise Meitner.

I felt better . . . a cold, stern pride, like Lucifer in *Paradise Lost*.

I recognized the red and silver of Jeff's wings while he was far off and I thought about slipping quietly away. But Jeff can overtake me if he tries, so I decided, "Holly, don't be a fool! You've no reason to run . . . just be coolly polite."

He landed by me but didn't sidle up. "Hi, Decimal Point."

"Hi, Zero. Uh, stolen much lately?"

"Just the City Bank but they made me put it back." He frowned and added, "Holly, are you mad at me?"

"Why, Jeff, whatever gave you such a silly notion?"

"Uh . . . something Mary the Mouth said."

"Her? Don't pay any attention to what *she* says. Half of it's always wrong and she doesn't mean the rest."

"Yeah, a short circuit between her ears. Then you aren't mad?"

"Of *course* not. Why should I be?"

"No reason I know of. I haven't been around to work on the ship for a few days . . . but I've been awfully busy."

"Think nothing of it. I've been terribly busy myself."

"Uh, that's fine. Look, Test Sample, do me a favor. Help me out with a friend—a client, that is—well, she's a friend, too. She wants to learn to use glide wings."

I pretended to consider it. "Anyone I know?"

"Oh, yes. Fact is, you introduced us. Ariel Brentwood."

" 'Brentwood?' Jeff, there are so many tourists. Let me think. Tall girl? Blonde? Extremely pretty?"

He grinned like a goof and I almost pushed him off. "That's Ariel!"

"I recall her . . . she expected me to carry her bags. But you don't need help, Jeff. She seemed very clever. Good sense of balance."

"Oh, yes, sure, all of that. Well, the fact is, I want you two to know each other. She's . . . well, she's just wonderful, Holly. A real person all the way through. You'll love her when you know her better. Uh . . . this seemed like a good chance."

I felt dizzy. "Why, that's very thoughtful, Jeff, but I doubt if she wants to know me better. I'm just a servant she hired—you know groundhogs."

"But she's not at all like the ordinary groundhog. And she does want to know you better—she *told* me so!"

After you told her to think so! I muttered. But I had talked myself into a corner. If I had not been hampered by polite upbringing I would have said, "On your way, vacuum skull! I'm not interested in your groundhog girl friends"—but what I did say was, "Okay, Jeff," then gathered the fox to my bosom and dropped off into a glide.

So I taught Ariel Brentwood to "fly." Look, those so-called wings they let tourists wear have fifty square feet of lift surface, no controls except warp in the primaries, a built-in dihedral to make them stable as a table, and a few meaningless degrees of hinging to let the wearer think that he is "flying" by waving his arms. The tail is rigid and canted so that if you stall (almost impossible), you land on your feet. All a tourist does is run a few yards, lift up his feet (he can't avoid it), and slide down a blanket of air. Then he can tell his grandchildren how he flew, really *flew*, "just like a bird."

An ape could learn to "fly" that much.

I put myself to the humiliation of strapping on a set of the silly things and had Ariel watch while I swung into the Baby's Ladder and let it carry me up a hundred feet to show her that you really and truly could "fly" with them. Then I thankfully got rid of them, strapped her into a larger set, and put on my beautiful Storer-Gulls. I had chased Jeff away (two instructors is too many), but when he saw her wing up, he swooped down and landed by us.

I looked up. "You again."

"Hello, Ariel. Hi, Blip. Say, you've got her shoulder straps too tight."

"Tut, tut," I said. "One coach at a time, remember? If you want to help, shuck those gaudy fins and put on some gliders . . . then I'll use you to show how not to. Otherwise get above two hundred feet and stay there; we don't need any dining-lounge pilots."

Jeff pouted like a brat but Ariel backed me up. "Do what teacher says, Jeff. That's a good boy."

He wouldn't put on gliders but he didn't stay clear, either. He circled around us, watching, and got bawled out by the flightmaster for cluttering the tourist area.

I admit Ariel was a good pupil. She didn't even get sore when I suggested that she was rather mature across the hips to balance well; she just said that she had noticed that I had the slimmest behind around there and she envied me. So I quit trying to get her goat, and found myself almost liking her as long as I kept my mind firmly on teaching. She tried hard and learned fast—good reflexes and (despite my dirty crack) good balance. I remarked on it and she admitted diffidently that she had had ballet training.

About mid-afternoon she said, "Could I possibly try real wings?"

"Huh? Gee, Ariel, I don't think so."

"Why not?"

There she had me. She had already done all that could be done with those atrocious gliders. If she was to learn more, she had to have real wings. "Ariel, it's dangerous. It's not what you've been doing, believe me. You might get hurt, even killed."

"Would you be held responsible?"

"No. You signed a release when you came in."

"Then I'd like to try it."

I bit my lip. If she had cracked up without my help, I wouldn't have shed a tear—but to let her do something too dangerous while she was my pupil . . . well, it smacked of David and Uriah. "Ariel, I can't stop you . . . but I should put my wings away and not have anything to do with it."

It was her turn to bite her lip. "If you feel that way, I can't ask you to coach me. But I still want to. Perhaps Jeff will help me."

"He probably will," I blurted out, "if he is as big a fool as I think he is!"

Her company face slipped but she didn't say anything because just then Jeff stalled in beside us. "What's the discussion?"

We both tried to tell him and confused him for he got the idea I had suggested it, and started bawling me out. Was I crazy? Was I trying to get Ariel hurt? Didn't I have any sense?

"*Shut up!*" I yelled, then added quietly but firmly, "Jefferson Hardesty, you wanted me to teach your girl friend, so I agreed. But don't butt in and don't think you can get away with talking to me like that. Now beat it! Take wing. Grab air!"

He swelled up and said slowly, "I absolutely forbid it."

Silence for five long counts. Then Ariel said quietly, "Come, Holly. Let's get me some wings."

"Right, Ariel."

But they don't rent real wings. Fliers have their own; they have to. However, there are second-hand ones for sale because kids outgrow them, or people shift to custom-made ones, or something. I found Mr. Schultz, who keeps the key, and said that Ariel was thinking of buying but I wouldn't let her without a tryout. After picking over forty-odd pairs I found a set which Johnny Queveras had outgrown but which I knew were all right. Nevertheless I inspected them carefully. I could hardly reach the finger controls but they fitted Ariel.

While I was helping her into the tail surfaces I said, "Ariel? This is still a bad idea."

"I know. But we can't let men think they own us."

"I suppose not."

"They do own us, of course. But we shouldn't let them know it." She was feeling out the tail controls. "The big toes spread them?"

"Yes. But don't do it. Just keep your feet together and toes pointed. Look, Ariel, you really aren't ready. Today all you will do is glide, just as you've been doing. Promise?"

She looked me in the eye. "I'll do exactly what you say . . . not even take wing unless you okay it."

"Okay. Ready?"

"I'm ready."

"All right. Wups! I goofed. They aren't orange."

"Does it matter?"

"It sure does." There followed a weary argument because Mr. Schultz didn't want to spray them orange for a tryout. Ariel settled it by buying them, then we had to wait a bit while the solvent dried.

We went back to the tourist slope and I let her glide, cautioning her to hold both alulae open with her thumbs for more lift at slow speeds, while barely sculling with her fingers. She did fine, and stumbled in landing only once. Jeff stuck around, cutting figure eights above us, but we ignored him. Presently I taught her to turn in a wide, gentle bank—you can turn those awful glider things but it takes skill; they're only meant for straight glide.

Finally I landed by her and said, "Had enough?"

"I'll never have enough! But I'll unwing if you say."

"Tired?"

"No." She glanced over her wing at the Baby's Ladder; a dozen fliers were going up it, wings motionless, soaring lazily. "I wish I could do that just once. It must be heaven."

I chewed it over. "Actually, the higher you are, the safer you are."

"Then why not?"

"Mmm . . . safer *provided* you know what you're doing. Going up that draft is just gliding like you've been doing. You lie still and let it lift you half a mile high. Then you come down the same way, circling the wall in a gentle glide. But you're going to be tempted to do something you don't understand yet—flap your wings, or cut some caper."

She shook her head solemnly. "I won't do anything you haven't taught me."

I was still worried. "Look, it's only half a mile up but you cover five miles getting there and more getting down. Half an hour at least. Will your arms take it?"

"I'm sure they will."

"Well . . . you can start down anytime; you don't

have to go all the way. Flex your arms a little now and then, so they won't cramp. Just don't flap your wings."

"I won't."

"Okay." I spread my wings. "Follow me."

I led her into the up-draft, leaned gently right, then back left to start the counterclockwise climb, all the while sculling very slowly so that she could keep up. Once we were in the groove I called out, "Steady as you are!" and cut out suddenly, climbed, and took station thirty feet over and behind her. "Ariel?"

"Yes, Holly?"

"I'll stay over you. Don't crane your neck; you don't have to watch me, I have to watch you. You're doing fine."

"I feel fine!"

"Wiggle a little. Don't stiffen up. It's a long way to the roof. You can scull harder if you want to."

"Aye aye, Cap'n!"

"Not tired?"

"Heavens, no! Girl, I'm living!" She giggled. "And mama said I'd never be an angel!"

I didn't answer because red-and-silver wings came charging at me, braked suddenly and settled into the circle between me and Ariel. Jeff's face was almost as red as his wings. "What the devil do you think you are doing?"

"Orange wings!" I yelled. "Keep clear!"

"Get down out of here! Both of you!"

"Get out from between me and my pupil. You know the rules."

"Ariel!" Jeff shouted. "Lean out of the circle and glide down. I'll stay with you."

"Jeff Hardesty," I said savagely, "I give you three seconds to get out from between us—then I'm going to report you for violation of Rule One. For the third time—*Orange Wings!*"

Jeff growled something, dipped his right wing, and

dropped out of formation. The idiot sideslipped within five feet of Ariel's wing tip. I should have reported him for that; all the room you can give a beginner is none too much.

I said, "Okay, Ariel?"

"Okay, Holly. I'm sorry Jeff is angry."

"He'll get over it. Tell me if you feel tired."

"I'm not. I want to go all the way up. How high are we?"

"Four hundred feet, maybe."

Jeff flew below us a while, then climbed and flew over us . . . probably for the same reason I did, to see better. It suited me to have two of us watching her as long as he didn't interfere; I was beginning to fret that Ariel might not realize that the way down was going to be as long and tiring as the way up. I was hoping she would cry uncle. I knew I could glide until forced down by starvation. But a beginner gets tense.

Jeff stayed generally over us, sweeping back and forth —he's too active to glide very long—while Ariel and I continued to soar, winding slowly up toward the roof. It finally occurred to me when we were about halfway up that I could cry uncle myself; I didn't have to wait for Ariel to weaken. So I called out, "Ariel? Tired now?"

"No."

"Well, I am. Could we go down, please?"

She didn't argue, she just said, "All right. What am I to do?"

"Lean right and get out of the circle." I intended to have her move out five or six hundred feet, get into the return down-draft, and circle the cave down instead of up. I glanced up, looking for Jeff. I finally spotted him some distance away and much higher but coming toward us. I called out, "Jeff! See you on the ground." He might not have heard me but he would see if he didn't hear; I glanced back at Ariel.

I couldn't find her.

Then I saw her, a hundred feet below—flailing her wings and falling, out of control.

I didn't know how it happened. Maybe she leaned too far, went into a sideslip, and started to struggle. But I didn't try to figure it out; I was simply filled with horror. I seemed to hang there frozen for an hour while I watched her.

But the fact appears to be that I screamed "*Jeff!*" and broke into a stoop.

But I didn't seem to fall, couldn't overtake her. I spilled my wings completely—but couldn't manage to fall; she was as far away as ever.

You do start slowly, of course; our low gravity is the only thing that makes human flying possible. Even a stone falls a scant three feet in the first second. But that first second seemed endless.

Then I knew I was falling. I could feel rushing air— but I still didn't seem to close on her. Her struggles must have slowed her somewhat, while I was in an intentional stoop, wings spilled and raised over my head, falling as fast as possible. I had a wild notion that if I could pull even with her, I could shout sense into her head, get her to dive, then straighten out in a glide. But I couldn't *reach* her.

This nightmare dragged on for hours.

Actually we didn't have room to fall for more than twenty seconds; that's all it takes to stoop a thousand feet. But twenty seconds can be horribly long . . . long enough to regret every foolish thing I had ever done or said, long enough to say a prayer for us both . . . and to say good-bye to Jeff in my heart. Long enough to see the floor rushing toward us and to know that we were both going to crash if I didn't overtake her mighty quick.

I glanced up and Jeff was stooping right over us but a long way up. I looked down at once . . . and I was overtaking her . . . I was passing her—*I was under her!*

Then I was braking with everything I had, almost pulling my wings off. I grabbed air, held it, and started to beat without ever going to level flight. I beat once, twice, three times . . . and hit her from below, jarring us both.

Then the floor hit us.

I felt feeble and dreamily contented. I was on my back in a dim room. I think mother was with me and I know daddy was. My nose itched and I tried to scratch it, but my arms wouldn't work. I fell asleep again.

I woke up hungry and wide awake. I was in a hospital bed and my arms still wouldn't work, which wasn't surprising as they were both in casts. A nurse came in with a tray. "Hungry?" she asked.

"Starved," I admitted.

"We'll fix that." She started feeding me like a baby.

I dodged the third spoonful and demanded, "What happened to my arms?"

"Hush," she said and gagged me with a spoon.

But a nice doctor came in later and answered my question. "Nothing much. Three simple fractures. At your age you'll heal in no time. But we like your company so I'm holding you for observation of possible internal injury."

"I'm not hurt inside," I told him. "At least, I don't hurt."

"I told you it was just an excuse."

"Uh, Doctor?"

"Well?"

"Will I be able to fly again?" I waited, scared.

"Certainly. I've seen men hurt worse get up and go three rounds."

"Oh. Well, thanks. Doctor? What happened to the other girl? Is she . . . did she? . . ."

"Brentwood? She's here."

"She's right here," Ariel agreed from the door. "May I come in?"

My jaw dropped, then I said, "Yeah. Sure. Come in."

The doctor said, "Don't stay long," and left.

I said, "Well, sit down."

"Thanks." She hopped instead of walked and I saw that one foot was bandaged. She got on the end of the bed.

"You hurt your foot."

She shrugged. "Nothing. A sprain and a torn ligament. Two cracked ribs. But I would have been dead. You know why I'm not?"

I didn't answer. She touched one of my casts. "That's why. You broke my fall and I landed on top of you. You saved my life and I broke both your arms."

"You don't have to thank me. I would have done it for anybody."

"I believe you and I wasn't thanking you. You can't thank a person for saving your life. I just wanted to make sure you knew that I knew it."

I didn't have an answer so I said, "Where's Jeff? Is he all right?"

"He'll be along soon. Jeff's not hurt . . . though I'm surprised he didn't break both ankles. He stalled in beside us so hard that he should have. But Holly . . . Holly, my very dear . . . I slipped in so that you and I could talk about him before he got here."

I changed the subject quickly. Whatever they had given me made me feel dreamy and good, but not beyond being embarrassed. "Ariel, what happened? You were getting along fine—then suddenly you were in trouble."

She looked sheepish. "My own fault. You said we were going down, so I looked down. Really looked, I mean. Before that, all my thoughts had been about climbing clear to the roof; I hadn't thought about how far down the floor was. Then I looked down . . . and got dizzy and panicky and went all to pieces." She shrugged. "You were right. I wasn't ready."

I thought about it and nodded. "I see. But don't worry —when my arms are well, I'll take you up again."

She touched my foot. "Dear Holly. But I won't be flying again; I'm going back where I belong."

"Earthside?"

"Yes. I'm taking the *Billy Mitchell* on Wednesday."

"Oh. I'm sorry."

She frowned slightly. "Are you? Holly, you don't like me, do you?"

I was startled silly. What can you say? Especially when it's true? "Well," I said slowly, "I don't dislike you. I just don't know you very well."

She nodded. "And I don't know you very well . . . even though I got to know you a lot better in a very few seconds. But Holly . . . listen please and don't get angry. It's about Jeff. He hasn't treated you very well the last few days—while I've been here, I mean. But don't be angry with him. I'm leaving and everything will be the same."

That ripped it open and I couldn't ignore it, because if I did, she would assume all sorts of things that weren't so. So I had to explain . . . about me being a career woman . . . how, if I had seemed upset, it was simply distress at breaking up the firm of Jones & Hardesty before it even finished its first starship . . . how I was *not* in love with Jeff but simply valued him as a friend and associate . . . but if Jones & Hardesty couldn't carry on, then Jones & Company would. "So you see, Ariel, it isn't necessary for you to give up Jeff. If you feel you owe me something, just forget it. It isn't necessary."

She blinked and I saw with amazement that she was holding back tears. "Holly, Holly . . . you don't understand at all."

"I understand all right. I'm not a child."

"No, you're a grown woman . . . but you haven't

found it out." She held up a finger. "One—Jeff doesn't love me."

"I don't believe it."

"Two . . . I don't love him."

"I don't believe that, either."

"Three . . . you say you don't love him—but we'll take that up when we come to it. Holly, am I beautiful?"

Changing the subject is a female trait, but I'll never learn to do it that fast. "Huh?"

"I said, 'Am I beautiful?' "

"You know darn well you are!"

"Yes. I can sing a bit and dance, but I would get few parts if I were not, because I'm no better than a third-rate actress. So I have to be beautiful. How old am I?"

I managed not to boggle. "Huh? Older than Jeff thinks you are. Twenty-one, at least. Maybe twenty-two."

She sighed. "Holly, I'm old enough to be your mother."

"Huh? I don't believe that, either."

"I'm glad it doesn't show. But that's why, though Jeff is a dear, there never was a chance that I could fall in love with him. But how I feel about him doesn't matter; the important thing is that *he* loves *you*."

"*What?* That's the silliest thing you've said yet! Oh, he *likes* me—or did. But that's all." I gulped. "And it's all I want. Why, you should hear the way he talks to me."

"I have. But boys that age can't say what they mean; they get embarrassed."

"But—"

"Wait, Holly. I saw something you didn't because you were knocked cold. When you and I bumped, do you know what happened?"

"Uh, no."

"Jeff arrived like an avenging angel, a split second behind us. He was ripping his wings off as he hit, getting his arms free. He didn't even look at me. He just stepped across me and picked you up and cradled you in his arms, all the while bawling his eyes out."

"He *did?*"

"He did."

I mulled it over. Maybe the big lunk did kind of like me, after all.

Ariel went on, "So you see, Holly, even if you don't love him, you must be very gentle with him, because he loves you and you can hurt him terribly."

I tried to think. Romance was still something that a career woman should shun . . . but if Jeff really did feel that way—well . . . would it be compromising my ideals to marry him just to keep him happy? To keep the firm together? Eventually, that is?

But if I did, it wouldn't be Jones & Hardesty; it would be Hardesty & Hardesty.

Ariel was still talking, ". . . you might even fall in love with him. It does happen, hon, and if it did, you'd be sorry if you had chased him away. Some other girl would grab him; he's awfully nice."

"But—" I shut up for I heard Jeff's step—I can always tell it. He stopped in the door and looked at us, frowning.

"Hi, Ariel."

"Hi, Jeff."

"Hi, Fraction." He looked me over. "My, but you're a mess."

"You aren't pretty yourself. I hear you have flat feet."

"Permanently. How do you brush your teeth with those things on your arms?"

"I don't."

Ariel slid off the bed, balanced on one foot. "Must run. See you later, kids."

"So long, Ariel."

"Good-bye, Ariel. Uh . . . thanks."

Jeff closed the door after she hopped away, came to the bed and said gruffly, "Hold still."

Then he put his arms around me and kissed me.

Well, I couldn't stop him, could I? With both arms broken? Besides, it was consonant with the new policy for the firm. I was startled speechless because Jeff never kisses me, except birthday kisses, which don't count. But I tried to kiss back and show that I appreciated it.

I don't know what the stuff was they had been giving me but my ears began to ring and I felt dizzy again.

Then he was leaning over me. "Runt," he said mournfully, "you sure give me a lot of grief."

"You're no bargain yourself, flathead," I answered with dignity.

"I suppose not." He looked me over sadly. "What are you crying for?"

I didn't know that I had been. Then I remembered why. "Oh, Jeff—I busted my pretty wings!"

"We'll get you more. Uh, brace yourself. I'm going to do it again."

"All right." He did.

I suppose Hardesty & Hardesty has more rhythm than Jones & Hardesty.

It really sounds better.

You may think the premise of this verse story is
fantastic. Yet if human beings can adapt to an
artificial environment, why not insects?

Metropolitan Nightmare

by Stephen Vincent Benét

It rained quite a lot, that spring. You woke in the morning
And saw the sky still clouded, the streets still wet,
But nobody noticed so much, except the taxis
And the people who parade. You don't, in a city.
The parks got very green. All the trees were green
Far into July and August, heavy with leaf,
Heavy with leaf and the long roots boring and spreading,
But nobody noticed that but the city gardeners
And they don't talk.
                         Oh, on Sundays, perhaps, you'd notice:
Walking through certain blocks, by the shut, proud houses
With the windows boarded, the people gone away,
You'd suddenly see the queerest small shoots of green
Poking through cracks and crevices in the stone
And a bird-sown flower, red on a balcony,
But then you made jokes about grass growing in the streets
And politics and grassroots—and there were songs
And gags and a musical show called "Hot and Wet."
It all made a good box for the papers. When the flamingo
Flew into a meeting of the Board of Estimate,
The new Mayor acted at once and called the photographers.
When the first green creeper crawled upon Brooklyn Bridge,
They thought it was ornamental. They let it stay.

That was the year the termites came to New York
And they don't do well in cold climates—but listen, Joe,
They're only ants and ants are nothing but insects.
It was funny and yet rather wistful, in a way
(As Heywood Broun pointed out in the *World-Telegram*)
To think of them looking for wood in a steel city.
It made you feel about life. It was too divine.
There were funny pictures by all the smart, funny artists
And Macy's ran a terribly clever ad:
"The Widow's Termite" or something.

                                        There was no
Disturbance. Even the Communists didn't protest
And say they were Morgan hirelings. It was too hot,
Too hot to protest, too hot to get excited,
An even, African heat, lush, fertile and steamy,
That soaked into bone and mind and never once broke.
The warm rain fell in fierce showers and ceased and fell.
Pretty soon you got used to its always being that way.

You got used to the changed rhythm, the altered beat,
To people walking slower, to the whole bright
Fierce pulse of the city slowing, to men in shorts,
To the new sun-helmets from Best's and the cops' white uniforms,
And the long noon-rest in the offices, everywhere.
It wasn't a plan or anything. It just happened.
The fingers tapped the keys slower, the office-boys
Dozed on their benches, the bookkeeper yawned at his desk.
The AT&T was the first to change the shifts
And establish an official siesta-room,
But they were always efficient. Mostly it just
Happened like sleep itself, like a tropic sleep.
Till even the Thirties were deserted at noon
Except for a few tourists and one damp cop.
They ran boats to see the big lilies on the North River
But it was only the tourists who really noticed
The flocks of rose-and-green parrots and parrakeets

Nesting in the stone crannies of the Cathedral.
The rest of us had forgotten when they first came.

There wasn't any real change, it was just a heat spell,
A rain spell, a funny summer, a weather-man's joke,
In spite of the geraniums three feet high
In the tin-can gardens of Hester and Desbrosses.
New York was New York. It couldn't turn inside out.
When they got the news from Woods Hole about the Gulf Stream,
The *Times* ran an adequate story.
But nobody reads those stories but science-cranks.

Until, one day, a somnolent city-editor
Gave a new cub the termite yarn to break his teeth on.
The cub was just down from Vermont, so he took the time.
He was serious about it. He went around.
He read all about termites in the Public Library
And it made him sore when they fired him.

                                        So, one evening,
Talking with an old watchman, beside the first
Raw girders of the new Planetopolis Building
(Ten thousand brine-cooled offices, each with a shower)
He saw a dark line creeping across the rubble
And turned a flashlight on it.
                          "Say, buddy," he said,
"You better look out for those ants. They eat wood, you know,
They'll have your shack down in no time."
                                The watchman spat.
"Oh, they've quit eating wood," he said, in a casual voice,
"I thought everybody knew that."
                           —and, reaching down,
He pried from the insect jaws the bright crumb of steel.

The idea of the city as a sovereign state able to wage war is older than the conflicts between Athens and Sparta. Obviously, loyalty to a city can go far beyond support of its football or baseball team. And, like nations, cities can reach a state in which war is essential to their way of life.

The Luckiest Man in Denv

by C. M. Kornbluth

May's man Reuben, of the eighty-third level, Atomist, knew there was something wrong when the binoculars flashed and then went opaque. Inwardly he cursed, hoping that he had not committed himself to anything. Outwardly he was unperturbed. He handed the binoculars back to Rudolph's man Almon, of the eighty-ninth level, Maintainer, with a smile.

"They aren't very good," he said.

Almon put them to his own eyes, glanced over the parapet and swore mildly. "Blacker than the heart of a crazy Angelo, eh? Never mind; here's another pair."

This pair was unremarkable. Through it, Reuben studied the thousand setbacks and penthouses of Denv that ranged themselves below. He was too worried to enjoy his first sight of the vista from the eighty-ninth level, but he let out a murmur of appreciation. Now to get away from this suddenly sinister fellow and try to puzzle it out.

"Could we?—" he asked cryptically, with a little upward jerk of his chin.

"It's better not to," Almon said hastily, taking the glasses from his hands. "What if somebody with stars happened to see, you know? How'd *you* like it if you saw some impudent fellow peering up at you?"

"He wouldn't dare!" said Reuben, pretending to be stupid and indignant, and joined a moment later in Almon's sympathetic laughter.

"Never mind," said Almon. "We are young. Someday, who knows? Perhaps we shall look from the ninety-fifth level, or the hundredth."

Though Reuben knew that the Maintainer was no friend of his, the generous words sent blood hammering through his veins; ambition for a moment.

He pulled a long face and told Almon: "Let us hope so. Thank you for being my host. Now I must return to my quarters."

He left the windy parapet for the serene luxury of an eighty-ninth-level corridor and descended slow-moving stairs through gradually less luxurious levels to his own Spartan floor. Selene was waiting, smiling, as he stepped off the stairs.

She was decked out nicely—too nice. She wore a steely hued corselet and a touch of scent; her hair was dressed long. The combination appealed to him, and instantly he was on his guard. Why had she gone to the trouble of learning his tastes? What was she up to? After all, she was Griffin's woman.

"Coming *down?*" she asked, awed. "Where have you been?"

"The eighty-ninth, as a guest of that fellow Almon. The vista is immense."

"I've never been . . ." she murmured, and then said decisively: "You belong up there. And higher. Griffin laughs at me, but he's a fool. Last night in chamber we got to talking about you, I don't know how, and he finally became quite angry and said he didn't want to hear another word." She smiled wickedly. "I was revenged, though."

Blank-faced, he said: "You must be a good hand at revenge, Selene, and at stirring up the need for it."

The slight hardening of her smile meant that he had scored and he hurried by with a rather formal salutation.

Burn him for an Angelo, but she was easy enough to take! The contrast of the metallic garment with her soft, white skin was disturbing, and her long hair suggested things. It was hard to think of her as scheming something or other; scheming Selene was displaced in his mind by Selene in chamber.

But what was she up to? Had she perhaps heard that he was to be elevated? Was Griffin going to be swooped on by the Maintainers? Was he to kill off Griffin so she could leech onto some rising third party? Was she perhaps merely giving her man a touch of the lash?

He wished gloomily that the binoculars problem and the Selene problem had not come together. That trickster Almon had spoken of youth as though it were something for congratulation; he hated being young and stupid and unable to puzzle out the faulty binoculars and the warmth of Griffin's woman.

The attack alarm roared through the Spartan corridor. He ducked through the nearest door into a vacant bedroom and under the heavy, steel table. Somebody else floundered under the table a moment later, and a third person tried to join them.

The firstcomer roared: "Get out and find your own shelter! I don't propose to be crowded out by you or to crowd you out either and see your ugly blood and brains if there's a hit. Go, now!"

"Forgive me, sir! At once, sir!" the latecomer wailed and scrambled away as the alarm continued to roar.

Reuben gasped at the "sirs" and looked at his neighbor. It was May! Trapped, no doubt, on an inspection tour of the level.

"Sir," he said respectfully, "if you wish to be alone, I can find another room."

"You may stay with me for company. Are you one of mine?" There was power in the general's voice and on his craggy face.

"Yes, sir. May's man Reuben, of the eighty-third level, Atomist."

May surveyed him, and Reuben noted that there were pouches of skin depending from cheekbones and the jaw line—dead-looking, coarse-pored skin.

"You're a well-made boy, Reuben. Do you have women?"

"Yes, sir," said Reuben hastily. "One after another—I *always* have women. I'm making up at this time to a charming thing called Selene. Well-rounded yet firm, soft but supple, with long red hair and long white legs—"

"Spare me the details," muttered the general. "It takes all kinds. An Atomist, you said. That has a future, to be sure. I, myself, was a Controller long ago. The calling seems to have gone out of fashion—"

Abruptly the alarm stopped. The silence was hard to bear.

May swallowed and went on: ". . . for some reason or other. Why don't youngsters elect Controller anymore? Why didn't you, for instance?"

Reuben wished he could be saved by a direct hit. The binoculars, Selene, the raid, and now he was supposed to make intelligent conversation with a general.

"I really don't know, sir," he said miserably. "At the time there seemed to be very little difference—Controller, Atomist, Missiler, Maintainer. We have a saying, 'The buttons are different,' which usually ends any conversation on the subject."

"Indeed?" asked May distractedly. His face was thinly filmed with sweat. "Do you suppose Ellay intends to clobber us this time?" he asked almost hoarsely. "It's been some weeks since they made a maximum effort, hasn't it?"

"Four," said Reuben. "I remember because one of my best Servers was killed by a falling corridor roof—the only fatality and it had to happen to my team!"

He laughed nervously and realized that he was talking like a fool, but May seemed not to notice.

Far below them, there was a series of screaming whistles as the interceptors were loosed to begin their intricate, double-basketwork wall of defense in a towering cylinder about Denv.

"Go on, Reuben," said May. "That was most interesting." His eyes were searching the underside of the steel table.

Reuben averted his own eyes from the frightened face, feeling some awe drain out of him. Under a table with a general! It didn't seem so strange now.

"Perhaps, sir, you can tell me what a puzzling thing, that happened this afternoon, means. A fellow—Rudolph's man Almon, of the eighty-ninth level—gave me a pair of binoculars that flashed in my eyes and then went opaque. Has your wide experience—"

May laughed hoarsely and said in a shaky voice: "That old trick! He was photographing your retinas for the blood-vessel pattern. One of Rudolph's men, eh? I'm glad you spoke to me; I'm old enough to spot a revival like that. Perhaps my good friend Rudolph plans—"

There was a thudding volley in the air and then a faint jar. One had got through, exploding, from the feel of it, far down at the foot of Denv.

The alarm roared again, in bursts that meant all clear; only one flight of missiles and that disposed of.

The Atomist and the general climbed out from under the table; May's secretary popped through the door. The general waved him out again and leaned heavily on the table, his arms quivering. Reuben hastily brought a chair.

"A glass of water," said May.

The Atomist brought it. He saw the general wash down what looked like a triple dose of XXX—green capsules which it was better to leave alone.

May said after a moment: "That's better. And don't look so shocked, youngster; you don't know the strain we're under. It's only a temporary measure which I shall discontinue as soon as things ease up a bit. I was saying that perhaps my good friend Rudolph plans to substitute one of his men for one of mine. Tell me, how long has this fellow Almon been a friend of yours?"

"He struck up an acquaintance with me only last week. I should have realized—"

"You certainly should have. One week. Time enough and more. By now you've been photographed, your fingerprints taken, your voice recorded, and your gait studied without your knowledge. Only the retinascope is difficult, but one must risk it for a real double. Have you killed your man, Reuben?"

He nodded. It had been a silly brawl two years ago over precedence at the refectory; he disliked being reminded of it.

"Good," said May grimly. "The way these things are done, your double kills you in a secluded spot, disposes of your body and takes over your role. We shall reverse it. You will kill the double and take over *his* role."

The powerful, methodical voice ticked off possibilities and contingencies, measures and countermeasures. Reuben absorbed them and felt his awe return. Perhaps May had not really been frightened under the table; perhaps it had been he reading his own terror in the general's face. May was actually talking to him of backgrounds and policies. "Up from the eighty-third level!" he swore to himself as the great names were uttered.

"My good friend Rudolph, of course, wants the five stars. You would not know this, but the man who wears the stars is now eighty years old and failing fast. I consider myself a likely candidate to replace him. So, evidently, must Rudolph. No doubt he plans to have your double per- petrate some horrible blunder on the eve of the election, and the discredit would reflect on me. Now what you and I must do—"

You and I—May's man Reuben and May—up from the eighty-third! Up from the bare corridors and cheerless bedrooms to marble halls and vaulted chambers! From the clatter of the crowded refectory to small and glowing res- taurants where you had your own table and servant and where music came softly from the walls! Up from the scramble to win this woman or that, by wit or charm or the poor bribes you could afford, to the eminence from which you could calmly command your pick of the beauty of Denv! From the moiling intrigue of tripping your fel- low Atomist and guarding against him tripping you to the heroic thrust and parry of generals!

Up from the eighty-third!

Then May dismissed him with a speech whose implica- tions were deliriously exciting. "I need an able man and a young one, Reuben. Perhaps I've waited too long looking for him. If you do well in this touchy business, I'll consider you very seriously for an important task I have in mind."

Late that night, Selene came to his bedroom.

"I know you don't like me," she said pettishly, "but Griffin's such a fool and I wanted somebody to talk to. Do you mind? What was it like up there today? Did you see carpets? I wish I had a carpet."

He tried to think about carpets and not the exciting contrast of metallic cloth and flesh.

"I saw one through an open door," he remembered. "It looked odd, but I suppose a person gets used to them. Perhaps I didn't see a very good one. Aren't the good ones very thick?"

"Yes," she said. "Your feet sink into them. I wish I had

a *good* carpet and four chairs and a small table as high as my knees to put things on and as many pillows as I wanted. Griffin's such a fool. Do you think I'll ever get those things? I've never caught the eye of a general. Am I pretty enough to get one, do you think?"

He said uneasily: "Of course you're a pretty thing, Selene. But carpets and chairs and pillows—" It made him uncomfortable, like the thought of peering up through binoculars from a parapet.

"I want them," she said unhappily. "I like you very much, but I want so many things and soon I'll be too old even for the eighty-third level, before I've been up higher, and I'll spend the rest of my life tending babies or cooking in the creche or the refectory."

She stopped abruptly, pulled herself together, and gave him a smile that was somehow ghastly in the half-light.

"You bungler," he said, and she instantly looked at the door with the smile frozen on her face. Reuben took a pistol from under his pillow and demanded, "When do you expect him?"

"What do you mean?" she asked shrilly. "Who are you talking about?"

"My double. Don't be a fool, Selene. May and I—" he savored it—"May and I know all about it. He warned me to beware of a diversion by a woman while the double slipped in and killed me. When do you expect him?"

"I really *do* like you," Selene sobbed. "But Almon promised to take me up there and I *knew* when I was where they'd see me that I'd meet somebody really important. I really do like you, but soon I'll be too old—"

"Selene, listen to me. Listen to me! You'll get your chance. Nobody but you and me will know that the substitution didn't succeed!"

"Then I'll be spying for you on Almon, won't I?" she asked in a choked voice. "All I wanted was a few nice things before I got too old. All right, I was supposed to be in your arms at 2350 hours."

It was 2349. Reuben sprang from bed and stood by the door, his pistol silenced and ready. At 2350 a naked man slipped swiftly into the room, heading for the bed as he raised a ten-centimeter poignard. He stopped in dismay when he realized that the bed was empty.

Reuben killed him with a bullet through the throat.

"But he doesn't look a bit like me," he said in bewilderment, closely examining the face. "Just in a general way."

Selene said dully: "Almon told me people always say that when they see their doubles. It's funny, isn't it? He looks just like you, really."

"How was my body to be disposed of?"

She produced a small flat box. "A shadow suit. You were to be left here and somebody would come tomorrow."

"We won't disappoint him," Reuben pulled the web of the shadow suit over his double and turned on the power. In the half-lit room, it was a perfect disappearance; by daylight it would be less perfect. "They'll ask why the body was shot instead of knifed. Tell them you shot me with the gun from under the pillow. Just say I heard the double come in and you were afraid there might have been a struggle."

She listlessly asked: "How do you know I won't betray you?"

"You won't, Selene." His voice bit. "You're *broken*."

She nodded vaguely, started to say something and then went out without saying it.

Reuben luxuriously stretched in his narrow bed. Later, his beds would be wider and softer, he thought. He drifted into sleep on a half-formed thought that someday he might vote with other generals on the man to wear the five stars —or even wear them himself, Master of Denv.

He slept healthily through the morning alarm and arrived late at his regular twentieth-level station. He saw his superior, May's man Oscar of the eighty-fifth level, Atomist, ostentatiously take his name. Let him!

Oscar assembled his crew for a grim announcement: "We are going to even the score, and perhaps a little better, with Ellay. At sunset there will be three flights of missiles from Deck One."

There was a joyous murmur and Reuben trotted off on his task.

All forenoon he was occupied with drawing plutonium slugs from hypersuspicious storekeepers in the great rock-quarried vaults, and seeing them through countless audits and assays all the way to Weapons Assembly. Oscar supervised the scores there, who assembled the curved slugs and the explosive lenses into sixty-kilogram warheads.

In mid-afternoon there was an incident. Reuben saw Oscar step aside for a moment to speak to a Maintainer whose guard fell on one of the Assembly Servers, and dragged him away as he pleaded innocence. He had been detected in sabotage. When the warheads were in and the Missilers seated, waiting at their boards, the two Atomists rode up to the eighty-third's refectory.

The news of a near-maximum effort was in the air; it was electric. Reuben heard on all sides in tones of self-congratulation: "We'll clobber them tonight!"

"That Server you caught," he said to Oscar. "What was he up to?"

His commander stared. "Are you trying to learn my job? Don't try it, I warn you. If my black marks against you aren't enough, I could always arrange for some fissionable material in your custody to go astray."

"No, no! I was just wondering why people do something like that."

Oscar sniffed doubtfully. "He's probably insane, like all the Angelos. I've heard the climate does it to them.

You're not a Maintainer or a Controller. Why worry about it?"

"They'll brainburn him, I suppose?"

"I suppose. *Listen!*"

Deck One was firing. One, two, three, four, five, six. One, two, three, four, five, six. One, two, three, four, five, six.

People turned to one another and shook hands, laughed and slapped shoulders heartily. Eighteen missiles were racing through the stratosphere, soon to tumble on Ellay. With any luck, one or two would slip through the first wall of interceptors and blast close enough to smash windows and topple walls in the crazy city by the ocean. It would serve the lunatics right.

Five minutes later an exultant voice filled most of Denv.

"Recon missile report," it said. "Eighteen launched, eighteen perfect trajectories. Fifteen shot down by Ellay first-line interceptors, three shot down by Ellay second-line interceptors. Extensive blast damage observed in Griffith Park area of Ellay!"

There were cheers.

And eight Full Maintainers marched into the refectory silently, and marched out with Reuben.

He knew better than to struggle or ask futile questions. Any question you asked of a Maintainer was futile. But he goggled when they marched him onto an upward-bound stairway.

They rode past the eighty-ninth level and Reuben lost count, seeing only the marvels of the upper reaches of Denv. He saw carpets that ran the entire length of corridors, and intricate fountains, and mosaic walls, stained-glass windows, more wonders than he could recognize, things for which he had no name.

He was marched at last into a wood-paneled room

with a great polished desk and a map behind it. He saw
May, and another man who must have been a general—Rudolph?—but sitting at the desk was a frail old man who
wore a circlet of stars on each khaki shoulder.

The old man said to Reuben: "You are an Ellay spy
and saboteur."

Reuben looked at May. Did one speak directly to the
man who wore the stars, even in reply to such an accusa-
tion?

"Answer him, Reuben," May said kindly.

"I am May's man Reuben, of the eighty-third level, an
Atomist," he said.

"Explain," said the other general heavily, "if you can,
why all eighteen of the warheads you procured today
failed to fire."

"But they did!" gasped Reuben. "The Recon missile
report said there was blast damage from the three that got
through and it didn't say anything about the others failing
to fire."

The other general suddenly looked sick and May
looked even kindlier. The man who wore the stars turned
inquiringly to the chief of the Maintainers, who nodded
and said: "That was the Recon missile report, sir."

The general snapped: "What I said was that he would
attempt to sabotage the attack. Evidently he failed. I also
said he is a faulty double, somehow slipped with great ease
into my good friend May's organization. You will find that
his left thumb print is a clumsy forgery of the real Reuben's thumb print and that his hair has been artificially
darkened."

The old man nodded at the chief of the Maintainers,
who said: "We have his card, sir."

Reuben abruptly found himself being fingerprinted
and deprived of some hair.

"The f.p.'s check, sir," one Maintainer said. "He's
Reuben."

"Hair's natural, sir," said another.

The general began a rearguard action: "My information about his hair seems to have been inaccurate. But the fingerprint means only that Ellay spies substituted his prints for Reuben's prints in the files—"

"Enough, sir," said the old man with the stars. "Dismissed. All of you. Rudolph, I am surprised. All of you, go."

Reuben found himself in a vast apartment with May, who was bubbling and chuckling uncontrollably until he popped three of the green capsules into his mouth hurriedly.

"This means the eclipse for years of my good friend Rudolph," he crowed. "His game was to have your double sabotage the attack warheads and so make it appear that my organization is rotten with spies. The double must have been under post-hypnotic, primed to admit everything. Rudolph was so sure of himself that he made his accusations before the attack, the fool!"

He fumbled out the green capsules again.

"Sir," said Reuben, alarmed.

"Only temporary," May muttered, and swallowed a fourth. "But you're right. You leave them alone. There are big things to be done in your time, not in mine. I told you I needed a young man who could claw his way to the top. Rudolph's a fool. He doesn't need the capsules because he doesn't ask questions. Funny, I thought a coup like the double affair would hit me hard, but I don't feel a thing. It's not like the old days. I used to plan and plan, and when the trap went *snap* it was better than this stuff. But now I don't feel a thing."

He leaned forward from his chair; the pupils of his eyes were black bullets.

"Do you want to *work?*" he demanded. "Do you want your world stood on its head and your brains to crack and do the only worthwhile job there is to do? Answer me!"

"Sir, I am a loyal May's man. I want to obey your orders and use my ability to the full."

"Good enough," said the general. "You've got brains, you've got push. I'll do the spade work. I won't last long enough to push it through. You'll have to follow. Ever been outside of Denv?"

Reuben stiffened.

"I'm not accusing you of being a spy. It's really all right to go outside of Denv. I've been outside. There isn't much to see at first—a lot of ground pocked and torn up by shorts and overs from Ellay and us. Farther out, especially east, it's different. Grass, trees, flowers. Places where you could grow food.

"When I went outside, it troubled me. It made me ask questions. I wanted to know how we started. Yes—started. *It wasn't always like this.* Somebody built Denv. Am I getting the idea across to you? *It wasn't always like this!*

"Somebody set up the reactors to breed uranium and make plutonium. Somebody tooled us up for the missiles. Somebody wired the boards to control them. Somebody started the hydroponics tanks.

"I've dug through the archives. Maybe I found something. I saw mountains of strength reports, ration reports, supply reports, and yet I never got back to the beginning. I found a piece of paper and maybe I understood it and maybe I didn't. It was about the water of the Colorado River and who should get how much of it. How can you divide water in a river? But it could have been the start of Denv, Ellay, and the missile attacks."

The general shook his head, puzzled, and went on: "I don't see clearly what's ahead. I want to make peace between Denv and Ellay, but I don't know how to start or what it will be like. I think it must mean not firing, not even making any more weapons. Maybe it means that some of us, or a lot of us, will go out of Denv and live a different kind of life. That's why I've clawed my way up. That's why I need a young man who can claw with the best of them. Tell me what you think."

"I think," said Reuben measuredly, "it's magnificent—the salvation of Denv. I'll back you to my dying breath if you'll let me."

May smiled tiredly and leaned back in the chair as Reuben tiptoed out.

What luck, Reuben thought—what unbelievable luck to be at a fulcrum of history like this!

He searched the level for Rudolph's apartment and gained admission.

To the general, he said: "Sir, I have to report that your friend May is insane. He has just been raving to me, advocating the destruction of civilization as we know it, and urging me to follow in his footsteps. I pretended to agree—since I can be of greater service to you if I'm in May's confidence."

"So?" said Rudolph thoughtfully. "Tell me about the double. How did that go wrong?"

"The bunglers were Selene and Almon. Selene because she alarmed me instead of distracting me. Almon because he failed to recognize her incompetence."

"They shall be brainburned. That leaves an eighty-ninth-level vacancy in my organization, doesn't it?"

"You're very kind, sir, but I think I should remain a May's man—outwardly. If I earn any rewards, I can wait for them. I presume that May will be elected to wear the five stars. He won't live more than two years after that, at the rate he is taking drugs."

"We can shorten it," grinned Rudolph. "I have pharmacists who can see that his drugs are more than normal strength."

"That would be excellent, sir. When he is too enfeebled to discharge his duties, there may be an attempt to rake up the affair of the double to discredit you. I could then testify that I was your man all along and that May coerced me."

They put their heads together, the two saviors of civilization as they knew it, and conspired ingeniously long into the endless night.

Many writers have imagined a city in which
computers control (or at least influence) every aspect
of existence, even the personal lives of its citizens.
It's not often, though, that the system works in an
entirely benevolent way. Or, is that really the point
here?

The City That Loves You
by Raymond Banks

They have never understood the city. They will never
understand it. Man recognizes one, himself, and he recognizes multiplicity, outside-self. Man thinks of himself as an
on-off switch. He is either-or. The more sophisticated
either-and-or . . .

How laughingly simple! Man is always less than one.
All his organizations are less than one. Fortunately, man
lives by his unconscious, which does not concern itself with
the sad lies of his conscious mind. Therefore, do not listen
to what men say, but watch what they do—if you care to
learn the secrets . . .

Wormser woke up with a start. His room was terribly
hot, suffocating. He felt sweaty, uneasy between his legs,
and his night jacket was plastered to his back.

THE CITY IS YOUR FATHER

That was the sign that greeted him every morning in this
little apartment in the City of Reflex. It was an ancient city
of an ancient, knowledgeable race, and he was here and
glad to be here. Except that it was too hot.

As soon as he got out of the bed, glad to leave its insufferable embrace but stumbling and thick-minded, the room began to cool. New York had nothing like this. Earth had nothing like this. The ridiculous, strained Earth colonies in space—on Mars, Saturn's moons, Pluto—had no real cities, only stockades against the hard arithmetic of space. But the Reflexians out near Alpha Centauri, on a planet of the double-star system—ahhhh, this was a City!

The room cooled rapidly, and his sweat disappeared. The windows opaqued, then cleared to reveal the bluish, startling cool dawn so delightful on Alpha. Gradually the windows turned sugary white and vanished; the pure air of Reflex poured in on him. It was a wine-cold, bracing air that urged the lungs to draw deeper morning breaths; he did. He was cleaned immaculately by his suit, ultrasonically, the pleasant vibrations shaking every flake of dirt from his skin—much cleaner than soap and water, without the temperature shock and drying effect of the latter.

By the time he had reached his breakfast table, his suit had been done for him just before he awakened; no use to spend waking hours in such a senseless waste of time. It was a device in the collar of his suit he wasn't sure how it worked. In the silver mirror across from his light wood table he looked refreshed, clear-eyed, sober, and sane. He felt quite good. For five years he had awakened thus, though on Earth he'd been a poor awakener, hating the mornings. But not on Reflex.

His breakfast was ready as he had imagined it, before saying the words aloud: "Execute breakfast." The bacon and eggs smelled good, looked good, and tasted good. Sick? He couldn't remember the last time in the City he had felt sick. Those same delicate, high-frequency radio waves that watched over all diagnosed any trouble in his body before he knew it himself and communicated with his city suit that led him to appropriate drugstores or doctors. Now *that* was the way to run medicare and keep down costs.

Psychological ills received the same sensitive attention, he reflected cozily, dialing his program for the day. Detecting neuroses in his thought, word, or deed, the City allowed him to gratify his wishes if they were harmless, or brought him to a corrective clinic if they were fantasies demanding rejection.

"Machine-dominated," his Earth friends would call him. Hah! Machine-supported! Why waste time on inconsequentials like maintenance errands or petty illnesses. Such waste in an unattentive City was neurotic.

He studied his work program for the day indifferently on the computer read-out. Expertly his eyes sought out the words LEISURE PERIOD wherever it appeared. He chuckled. Even in Reflex a certain amount of loafing was good, necessary, and accepted.

Then he saw the brand new REJECT button on the machine; full-memory flooded back. Today, at the five-year mark, he was a full-fledged citizen of Reflex. He had passed his novitiate.

Fascinated, he pushed the REJECT button and watched his program disappear. His plate was empty; he rose, stretched luxuriously, and yawned. He felt the missing support of his daily program, but knew this was expected of new citizens.

He went to the deep-space radio and dialed the Saturn mission, knowing that his eyes danced and a smile lurked at the edge of his lips. It took a while for the screen to clear and for contact with Saturn to be made, so many parsecs from here. But there was Butler, older and grayer and looking astonished as Wormser knew he would.

"Robert Wormser, Sociologist First Class, Saturn Mission, reporting," he said.

"For God's sake," said Butler. "After all this time!"

"I told you I'd call in a couple of years," said Wormser. "On the day they made me a citizen of Reflex. It happened last night."

"Man!" said Butler. "This is a red-letter day! You're the first to report back in months and months out of the ten people on the last mission."

"I rather thought so. I've seen some of the others, talked to them. We have a club here. Around Reflex you get interested in other things besides the Saturn mission."

"Are you coming back?" asked Butler anxiously. "Are we going to get that report we sent the expedition for? Or will they stop you?"

Wormser smiled. "You're naïve. There isn't any 'they.' Just the City of Reflex. It's not a political party, or bureaucracy—it's just an intelligent, well-run City. I can leave whenever I want and come back whenever I want, now that I'm a citizen."

"You're coming back, then."

"Of course I'm coming back. I told you two years ago I'd come back when I got my citizenship."

"Others have promised," said Butler darkly. "Something always happened. Not a single man or woman ever came back."

"Tomorrow for sure," said Wormser.

"Oh, sure," said Butler. "Williams promised to come back. He was leaving tomorrow, but we never saw him. Nor any of the others."

"Oh, Williams is around," said Wormser. "He may come back someday. Butler, you just don't understand either me or the City. The others thought they'd make a quick study and come back; they're still here, or dead. Ours and those of earlier expeditions. But I came to experience Reflex through every sense and nerve. I entered it with as blank a mind as one can have. I gave myself to the City, and the City gave itself to me. Now it doesn't matter whether I leave or not. I am the City, it is me, and I will come back to make a full, detailed report with film, statistics, books, recordings, and personal observations. I've already packed the spaceship."

"I'll believe it when you get here," said Butler, obviously impressed nevertheless.

"Tomorrow," said Wormser. "Maybe tonight." He chuckled as he broke the connection.

Ominous? Dangerous? The incredible phalanx and array of uprising apartments, level upon level, swept away from his feet above him, where the topmost apartments blended into a gray sky. His dawn was a sunlight ricocheted down a million morning windows, past gaily colored stone and somber aluminum. Now people already moved on the levels outside.

Wormser went to the table and his programmer. He punched out the message carefully, T-R-I-P.

Hold him? Subvert him? Imprison him? Now that his novitiate was past, now that he was a citizen, why would the City do this?

The white buttons snapped up, the programmer made a light, whirring sound and was still. Message received. Robert Wormser went to the door of his apartment and out into the City to see what it had in store for him.

He moved in luxury at a leisurely pace, with no schedule to fulfill, without the subtle pressuring of the great machine City to urge him to work. In the City idleness was a pain, like a dull toothache that nagged you until you fulfilled your schedule. You fell into the habit of work because then you felt good.

Today, as a citizen, he enjoyed the pleasure of stopping for a morning drink in a bar where a few other citizens dallied. The liquor tasted unfamiliar, sweet at such an unaccustomed time. But good. Now if there were only someone to . . .

"Hello, Wormser!"

He turned and recognized Snell, an Earthman, one of the ten who had come on Wormser's sociological expedition. Or was it the one before that? Snell was also a citizen; they fell into a pleasant chat about the City and its affairs.

"By the way, I hear you're going on a trip," said Snell.

Wormser lazily lifted his apricot brandy. Delicious! He smacked his lips. "Yes. Going back to Saturn. Going back to report."

Snell looked uneasy. "Wormser—none of us ever have, you know. The thirty from the first expedition. The twenty on the second. The ten on the last. Not one."

"Well, you can't blame the City. It has its rules. Once they let you in, it has its rules. A five-year novitiate. They can't have people running in and out all of the time. The natives are born here and die here; they do not leave. So why should the City waste the energy-money to set up a come-and-go routine for sixty Earthmen or the other strays that come by occasionally?"

"It's best not to leave at all," said Snell. "We talked about you at the last meeting of the Former Earthmen's Club. Everybody was happy to see you make citizen status. They'd be shocked if you left."

"Oh, I shall return, as they say."

Snell was apparently not made easy by the statement. "It would embarrass the club if you left."

"Yes," said Wormser. "Still, none of us gets through life without little embarrassments, even in such a fine City as Reflex."

Snell struck his palm, a lecturer making a point to a student. "The whole point of having a City is to make it a place that you would prefer to any other place. Therefore to leave the City is to deny the City."

"Well, one man leaving the City in all eternity won't make much difference, I expect," said Wormser easily. He held up another finger and the light-sensitive, automatic bartender yielded more delicious brandy.

"It's precedent," said Snell.

"Especially to one who wasn't born here," Wormser said.

"The City is very proud that no one has ever left it, even the foreigners. For us it is much more important not to leave."

"I can see that," nodded Wormser, cutting happily into his second brandy. "The ultimate City offering the ultimate scope of human affairs to any man would be downgraded to penultimate if anybody left. Even one man."

"Now you've got it!" said Snell. "For you to leave—this could destroy the City. Twenty million human lives, including your former Earthman friends. Incidentally, the club would like to ask you to be vice-chairman next term. You have many admirers in the club."

"They don't admire me as much as I do them," said Wormser. "All fine fellows. When I get back from Saturn, I'd be glad to serve."

Snell protested: "Wormser, for God's sake, why—"

"Because the City isn't one," said Wormser. "That's all." He paid and left.

Wormser sped down the endless levels of streets and walkways—purples, mauves, greens, yellows—meanings piled upon subtle meanings; one could study for a century and not learn all of the things that the City encompassed. He floated downward in a two-place drifting machine that one used to reach the foundations, slipping pleasantly from level to level, much like a lazy paper airplane Wormser had once shot out of the fourth floor of his college dorm and watched fall gently.

Now he was down to the apartments of the families. His own level was reserved for the young and unmarried.

Down here were all the wide parkways, schools, playgrounds, children's vehicles. Women moved with their shouting children, kids raced, ran, fell, cried, laughed, shouted, as children have done since the world began. If one preferred marriage, one could be happy here, thought Wormser, waving to a blond boy who might have been himself years back. If one did not prefer marriage, one was not forced.

He saw an attractive redheaded wife and thought back to his own sexual experiences on coming to the City. It had been hard to get used to. The City rather preferred that a novitiate not neglect his private life. But it was too sophisticated to believe that it could thrust any girl into his arms.

Consequently, he met girls in usual and unusual ways; but when he was lonely, it was somehow never for long. Nor was there a need to make a spectacle of it. A direct look and a gesture from a man's repertoire, a smile if accepted, an averted face if not. Just like back home. But the similarities ended there. Sometimes the girl was forward; sometimes the results were quick. At other times she was hard to reach, hard to convince.

The one thing you could count on was that no two experiences were alike, but all relationships ended successfully. Somehow, whether the girl was short or tall, cute or stately, quick or slow, she always revealed a compatibility. True, for Wormser, affairs never lasted long; they followed their sine wave—passion rose to a peak, diminished, and then one day he didn't think about her anymore.

There was pleasure at the meeting, pain in the parting. Sometimes your nose was put a little out of joint. But always underneath was the sure knowledge that the pain of the old would be followed by the pleasure of the new.

His speculations, pleasant and relaxing, had brought him to the very floor of the plain of the planet upon which the huge City rested. Here, five years ago, the Saturn-based ship had landed with its crew, of which Wormser was not the head, but the third leader of the ten. Here also was the parking lot for the other Earth ships that had brought earlier expeditions. And the ships from other worlds, which had likewise disgorged aliens who had entered the City never to return.

Wormser's robots were busy preparing the small spacecraft for flight, as he had ordered them to do. As he watched the willing, skillful robots, manlike machines over ten-feet tall, he wondered how often this ship had been prepared for the flight to Saturn. Dozens, perhaps hundreds of times. And the other ships too. During the novitiate, all citizen-prospectives had come outside the City to prepare their machines to leave many times. But none had ever left. Wormser put that knowledge out of his mind; he had no quarrel with the City. Out here, Wormser felt uncomfortable. His all-purpose suit had ceased to function so far from the broadcast power sources. He felt sweaty; his lungs breathed pungent, unwashed air. There was a laziness, a chaotic mixture of things—dust, old tree branches, dead grass mixed with living, the usual poor assortment of what men called nature and had immeasurably improved upon in Reflex.

A slatternly native approached him. Wormser took out his small gun and waved it at her. There were nomadic tribes on the planet who did not belong to the City. They never had and never would. Subhuman, they lived in tents and huts, ate raw meat, were ridden with disease and were slaves to quixotic mythologies. In the beginning, you came out to study the tribes. Free men living in a free nature. Reflex was glad to have you do this; you lost interest soon enough. They hated Citymen and would steal from them, attack, subvert. They understood only the gun. Reflex did not deny them. There was a section of the City to which they could be admitted, but their novitiate was sixty or eighty years. They died before ever becoming citizens in a sort of semi-City limbo. Their children became useful citizens, but there was nothing to be done about these uncomprehending animals that walked like men.

The woman made gibbering speech sounds, offering Wormser a grin from a dirty face and digging two round, sun-tanned breasts out of her animal-skin jacket. Her hips moved to suggest sex. If he hadn't felt sorry for this basic, pleading creature he might have laughed. If one accommodated a forest maiden, one would find a knife in one's back at some moment.

Wormser waved her off; she went at a wolf-lope, her short attention span captured by a sight or a sound or a smell beyond his senses, having failed the fruits of his person and possessions.

During the encounter a monitor had quietly driven up to Wormser's ship. These were the police of the City. The delicate radar connected to the giant computer took care of most crime before it got started, reading dangerous thoughts, so the monitors were all that was required.

"You are planning a space trip?" asked the man.

"Yes. Going to Saturn," said Wormser.

The monitor looked worried. "I don't believe that would be a good idea," he said.

"Perhaps not," said Wormser. "Still, in a less than perfect universe one follows one's ideas, good or bad."

The monitor nodded. Wormser was a full-fledged citizen and not to be treated carelessly.

"You will have to appear before the city council, of course."

"It is required of a citizen?" said Wormser sharply, letting surprise show in his voice. The man caught the nuance and blushed.

"I mean—it is customary before one does such a thing," he said.

"Naturally," said Wormser. The man relaxed; he went to his craft and dialed the computer. His little task was done. He drove politely behind Wormser as the Earthman regained his city sailer and headed back into Reflex.

It did not seem to Wormser that the city council met very often from the way they shifted in their chairs and stared about their chamber as if it were almost as unfamiliar to them as to him. There was a moment of laughable confusion when it became obvious that none of the seven men were quite sure which was the mayor and was to have the big, white leather chair in the center of the table, but one of the number was eventually thrust forward. He now faced Wormser, who sat in a sort of witness box facing the seven on a very comfortable, dark leather chair.

"You wish to leave the City, citizen?" asked the mayor. He looked disappointed.

"Yes. For a short time. I believe there is no law against it."

"There are no laws at all on Reflex, as you well know," said the mayor testily. "Only the semi-civilized have laws. They merely serve as a point of endless dispute and challenge to activate man's hostility."

"The computer ranks you high as a citizen," said a white-haired man down at the end.

The computer rested beneath the City. It took care of ninety percent of the needs and ran the machines that made everything fit together so comfortably. It was a slave to the people, but well respected.

"I have a high regard for the computer," said Wormser. "In my former world, machines were distrusted. My own thought is that machines embody the perfections men cannot build in themselves and are useful extensions of man's finer drives."

They all nodded solemnly. The eight men in the room felt comfortable and useful and close to one another. Wormser liked that.

"However," said Wormser. "The City is less than one."

The feeling of good fellowship seemed to dissolve. The mayor shifted uneasily. The six others reacted in various ways—startled, unbelieving, amused. But they all reacted.

"I fail to see your point."

"If you cannot see my point," said Wormser, "you cannot understand why I want to go to Saturn for a while."

One of the men got up and dialed the computer from a telephone switchboard. "The machine will probably call your statement nonsense," he said. "The machine is programmed to handle nonsense statements—they have been tried many times."

"The machine will understand," said Wormser. "Itself, it operates on a range between minus one and plus one. Death is one. The time before birth is one. But life is always less than one."

"You've heard the citizen's statements," said the mayor. "How do you vote?"

The city council voted against Wormser leaving Reflex. "You understand," the mayor said, "we have nothing against leaving. We are merely advising you of our opinion, seven good citizens to one good citizen."

"These differences of opinion do arise," said Wormser affably.

"You reject our advice?"

"Oh, yes," said Wormser. "I must reject your advice. I plan to go to Saturn."

The council stood up. "We are going to program a vote of all of the twenty million people of the city on this trip tonight," said the mayor. "This will occur at dinner-time when everyone is home. How do you think your twenty million fellow citizens will react?"

"I expect they will vote against me."

The mayor nodded. "All except the small nuisance vote. Every human society has its negative people. How will you react then when both the officers of your City and the people themselves advise you against leaving?"

"I couldn't say," said Wormser. "It isn't even lunch-time, but the vote doesn't take place until tonight."

They called him at the apartment at about eight o'clock that night. It was the mayor himself to tell him that the dinner-time vote had gone against him with ninety-nine percent taking that position, one-half voting for him, and one-half percent declining any opinion.

"And one not voting," said Wormser. "The computer is very accurate. It deleted the question on my dinner-time vote display out of a sensitivity to my position. I appreciate that."

"You will give up the project?" asked the mayor.

"No," said Wormser. "But you must thank the citizens for having shown enough interest to participate in the vote on my project."

The mayor was silent, staring at Wormser on the tele-vision plate. The old man pulled at his lip. "Your statement about your reasons has gone to the computer," he said, in a voice with the echo of a threat. "It is in the hands of the ma-chine now. The machine understands ethical logic, but it has no emotions."

"How will it react?"

"One of three ways," said the mayor. "It will remain silent, showing that it has no opinion. Or it will agree with your reason and that would be a miracle, because this mat-ter has come up a hundred thousand times before with other citizens. Always it has disagreed, destroyed their logic. Or it will find you emotionally disturbed, in which case it will insist on corrective therapy rather than your trip. In the parlance of your former tradition, the machine is our Supreme Court."

Wormser thanked him and hung up. At ten o'clock the computer itself called, and its interrogative voice asked him for further information on his less-than-one statement. With lights going off and the City retiring, it had many circuits available to work on the problem. Wormser sat at his keyboard and typed for over an hour, setting forth his argument from every position. Then he took a chilled glass of pink wine and fell into a deep, restful sleep.

The overnight poll had made Wormser a temporary celebrity—not a large one, just an average one. There were about one hundred thousand citizens out to watch him depart, or attempt to depart, on his trip on the following morning.

They clustered along the foundation road that led out of the City, bunched on the open fields and covered the area where the spaceships rested, leaving a polite circle around his own vehicle. A helio platform bore a newspaperman, the glassy eye of the television pointing on him. The city council was all present, standing high above the crowd on a temporary platform. Small children played about the feet of their parents; hawkers sold drinks and ice cream; it was definitely an event of some interest. Along one edge of the crowd were the members of the Former Earthmen, their banner raised over their heads and a large placard which read: NO, WORMSER, NO!

Wormser felt very much like a political candidate who faces an unenthusiastic audience. When he appeared, there was a scattering of applause and a few faint cheers. These were balanced by some jeers and boos. But most of the audience stared at him sullenly, interested but removed, curious, as if he were a strange beast beyond knowing. No one had ever left the City in recorded history. The City had driven out a few—a very few—but this was the voluntary act of a full-fledged valuable citizen, man with a good work record, pleasant personality, a community asset, as important as every other one. If one could believe, what would be the effect on those less willing to brave popular opinion but nevertheless curious?

The most disheartening sight was the full-fledged soldier standing next to the mayor. He held a submachine gun at ready. The sun made the purposeful weapon glitter with real and shocking seriousness.

Wormser knew that the City kept one full-fledged soldier on its payroll, fully equipped, but he had never thought to meet the man. From the way the man moved, shuffling his feet, checking his gun as if getting ready to use it, Wormser felt at last the hard edge of reality.

The newsmen caught up with him at the side of his ship, inviting him on the platform. "Will you say a few words about your project, citizen?"

Wormer stepped up on the platform, aware of the new sweat beginning. "If I had known so many were interested, I wouldn't have promised to bring back Saturn souvenirs," he said. The thin joke brought forth no laughter. His voice howled and echoed off the walls of the City behind him. "I am going to Saturn," he went on. "I was sent from Saturn to study the City and report back on it. I've lived and worked here five years. I love the City. I shall return when my report to Earth officials on Saturn is finished. Don't let anything happen to the City while I'm gone."

He felt light-headed at this point. The question was whether they'd let him enter his vehicle. Once inside, the submachine gun could do no harm, although he supposed they had rockets to shoot him down in space. But the sky looked blue, sunny, and friendly, and there were no ships aloft. There were no rocket launchers that he could see— just the uniformed soldier with the gun. The man now stepped forward and the city council and the mayor fell back in a polite circle against the executing blast of the gun. The white-haired fellow whom Wormser remembered from yesterday made a point of stuffing cotton in his ears.

The mayor had his own bullhorn. "Wormser, I beseech you to abandon your project. It is not popular with your officials or the majority of the citizens."

Wormser still had the PA mike from the newsmen. He still stood on the platform. "Men make decisions that are sometimes not popular," he said. "Men seek atonement, harmony. Men seek oneness. A place like Reflex comes close to unity, to providing each small and large thing that satisfies a man. But to me, unity is not quite reached on Reflex, or anywhere else. Unity may turn out to be the time before birth and the time after death. But for me there is still a small gap. So I search. I am sorry to upset you all."

There was a painful silence now as he put down the microphone. The silence was broken by several yells and calls for the last restraint. "The computer!" called many.

The computer would reject his argument, and he would be shot if he were found sane but destructive in his act. The computer would reject his argument, and he would be sent to a hospital if he were found insane. His only hope was that the computer had made or would make no statement at all.

Wormser felt that he walked on cotton; his legs were not his as he moved down to the ground and walked to his entrance ramp. The sound of the submachine gun being cleared and the magazine slamming home made him jump; his neck tingled and his back cringed.

He remembered the call from Saturn early this morning. "Don't come back," Butler had said. "Stay in Reflex.

We can continue to get reports by communications as we have before."

"Snell has called you."

"Snell and a few others," said Butler. "If you try to leave, it seems certain that you will lose your life. It will probably also result in a break in diplomatic relations for us. Much better to stay there and see if a few more years won't change things."

"You've never debriefed a Cityman in person back on Saturn."

Butler sighed. "I don't expect to in my lifetime. You stay there."

Now his hand on the door handle. It trembled. He turned; he saw the soldier and saw the small hole of the submachine gun barrel pointing at him. His heart gave a jump, his breath felt hot and cold in his lungs. The crowd was extremely silent. His unamplified voice was heard.

"There is no law," he said. "The machine has remained silent. Good-bye."

He started in. He heard the shocking clatter of the submachine gun.

Then inexplicably, despite the ear-smashing roar of the gun, he was inside the ship. He closed the door; he walked up to the pilot compartment, nodded to his robot assistant and punched the START buttons with sweating hands. He expected to feel the pain of the bullets in his back . . .

But outside the ship, the soldier had stepped back to parade rest, holding the gun aloft. The platform around the soldier's feet was sprinkled with spent shell casings. The mayor and the city council smiled and waved. Most of the crowd moved back now, waving, breaking up.

The sky blackened as he reached deep space. There was no sign of pursuit by ship or rocket.

"Reflex. City computer calling."

"Wormser," said Wormser into the mike, thinking that the machine sounded almost human in radio communication where all men sounded like machines through space static. "That submachine gun of the soldier's," he went on in a compulsive rush of words. "Those were blanks."

"Of course," said the City computer. "The soldier had to be convinced you were not stunting for attention."

"Thank you."

"You are two degrees off course for Saturn," said the machine. "You'll miss a bit if you don't correct."

He broke off, corrected his course and sat there traveling in space, feeling good, relieved, and then sad, eventually. He hoped they wouldn't hold him too long on Saturn. He missed the City already.

In the previous story the principal problem was to get out of a city no one was supposed to wish to leave. Here we have the opposite situation. A man wishes to enter a city where no one else would care to go.

The Place Where Chicago Was

by James Harmon

I

It was late December of 1983. Abe Danniels knew that the streets and sidewalks of Jersey City moved under their own power, and that half the families in America owned their own helicopters. He was pleased with these signs of progress, but he was sweating. He thought he was getting athlete's foot instead of athletic legs from walking from the New Jersey coast to just outside of Marshall, Illinois.

The heat was unbearable.

The road shimmered before him in rows of sticky black ribbon, on which nothing moved. Nothing but him.

He passed a signal post that said CAUTION—SLOW in a gentle but commanding voice. He staggered on toward a reddish metallic square set on a thin column of bluish concrete. It was what they called a sign, he decided.

Danniels drooped against the sign and fanned his face with his sweat-ringed straw cowboy hat. The thing seemed to have something to say about the mid-century novelist, James Jones, in short, terse words.

The rim of the hat crumpled in his fist. He stood still and listened.

There *was* a car coming.

It would almost *have* to stop, he reasoned. A man couldn't stand much of this Illinois winter heat. The driver might leave him to die on the road if he didn't stop. Therefore, he would stop.

He jerked out the small pouch from the sash of his jeans. Inside the special plastic the powder was dry. He rubbed some between his hands briskly, to build up the static electricity, and massaged it into his hair.

The metal of the Jones plaque was fairly shiny. Under the beating noon sun it cast a pale reflection back at Danniels. His hair looked a reasonably uniform white now.

He started to draw the string on the pouch, then dipped his hand in and scooped his palm up to his mouth. He chewed on the stuff while he was securing the nearly flat bag in his sash. He swallowed the dough; the powder had been flour.

Danniels took the hat from beneath his arm, set it to his head, and, at last, faced the direction of the engine whine.

The roof, hood, and wheels moved over the curve of the horizon, and Danniels saw that the car was a brandless classic that probably still had some of the original, indestructible Model A left in it.

He pondered a moment whether to thumb or not to thumb.

He thumbed.

The rod squealed to a stop exactly even with him. A door unfolded and a voice like a stop signal said flatly, "Get in."

Danniels got in. The driver was a teen-ager in a loose scarlet tunic and a spangled WPA cap. The youth wouldn't have been bad-looking except for a sullen expression and a rather girlish turn of cheek, completely devoid of beard line. Danniels wrote him off as a prospective member of the Wolf Pack in a year or two.

But not just yet, he fervently hoped.

"Going far? I'm not," said the driver.

Danniels adjusted the knees of his trousers. "I'm going to—near where Chicago used to be."

"Huh?"

Danniels had forgotten the youth of his companion. "I mean I'm going to where you can't go any farther."

The driver nodded smugly, relieved that the threat to the vastness of his knowledge had been dismissed. "I get you, Pop. I guess I can take you close to where you're headed."

They rode on in silence, both relieved that they didn't have to try to span the void between age and position with words.

"You aren't anywhere near starvation, are you?" the driver said suddenly, uneasy.

"No," Danniels said. "Anyway I've got money."

"Woodrow Wilson! I'll pull in at the next joint."

The next joint was carved out of the flat cross section of hill that looked unmistakably like a strip ridge of a Colorado copper mine, but wasn't . . . even barring the fact that this was Illinois. The rectangle of visible diner was color-fused aluminum from between No. Two and Korea.

Danniels was glad to get into the shockingly cold air conditioning. It was constant, if unhealthy. The chugging unit in the car failed a heartbeat every now and then for a sickening wave of heat.

The two of them pulled up wire chairs to a linoleum-top table in a mirrored corner. A faint, purple-hectographed menu was stuck between appropriately colored plastic squeeze bottles labeled MUSTARD and BLOOD.

Danniels knew what the menu would say but he unfolded it and checked.

Steaks

Plankton	.90
Juicy, rich-red tantalizing hamburger	.17

Accessories

Mashed potatoes	.40
Delectable oysters, all you can eat	.09
Peas	.35
Rich, fragrant cheese, large slice	.02

Drinks

Coke	.50
Milk, the forbidden wine of nature	.01
Coffee (without)	.50
Coffee (with)	.02

A fat girl in white came to the table.

Danniels tossed the menu on the table. "I'll take the meat dinner," he said.

The teen-ager stared hard at the tabletop. "So will I."

"Good citizens," the waitress said, but revulsion crept into her voice over the professional hardness.

Danniels looked carefully at his companion. "You aren't used to ordering meat."

"Pop," the youth began. Danniels waited to be told that being short of cash was none of his business. "Pop, on my leg. Kill it, kill it!"

Danniels leaned over the table startled and curious. A cockroach was feeling its way along a thin meridian of vari-colored jeans. Danniels pinched it up without injuring it and deposited it on the floor. It scurried away.

"Your kind make me sick," the driver said in lieu of thanks. "You act like a Fanatic but you're a Meat-Eater. How do you blesh that?"

Danniels shrugged. He did not have to explain anything to this kid. He couldn't be stranded.

The kid was under the same encephalographic inversion as the rest of the world. No human being could directly or indirectly commit murder, as long as the broadcasting stations, which every nation on earth maintained in self-defense, continued to function.

These mechanical brain waves coated every mind with enforced pacifism. They could have just as easily broadcast currents that would have made minds swell with love or happiness. But world leaders had universally agreed that these conditions were too narcotic for the common people to endure.

Pacifism was vital to the survival of the planet.

War could not go on killing; but governments still had to go on winning wars. War became a game. The International War Games were held every two years. With pseudo-H-bombs and mock germ warfare, countries still effectively eliminated cities and individuals. A "destroyed" city was off-limits for twenty years. Nothing could go in or out for that period. Most cities had provided huge food deposits for emergencies.

Before the Famine.

Some minds were more finely attuned to the encephalographic inversion than others. People so in tune with the wavelength of pacifism could not only not kill another human being, they could not even kill an animal. Vegetarianism was thrust upon a world not equipped for it. Some— like Danniels—who could not kill, still found themselves able to eat what others had killed. Others who could not kill or eat *any* once-living thing—even plants—rapidly starved to death. They were quickly forgotten.

Almost as forgotten as the Jonahs.

The war dead.

Any soldier or civilian "killed" outside of a major disaster area (where he would be subject to the twenty years) became a man without a country—or a world. They were tagged with green hair by molecular exchange and sent on their way to starve, band together, reach a disaster area (where they would be accepted for the duration of the disaster), or starve.

Anyone who in any way communicated with a Jonah, or even recognized the existence of one, automatically became a Jonah himself.

It was harsh. And if it wasn't better than war it was quieter.

And more permanent.

The counterman with a greasy apron and hairy forearms served the plates. The meat had been lightly glazed to bring out the aroma and flavor, but the blood was still a pink sheen on the ground meat. There were generous side dishes of cheese and milk. Even animal by-products were passed up by the majority of vegetarians. Eggs had been the first to be dropped—after all, every egg was a potential life. Milk and associated products came to be spurned through sheer revulsion by association. Besides, milk was intended only to feed the animal's own offspring, wasn't it?

Danniels squirted blood generously from its squeeze bottle. Even vegetarians used a lot of it. It gave their plankton the gory look the human animal craved. Of course it was not really blood, only a kind of tomato paste. When Danniels had been a boy people called it catsup.

He tried to dig into his steak with vengeance but it tasted of ashes. Meat was his favorite food; he was in no way a vegetarian. But the thought of the Famine haunted him. Vegetable food was high in price and ration points. Most people were living on 2500 calories a day. It wasn't quite starvation and it wasn't quite a full stomach. It was hard on anybody who did more than an average amount of work. It was especially hard on children.

The Meat-Eaters helped relieve the situation. Some, with only the minimum of influence from the Broadcasters, ate nothing but meat. They were naturally aggressive morons who were doing no one favors, potential members of a Wolf Pack.

Danniels knew how to end the Famine.

The mob that was the men he had commanded had hunted him in the hills below Buffalo, and he had been hungry, with no time to eat, or rest, or sleep. Only enough time to think. He couldn't stop thinking. Panting over a smothered spark of campfire, smoldering moss and leaves, he thought. Drinking sparkling but polluted water from a twisting mountain stream and trying unsuccessfully to trap silver shavings of fish with his naked hands, he thought.

His civilian job was that of a genopseudoxenobeastimacroiologist, a specialized field with peacetime applications that had come out of the War Games—specialized to an almost comic-opera intensity. He knew virtually everything about almost nothing at all. Yet, delirious with hunger, from this he fashioned in his mind a way to provide food for everybody, even Jonahs.

After they caught him—weeks before the tag spot would have faded off—he wasn't sure whether his idea had been a sick dream or not. But he intended to find out. He wouldn't let any other mob stop him from that.

Danniels had decided he was against mobs, whether their violence and stupidity was social or antisocial. People are better as individuals.

The driver of the hot rod was also picking at his food uncertainly. Probably a social vegetarian, Danniels supposed. An irresponsible faddist.

The counterman stopped staring and cleared his throat apologetically. "This ain't the Ritz but it don't look good for customers to sit with hats on."

Danniels knew that applied to only nonvegetarians, but he put his Stetson, reluctantly, on an aluminum tree.

The teen-ager looked up. And did not go back to the food.

Danniels knew that he had been found out.

The counterman went back to wiping down the bar.

The youth was still looking at Danniels.

"You better eat if you don't want me to be discovered," Danniels said gently.

Young eyes moved back and forth, searching, not finding.

"It won't do you any good to run," Danniels continued. "The waitress and the counterman will swear they had nothing to do with me. But you were driving me, eating with me."

"You can't let even a Jonah die," the youngster said in a hoarse whisper that barely carried across the table.

Danniels shook his head sadly. "It won't work. You might have slowed down enough to let me grab onto the rear bumper or tossed me out some food. But you took me into your car, sat down at a table with me."

"And this is the thanks I get!"

Danniels felt his face flush. "Look, son, this isn't a game where you can afford to play by good sportsmanship. That's somebody else's rules, designed to make sure you get at least no better a break than anyone else. You have to play by your rules—designed to give *you* the best possible break. Let's get out of here."

He wolfed the last bite and jammed his hat back on his head, pulling it down about his ears. The sweat band had rubbed the flour off his hair in a narrow band. A band of green. The mark of the Jonah.

In the last War Games, Danniels had come into the sights of a Canadian's diffusion rifle. For six months he had worn a cancerous badge of luminosity over his heart. Until his comrades had trapped him and, through a system similar to the one their rifles employed, turned his hair to green and cast him out.

Danniels scooped up both checks and with deep pain paid both of them to save time. He wanted to get his companion out of there before he broke.

The heat struck at their faces like jets of boiling water. The authorities said nuclear explosion had had nothing to do with changing climatic conditions so radically, but *something* had.

The two of them were walking toward the parked car when the Wolf Pack got to them.

II

The horrible part was that Danniels knew they wouldn't kill him. No one could kill.

But the members of the Wolf Pack wanted to. They were the professional soldiers, policemen, prizefighters, and gangsters of a society that had rejected them. They were able to resist some of the pacifism of the Broadcasters. In fact, they were able to resist quite a lot.

The first one was a round-shouldered little man with silver spectacles. He kicked Danniels in the pit of the stomach with steel-shod toes. A clean-cut athletic boy grabbed the running teen-ager and ripped the red tunic halfway off. From the pavement Danniels at last isolated the doubt that had been nagging him. His companion wore a tight tee-shirt under the coat. She was a girl.

Danniels saw a heavy shoe aimed at his face but it went far afield. Running feet went completely past him.

He was left alone, unharmed, with only the breath knocked out of him momentarily.

They were closing in on the girl who had picked him up.

This Pack was all men, although there were female and coed groups just as vicious. Beating up a girl, Danniels knew, would give an added sexual kick to their usual sado-masochism.

They were a Pack. A mob. They were like the soldiers who had hunted him down and had him permanently tagged a Jonah. His men had been looked upon favorably by his society, while the Wolf Pack was so ill-favored it was completely ignored in absolute contempt. But they were the same in the essentials: a mob.

And once again Danniels, who was incapable of harming the smallest living creature, wanted to kill men. But he couldn't.

All his life he had experienced this mad fury of desire and it shamed him. He wanted to destroy men of stupidity, greed, and brutality on sight. Any other kind of conflict with them was weak compromise.

At times, he wondered if this atavistic if prosurvival trait had not shamed him so much that he overcompensated for it by violently refusing to take any kind of life. Like all men of his time, he asked himself: how much of my mind is the Broadcasters' and how much is mine?

If he couldn't destroy, he could defend.

With the idea still only half-formed, he lurched to his feet and stumbled into the side of the hot rod. He fumbled open the heated metal door and slid under the wheel.

He thumbed the drive on savagely and roared down on the mob.

Rubber screamed, whined, and smelled as he applied the brakes just soon enough for the men to jump out of the way—away from the girl.

He folded back the door he hadn't latched, leaned down, grabbed the teen-ager by the leg, and dragged her bruised form, bumping up into the car.

The little man with silver glasses tried to reach into the car.

Danniels swung the door back into his face.

The glasses didn't break; but everything else did.

With one foot under the girl and the other on her, Danniels tagged the illegal acceleration wire most cars had rigged under the dashboard and raced away into the brassy sunshine.

She was slouched against his shoulder when the stars blazed out in the moonless night.

Tires hummed beneath them and their headlights ate up the white-striped typewriter ribbon before them.

The girl opened her eyes, hesitated as they focused on the weave pattern of denim in his shirt, and said, "Where are they?"

"Back there someplace," Danniels told her. "They followed in their cars, a couple on motorcycles. But they must have been scared of traffic cops on the main highway. They dropped out."

She sat up and ran her fingers through her cropped mouse-colored hair. Her quick glance at him was questioning; but she answered her own question and reluctantly absorbed the truth of it. She knew he knew.

The girl huddled in the tatters of her bright tunic. "Just what do you expect to get out of helping me?" she asked.

Danniels kept his eyes on the road. "A free trip to Chicago."

"You'll get us both arrested!" she shrilled. "Nobody can get past those roadblocks."

He nodded to himself, not caring if she saw the gesture in the uncertain light from the auto gauges.

"All right," she admitted. "I know what Chicago is. That's no crime."

"You ought to," Danniels said. "You're from there."

She was tired. It was a moment before she could continue fighting. "That's foolish—"

He hadn't been sure. If she hadn't hesitated he might have given up the notion.

"That getup was what was foolish," Danniels snorted.

"Anybody would know you were trying to hide something as soon as they found out the masquerade."

"You wouldn't have found it out," she said, "if one of that Pack hadn't torn my jacket off."

"I really don't know. It might be animal magnetism, if there is such a thing. But I can't be around a woman for long without knowing it. I repeat: why?"

"I—I didn't know what they would do to a girl outside."

"For peace' sake, why did you have to come out at all?"

The girl was silent for a mile.

"Most Chicagoans think the rest of the world has reverted to barbarism," she told him.

"A common complaint of city dwellers," he observed.

"Don't joke!" she demanded. "Our food is running out. We have enough to last five more years if the present birth-death cycle maintains itself."

Danniels whistled mournfully.

"And you have—let's see—about seven more years to go."

She nodded. "I came out to see what chance there was of ending this senseless blockade."

"None at all," he snapped. "No one is going to risk breaking the rules of the War Games just to save a few million lives."

"But they will have to! The Broadcasters will make them."

"You would be surprised at how much doublethink people can practice about not killing," he assured her from bitter, personal experience. "They don't *know* for certain that you will be starving in there, so they will be free to keep you inside."

The girl straightened her shoulders, emphasizing the femininity of her slender form.

"We'll tell them," she said. "*I'll* tell them."

Danniels almost smiled, but not quite. His hands tightened on the steering wheel and he kept his eyes to the moving circle of light against the night.

"You open your mouth about Chicago to the authorities or anyone else and they will slap you under sedation and keep you there until you die of old age. They used to drop escapees back into the Cities by parachute. But too many of them were inadvertently killed; they are more subtle these days. By the way," he said very casually, "how *did* you escape?"

She told him where to go in a primitive, timeless fashion.

"No," Danniels said. "I'm going to Chicago."

"Not with me," the girl assured him quietly. "We have enough to feed without bringing in another Jonah. Besides you might be an FBI man or something trying to find our escape route."

"I'd be a Mountie then. The FBI has deteriorated pretty badly; spent itself on political security. The Royal Canadian Mounted Police lends us men and women during peacetime. Up until the War Games anyway—even though Britain would like to see us *constantly* disrupted. But," he said heavily, "I am not a government agent of any kind. Just the Jonah I appear to be."

She shivered. "I can't take the responsibility. I can't either expose our escape route—or bring in another mouth, to bring starvation a moment closer."

"Look, what can I call you?" he demanded in exasperation.

"Julie. Julie Amprey."

"Abe Danniels. Look, Julie—"

"You were named after Lincoln?" she asked quietly.

"A long time after. Look, Julie, I want to get into Chicago because of the old Milne Laboratories." He caught his breath for a long second. "They are still standing?"

Julie nodded and looked ahead, through the insect-spotted windscreen. "Partial operation, when I left."

Danniels gave a low whistle. "Lord, after all these years!"

"We manage."

"Fine! Julie, I'm sure that if I can get back in a laboratory I can find a way of ending this condemned Famine—inside Chicago and outside."

"That sounds a little like delusions of grandeur to me," the girl said uncertainly.

"It was my field for ten years. Before the last War Games. I had time to think while my platoon was hunting me down, after I had been tagged out. I thought faster than I ever thought before."

Julie studied his face for a long moment.

"What was your idea?"

"The encephalographic inversion patterns of the Broadcasters," he said quickly, "can be applied to animals as well as human beings, on the right frequencies. Even microscopic animals. Bacteria. If you control the actions of bacteria, you control their reproduction. They could be made to multiply and assume different forms—the form of food, for example."

Danniels took a deep breath and plunged into his idea as they drove on through the deepening night. He talked and explained to her, and, in doing so, he clarified points that he hadn't been sure of himself.

He stopped at last because his throat was momentarily too dry to continue.

"It's too big a responsibility for me," Julie said.

Defeat stung him so badly he was afraid he had slumped physically. But it won't be permanent defeat, he told himself. I've come this far and I'll find some other way into Chicago.

"I haven't the right to turn down something this big,"

Julie said. "I'll have to let you put it to the mayor and the city council."

He relaxed a trifle, condemning himself for the weak luxury. He couldn't afford it yet. He ran his fingers through his flour-dusted green hair and the electricity of the movement dragged off much of the whiteness. His skin, like that of most people, had been given a slight negative charge by molecularization to repel dirt and germs. The powder was anxious to remove itself, and dye or bleach refused to take at all.

"We're nearing the rim of the first blockade zone," Danniels told the girl. "Where to?"

"Circle around to the first unrestricted beach of the lakeshore."

"And then."

"Underwater."

Illegal traffic in and out of Disaster Areas was not completely unheard of. There was a small but steady flow both ways that the authorities could not or would not completely check. The patrols seemingly were as alert as humanly possible. Capture meant permanent oblivion for Disaster Residents under sedation, while Outsiders got prescribed periods of morphinvert-induced antipode depression of the brain, a rather sophisticated but effective form of torture. A few minutes under the drug frequently had an introspective duration of years. Therefore, under the typical sentence of three months, a felon lived several lifetimes in constant but varying stages of acute agony and posthysteric terror.

While few personalities survived, many useful human machines were later salvaged by skillful lobotomies.

Lake Michigan beaches were pretty good, Danniels observed. Better than at Hawaii. This one had been cleaned up for a subdivision that had naturally never been completed. It had been christened Falstaff Cove, although it was almost a mathematically straight half-mile of off-white sand.

He had shifted to four-wheel drive at the girl's direction and bored through the sand to the southernmost corner of the beach, where it blurred into weeds, rocks, dirt, and incredible litter. He braked. The car settled noticeably.

"There's a two-man submarine out there in the water under the overhang," Julie said without prompting. "We got it from the Armed Forces Day display at Soldiers' Field."

"What I'd like to know is how you get the car in and out of it?" Danniels said.

Anger, disgust, and fatigue crossed the girl's face. It was, after all, a very young face, he thought. "We have Outside contacts of sorts," she said. "Nobody trusts them very much."

He nodded. There was a lot of money in the Federal Reserve vaults inside the city.

The two of them got out of the car.

Julie stripped off her jeans, revealing the bottom half of a swimsuit and nicely turned, but pale, legs. "We'll have to wade out to the sub."

"What about the car?" Danniels asked. "Is your friend going to pick it up?"

"No! They don't know about this place."

He reached in the window and turned the ignition. "Want me to run it off into the water? You don't want to tag this spot for the authorities."

"No, I—I guess not. I don't know what to do! I'm not used to this kind of thing. I don't know why I *ever* come. We paid an awful lot for the car . . ."

He found the girl's wailing unpleasant. "It's your car, but take my advice. Let me get rid of it for you."

"But," she protested, "if you run it into the water they

can see from the air in daylight. I know. They used to spot our sub. Why not run it off into those weeds and little trees? They'll hide it and maybe we could get it later."

It wasn't a bad idea but he didn't feel like admitting it. He gunned the rod into the tangle of undergrowth.

Danniels came back to the girl with his arms and face laced with scratches from the limbs.

He tried to roll his trousers up at the cuff but they wouldn't stay. So he would spend a soggy ten minutes while they dried.

He told the girl to go ahead and he went after her, marking the spongy wet sand and slapping into the white-scummed, very blue water.

The tiny submarine was just where Julie had said it would be. He waited impatiently as she worked the miniature airlock.

They squeezed down into the metallic hollowness of the interior and Julie screwed the hatch shut, a Mason lid inappropriately on a can of sardines.

There were a lot of white-on-black dials that completely baffled Danniels. He had never been particularly mechanically minded. His field was closer to pure science than practical engineering. Because of this, rather than in spite of it, he had great respect for engineering.

It bothered him being in such close quarters with a woman after the months of isolation as a Jonah, but he had enough of the conventions of society fused into him and enough other problems to attempt easing his discomfort.

"It isn't much farther," Julie at last assured him.

He was becoming bored to the point of hysteria. For the past several months he hadn't had much diversion, but he had not been confined to what was essentially an oil drum wired for light and sound.

One of the lights changed size and pattern.

He found himself tensing. "That?" He pointed.

"Sonadar," Julie hissed. "Patrol boat above us. Don't make any noise."

Danniels pictured the heavily equipped police boat droning past above them and managed to keep quite silent.

Something banged on the hull.

It came from the outside and it rang against the port side, then the starboard. The rhythm was the same, unbroken. Danniels knew somehow the noise from both sides was made by the same agency. Something with a twelve-foot reach.

Something that knew the Morse code.

Da-da-da. Dit-dit-dit. Da-da-da.

SOS.

Help.

"It's not the police," Julie said. "We've heard it before." She added, "They used to dump nondangerous amounts of radioactives into the lake," as she decided the police boat had gone past and started up the engines again.

Danniels never forgot that call for help. Not as long as he lived.

III

The electron microscope revealed no significant change in the pattern of the bacteria.

Danniels decided to feed the white mice. He got out of his plastic chair and took a small cloth bag of corn from the warped, sticking drawer of the lab table.

Rationing out a handful of the withered kernels, he went down the rows of cages. A few, with steel instead of aluminum wiring, were flecked with rust. The mice inside were all healthy. Danniels was not using them in experiments; he was incapable of taking their lives. But some experimenter after him might use them. In any case, he was also incapable of letting them starve to death.

He had been out of jail less than two weeks.

The city council had thrown him into the Cook County lockup until they decided what to do with him. He hadn't known what happened to the girl, Julie Amprey, for bringing him back with her.

He was surprised to see Chicago functioning as well as it was after thirteen years of isolation. There were still a few cars and trucks running here and there, although most people walked or rode bicycles. But the atmosphere seemed heavy and the buildings dirtier than ever. The city had the aura of oppression and decay he thought of as belonging to nineteenth-century London.

Danniels had waited out New Year's and St. Valentine's Day in a cell between a convicted burglar and an endless parade of drunks. Finally, two weeks ago, the mayor himself came, apologizing profusely but without much feeling. Danniels was escorted to the old Milne Laboratory buildings and told to go to work on his idea. He had, they said, two weeks to produce. And he was getting nowhere.

His deadline was up. The deadline of the real world. But the one he had given himself was much, much more pressing.

"You'll kill yourself if you don't get some sleep," the girl's voice said behind his back.

Danniels closed the drawer on the nearly depleted sack of grain. It was the girl, Julie Amprey. He had been expecting her but not anticipating her. He didn't like her very much. The only reason he could conceive for her venture Outside was a search for thrills. He might find it understandable, if immature, in a man, but considered it unattractive in a woman. He had no illusions about masculine superiority, but women were socially, if not physically and emotionally, ill-equipped for simple adventuring.

Julie was more attractive dressed in a woman's clothes, even if they were a dozen years out of style. Her hair had a titian glint. She was, perhaps, really too slender for the green knit dress.

"It's a big job," he said. "I'm beginning to think it's a lifetime job."

He half-turned and motioned awkwardly at the lab table and the naked piece of electronics.

"That's the encephalographic projector I jury-rigged," he explained.

"You can spare me the fifty-cent tour," Julie said.

He wondered how she had managed to get so irritating in such a short lifetime. "There's not much else to see," Danniels grunted. "I've got some reaction out of the bacteria, but I can't seem to control their reproduction or channel them into a food-producing cycle."

Julie tossed her head. "Oh, I can tell you why you haven't done that," she said.

He didn't like the way she said that. "Why?"

"You don't *want* to control them," Julie said simply. "If you really control them, you'll cause some to be recessive. You'll breed some strains out of existence. You'll *kill* some of them. And you don't want to kill any living thing."

She was wrong.

He wanted to kill her.

But he couldn't. She was right about the bacteria. He should have realized it before. He had planned for almost a year and worked for two weeks; and this girl had walked in and destroyed everything in five minutes. But she was right; he spun toward the door.

"Where are you going?" she demanded.

"I'm leaving. See what somebody else can do with the idea."

"But where are you going?" Julie repeated.

"Nowhere."

And he was absolutely right.

Danniels walked aimlessly through the littered streets

for the rest of the day and night. He couldn't remember walking at night, but neither could he remember staying anywhere when he discovered dawn in the sky.

It was that time of dawn that looks strangely like an old two-color-process movie that they show on TV occasionally—all orange and green, with no yellow to it at all, when even the truest black seems only an off-brown or a sinister purple.

He shivered in the chill of morning and decided what to do.

He would have to walk around for a few hours even yet.

The drink his friend, Paul, placed before him was not entirely distinct. Neither were the bills he had in his hand. It was money the mayor's hireling had given him to use for laboratory supplies. Danniels peeled off a bill of uncertain denomination and gave it to his friend. Paul seemed pleased. He put it into the pocket of his white shirt, the pocket eight inches below and slightly to the left of the black bow tie, and polished the bar briskly.

Danniels picked up the glass and sipped silently until it was empty.

"Do you want to talk about anything, Abe?" Paul asked solicitously.

"No," Danniels said cheerfully. "Just give me another drink."

"Sure thing."

Danniels studied his green hair in the glass. Here, the mark of the Jonah wasn't important. Not yet. But he would be unwelcome even here after the time of Disaster ran out. He would have to move on sooner or later. Eventually—why not now? That slogan went better than the one in pink light over the mirror. THE BEER THAT MADE MILWAUKEE FAMOUS. There hadn't been any

Milwaukee beer here for thirteen years. Most of the stuff came out of bathtubs.

Why not now?

He smoothed another bill on the damp polished wood and negotiated his way through the hazy room.

Outside, he turned a corner and the City dropped away from him. He seemed to be in a giant amusement park with acres of empty ground patterned off in squares by unwinking dots of light.

He grinned to himself, changed direction with great care, and started down the one-way street to the lakefront.

He heard the footsteps behind him.

Danniels put his palm to the brick wall, scaling posters, and turned.

The clean-cut young man smiled disarmingly. "I saw you at Paul's. You'll never make it home under your own power. Better let me take you in my cab."

Danniels knocked him out on his feet with a clean right cross.

He blinked down at the boy. Self-preservation had become instinctive with him during his months as a wandering Jonah.

Gnawing at his underlip, he studied the twisted way the supposed cabbie lay. If he really were . . . Danniels patted the man down and brought something out of a hip pocket.

He inspected the leather blackjack, weighing it critically in his hand.

It slid out of his palm and thudded heavily on the cracked sidewalk.

Danniels shrugged and grinned and moved away unsteadily. Toward the lake.

The lake looked gray and winterish.

There was no help for it.

Danniels swung his leg over the rust-spotted railing and looked down to where the water lapped at crumbling bricks blotched with green. He peered out over the water. Only a few miles to the beach where he had left the car parked in the undergrowth. He would have preferred to use the little sub, but he could swim if he had to.

The surface below showed clearly in the globe lights. Danniels dived.

Before he hit the water, he remembered that he should have taken off some of his clothes.

When he parted the icy foam with his body, he knew he had committed suicide. And he realized that that had been what he intended to do all along.

There was something in the lake holding him, and it had a twelve-foot reach.

It kept holding on to him under the surface of green ice and begging him for help. He couldn't breathe, and he couldn't help. Of the two, not being able to help seemed the worse. Not breathing wasn't so bad. . . . It hurt to breathe. It choked him. It was very unpleasant to breathe. He had much preferred not breathing to this . . .

Some time later, he opened his eyes.

A small, round-faced man was staring down at him through slender-framed spectacles. For a moment he thought it was the man in whose face he had smashed the car door at the diner weeks before. But this man was different—among other things his glasses were gold, not silver. Yet he was also the same. Danniels knew the signs of the Wolf Pack.

"How's your foot?" the little man asked in a surprisingly full-bodied voice.

Danniels instantly became aware of a dull subpain sensation in the toes of his left foot. He looked over the crest of his chest and saw the foot, naked below the cuff of his wrinkled trousers. The three smaller toes were red. No, maroon. A red so dark it was almost black. Fainter streaks of red shot away from the toes, following the tendon.

Danniels swallowed. "The foot doesn't *feel* so bad, but I think it *is*."

"We may have to operate," the small man said eagerly.

"How did I get out of the lake?"

"Joel. The man you knocked out. He came to and followed you. Naturally, he had to save your life. He banged your foot up, dragging you ashore."

Or afterward, Danniels thought.

Abruptly, the stranger was gone and a door was closing and latching on the other side of the room.

Danniels tried to rise and fell back, his head floating around somewhere above him. Maybe a Wolf Pack member would have to save his life but he wouldn't have to bring him home and nurse him back to health.

Why?

He fell asleep without even trying to guess the answer.

He woke when they brought food to him.

Danniels finished with the tray and set it aside.

The small man, who had identified himself as Richard, beamed. "I think you are strong enough to attend the celebration tonight."

Danniels did feel stronger after rest and food, but at the same time he felt vaguely dizzy and his leg was beginning to hurt. "What kind of a celebration?" he asked.

Richard chuckled. "Don't worry. You'll like it."

Danniels had seen the same expression on the faces of hosts at stag dinners; but with a Wolf Pack it was hard to know what to expect.

IV

The place he was in did not seem to be a house after all.

Danniels leaned on the shoulder of Richard, who helped him along solicitously. They entered a large chamber nearly a hundred feet wide. There were people there. It wasn't crowded but there were many people standing around the walls. A lot of them were holding three-foot lengths of wood.

Richard led him to a chair, the only one apparent in the room.

"I'll go tell them we're ready now," the small man said, chuckling.

Danniels looked around slowly at the shadowed faces. Of those holding clubs, he knew only the man Richard had told him was Joel, the man who had pulled him from Lake Michigan. Apparently the ones with the clubs were members of the Pack, while the others were observers and potential members. Among these, he spotted a member of the city council.

And Julie.

She stood in a loose sweater and skirt, her hands hugging her elbows, eyes intent on the empty center of the room. Danniels was reminded of some of the women he had seen at unorthodox political meetings.

Danniels was surprised to find that he wanted to talk to her. He might try hobbling over to her or calling her over to him. But with the instinct he had developed while being hunted, he knew it was wrong to call attention to the two of them together.

He noticed that he was in line with the door. Julie would have to pass by him when she left—after the celebration.

"The celebration begins in five minutes."

Someone he hadn't seen had shouted into the big room. The words bounced back slightly and hung suspended.

The people's waiting became an activity. Tension lived in the room.

And then the cat was released.

The Pack members moved apart from the rest and

struck at the scrawny yellow beast. The cat didn't make it very far down the line. The men from the other end of the room moved up quickly to be in on the kill.

The clubs rose and fell even after it was clear there was no reason for it.

Their ranks parted and they left their handiwork where it could be admired.

It must be hard to find animals in a closed city like this, Danniels thought. It must be quite a treat to find one to beat to death.

He sat and waited for them to leave. But he found the celebration was just beginning. The group was laughing and talking. Now that it was over they wanted to talk about it the rest of the evening. They had created death.

He searched out Julie Amprey again. She was looking at what they did. He thought she was sick at first. His lips thinned. Yes, she was sick.

Her eyes suddenly met his. Shock washed over her face, and in the next moment she was moving to him.

"So," she said coolly, "you found out my little secret. This is where I get my kicks."

He nodded, thinking of nothing to say.

"Did you ever read them?" she asked breathlessly. "All the old banned books—Poe and Spillane and Proust. The pornography of death. I grew up on them, so you see there's no harm in them. Look at me."

"You want to kill?" Danniels asked her.

She lit an expensive, king-size cigarette. "Yes," she exhaled. "I thought I might join a Pack on the Outside. But, you'll remember, I didn't quite make it. I couldn't even kill a cockroach. I want to, but the damned Broadcasters keep interfering with me."

Richard came back, smiling broadly. "Well, Abe, has Miss Amprey been telling you of our plans to ruin the planet?"

Danniels was incredibly tired. He had been listening and arguing for hours.

"You're a scientist," Joel persisted. "Help us."

"There are different kinds of scientists," Danniels repeated. "I'm not a nuclear physicist."

"Right there." Richard tapped the pink rubber eraser of his pencil against the map of Cook County. "Right there. An armory no one else knows anything about. Enough H-bombs to wipe out human life on the planet. And rockets to send them in."

"The councilman may be lying," Danniels said. "How do you think he should happen to find it and no one else?"

"The information was in the city records," Richard said patiently, "but buried and coded so it would take twenty years to locate. Bureaucracy is an insidious evil, Abe."

Danniels rubbed his face with his palms. "I'm not even sure if I understand what you mean to do. You want to rocket the H-bombs out almost but not quite beyond Earth's gravitation and explode them so that the fallout will be evenly distributed over the surface of the planet. You think it will cause no more than injury and destruction—"

"That's all," Joel said sharply.

Richard gave an eager nod.

They had had to convince themselves of that, Danniels knew. "But why do you want to do anything as desperate as that?"

"Simple revenge." Richard's tone was even and cold. "And to show them what we can do if they don't cut off the Broadcasters." The small man's liquid brown eyes softened. "You've got to understand that we really don't want to kill people. Our actions are merely necessary demonstrations against insane visionary politics. I only want the Broadcasters shut off so I can do efficient police work—

Joel, so that he can fight in the ring with the true will of a sportsman to win. The rest of us have equally good reasons."

"I think I understand," Danniels said. "I'll do what I can to help you."

Danniels was not surprised when Julie Amprey was in the raiding party. He was past the capacity for surprise.

He was getting around on his own today only because he was learning to stand the pain. It was worse. And he was weak and dizzy from a fever.

They had all managed to produce bicycles. Richard had even managed to find one for him with a tiny engine powered by solar-charged batteries.

Julie looked crisp and attractive in sweater and jeans. Joel was strikingly handsome in the clear sun, and even Richard looked like a jolly fatherly type.

As they wheeled down the street, Danniels was afraid only he with his wet, tossed green hair and drooping cheeks warped the holiday mood of those who, in some other probability sequence, were happy picnickers.

When they reached the place, Richard giggled nervously. "It takes a code to open the hatch," he explained. "If Aldrich didn't decode it correctly there will be a small but effective chemical explosion in this area."

Danniels leaned against a maple, watching. The bicycles were parked in the brush and a shallow hole had been dug at an exact spot in the suburban park. Only a few inches below ground was the gray steel door flush with the level of grass.

Richard hummed as he worked a prosaic combination dial.

Finally there was a muffled click and a churning whine began.

The hatch raised jerkily and latched at right angles.

The Pack milled about the opening, excited. Joel got the honor of going down first. Richard seemed to fumble his chance for the glory, Danniels observed. The other men went down, one by one. And finally only Julie and Richard were left. He supposed that this meant the girl had been accepted as a full member of the Wolf Pack. That would change the whole character of the organization. He vaguely wondered who her sponsor was. Joel?

Julie and the little man came to him. They started to help him down into the opening and suddenly he was at the bottom of a ladder. Things were beginning to seem to him as if they were taking place underwater.

They walked down a corridor of shadow, lit only by tarnished yellow from red sparks caught on the tips of silver wire inside water-clear bulbs recessed in the concrete ceiling.

When they passed a certain point sparks showered from slots in opposite walls. They burned out ineffectively before they reached the floor of cross-hatched metallic mats.

"Power failing," Richard observed with a chuckle. "Congress should investigate the builders."

There was a large, sliding door many feet thick but so well-balanced it slid open easily. And they were there.

It was a big room full of many little rooms. Each little room had a door that a man could enter by stooping and a chair-ledge inside for him to sit and read or adjust instruments. The outside of the rooms were finished off cleanly in shining metal with large, rugged objects fitted to all sides. There were hydrogen bombs.

The Wolf Pack ranged joyously through the maze.

Danniels found one of several stacks of small instruments and sat down on it. The things looked like radios, but obviously weren't.

Richard came to him, wringing his hands. "These bombs seem to be designed to be dropped from bombers.

There are supposed to be rockets here too. I hope the H-bombs will fit. They seem so bulky . . ."

"Perhaps the rockets have self-contained bomb units," Danniels suggested.

"Perhaps. We're all going off and try to find the rockets. You'd be amazed at all the cutoffs down here. I'll leave Joel here to look after you."

Danniels sat on the instruments. Joel stayed several hundred feet away, an uncertain shadow in the light, smoking a red dot of a cigarette. Somehow Danniels associated fire with munitions instead of atomics and felt uneasy.

He discovered Julie Amprey at his side. She didn't say anything. She seemed to be sulking. Like a spoiled brat, he thought.

He fingered one of the portable instruments from an open crate beside him. "Wonder what these are?" he said to break up the heavy silence.

"Pseudo-H-bombs," the girl snapped.

Of course. Just as money had to be backed by gold or silver reserves, every pseudo-bomb or mock-gas had to be backed by the real thing which, after its representative had been used, was dismantled, neutralized, or retired. International inspection saw to that.

"There's enough here to blow up the whole world . . . if they were real," Danniels said.

The girl pointed out into the chamber. "Those *are* real."

Each nation had many times over the nuclear armament necessary to destroy human life. There was enough for that right in this vault—both in reality and in the Games.

Danniels stopped drifting and took a course. He stopped observing and began to act. There was a mob in action.

Even if they did somehow manage not to kill off the

population with the fallout they were engineering, they would ruin farmland, create new recessive mutations.

Famine would cease to be a psychological affliction for half the world and become a physiological reality instead . . . for all the world.

He had failed in his plans to end the psychological Famine because of his own attunement to the Broadcasters. He wouldn't fail in stopping the new physiological Famine.

V

"Put that thing down," Joel said. "I don't trust you any farther than I can spit, and that looks like a radio. You trying to warn the city council?"

Danniels put down the instrument. One wouldn't do it, and he could tell from Joel's eyes that he would have a very bad experience by disobeying him.

"You were going to do something," Julie said. "What were you trying to do with that pseudie?"

"How do you know so much about this stuff?" Danniels demanded.

"My father told me all he found out from the records. He's Councilman Aldrich."

He rested his eyes for a second. "But your name?—" he heard himself say.

"My stepfather, I should have said. Mother married him when I was two. *What were you going to do?*"

"I," he said, "intended to end it all. All of this. All of it Outside. End everything."

The girl turned from him. "Then why don't you do it?"

"You mean you don't want our friends to succeed in torturing a sick world?"

"I don't like pain," she said. "There's something clean,

positive, and challenging about killing. I'd like to kill. But pain seems so pointless. If you can stop them, go ahead. I'll help you."

He was exhausted and in fever. "Joel won't let me."

"Then—kill him," she said.

He knew it was all useless, tired, stale, unrewarding. It was done. He was nothing, and the girl was less. The Pack would succeed and a tortured world would die of a greater Famine because he had failed all down the line. And he blamed himself for making a mistake that actually was unimportant. For a moment, he had trusted the girl.

"You *can* kill him." Julie turned back and faced him. "How much do you think those Broadcasters can really control human beings? We aren't fighting wars because we don't want to. We've finally seen what war can do and we're scared. We've retreated. The human race is hiding just like you are now."

Danniels laughed.

She lunged forward, tense. For a moment he thought she had actually stamped her foot. "It's true, you fool! Don't the actions of these men prove it to you? They are going to risk destroying the planet. If pacifism really controlled them do you think they could do that?"

He mumbled something about Wolf Pack members.

"There's never been any law or moral credo that human beings couldn't break and justify within themselves some way," Julie intoned carefully. "People can do the same with the induced precepts of the Broadcasters. If you really want to stop them, you can—by killing Joel and going ahead."

"Maybe later," Danniels mumbled. "I'll think about it."

Julie slapped his face. He wondered why he didn't feel it.

"You don't have much time left," Julie whispered. "Don't you know what's wrong with your foot? *Gan-*

grene. You have to get those toes amputated soon or you'll die."

"Yes," he said numbly. "Must get amputation." But it didn't seem urgent. He felt he should get some rest first.

"It's too bad you can't allow the operation," the girl said sweetly. "You can't allow lives to be destroyed just to save your own personality."

"What lives?" he demanded.

"All the cells and microorganisms in your toes," Julie told him. "You know they'll *die* if you are operated on. Are they any worse than the little bacteria you refused to murder? I suppose it's just as well that you die. How can you stand it on your conscience to breathe all the time and burn up innocent germs in your foul breath?"

Danniels understood; to live was to kill.

Every instant he lived his old cells were dying and new ones were being born. So Danniels, who thought he could not kill any living thing, finally accepted himself as a killer. It wasn't human life he was taking . . . but it was life.

If he could be wrong about taking any life at all—and he had always believed himself unable to kill anything—he might be wrong about being able to kill men, in spite of everything he had been taught and what he believed about the influence of the Broadcasters.

He studied Joel in the gloom. The man represented everything he loathed—stupidity, brutality, the mob. If I can kill anyone, he told himself, it should be Joel.

He could try. Yes, he could. And that was a victory in itself.

He moved, and that was another triumph over the physical defeat that was already upon him.

Joel looked up, narrow eyes widened, as Danniels came down on him.

Danniels caught him in the stomach with the flat of his palm and shoved up.

Joel gargled in the back of his throat and rammed his thumbs for the prisoner's eyes. Danniels nodded and caught the balls of the thumbs on his forehead. He brought his fist up sharply and hit Joel on the point of the chin. His head snapped but righted itself slowly. He lashed into Danniels's body with both eager hands and Danniels, weakened, went down before he had time to think about it.

From the crazy angle of the floor he saw far above him Joel's lips curl back and closer, further down, a shoe was lifted to kick. It was aimed at Danniels's swollen foot.

Danniels smiled. He shouldn't have done that. If he had acted like a man instead of an animal he would have been fine. But now . . . Danniels rolled over quickly against the one leg of Joel's firmly on the floor. Off balance, Joel fell backward with a curse, the back of his skull ringing against the side of one of the bombs.

Exertion was painting red lines across his vision, but Danniels climbed to his knees, put his hands to Joel's corded throat, and squeezed.

Yes. He knew he could kill. A few more seconds and he would be dead.

Danniels stopped.

There was no need to kill the boy. He would be unconscious long enough for him to do his job. And he found that fear had left him. He was no longer afraid of killing small things, because he was no longer afraid of killing men.

He had been able to kill when he had to, but more important, he had been able to keep from killing when it wasn't needed. He didn't need to be afraid of the old blood-lust—because he knew now he could beat it.

And Julie had seen. She had seen something she had never believed was possible. That a man could keep from being a savage without the restraints of the Broadcasters or of society.

He limped to the stacked pseudies and sat down.

"Now we can make it clean, Julie. We can end the whole mess. Ready?"

"Yes," she told him.

He picked up a pseudie and threw the switch.

The radio signal went out, and all over the world receivers noted a pseudoexplosion in the heart of a Disaster Area. Danniels could imagine the men in the council room in the heart of the City seeing the flash and feeling the doom of a renewed twenty years of isolation, and heading for the exact spot of the flash.

More signals flashed. And flashed. And flashed.

And he thought of the people all over the world wondering about the devastating sneak attack on the United States, and the incredible readings of the instruments.

"Keep working," Danniels said. "The Wolf Pack or the officials from the City will be here soon. I hope it's a dead heat. But," he said, "I think we've done it. But we can keep working on the safety margin."

"What have we done, Abe?" Julie asked trustingly.

He was going to feel foolish saying it. "We have just blown up the world according to the official records of the War Games."

"Then they'll have to start over," she said.

"Maybe," Danniels whispered. "If they do, we'll all start even. Everybody's a Jonah. The world is a Disaster Area. Maybe they'll start the War Games over. Or maybe they'll try the real thing again, now that they've seen how easy it is with pseudies."

He felt the numb foot and knew he would have to have an emergency operation if he survived the mobs that were coming. But he had a way of surviving mobs. He looked at Julie. He would see that their children could eat.

"At least," he said, triggering another H-bomb for the world's records, "it isn't a bad day when the world has been given a fresh slate, a new start."

There were footsteps outside, coming closer.

The antagonism between city and country dwellers is by now a familiar theme. But what if one side regards the other not merely with distrust but with horror and disgust? And what if the highest form of patriotism for a city dweller is to volunteer for duty in the country?

Natural State

by Damon Knight

I

The most promising young realie actor in Greater New York, everyone agreed, was a beetle-browed Apollo named Alvah Gustad. His diction, which still held overtones of the Under Flushing labor pool, the unstudied animal grace of his movements and his habitually sullen expression enabled him to dominate any stage not occupied by an un-clothed woman at least as large as himself. At twenty-six, he had a very respectable following among the housewives of Manhattan, Queens, Jersey, and the rest of the seven boroughs. The percentage of blown fuses resulting from subscribers' attempts to clutch his realized image was extraordinarily low—Alvah, his press agents explained with perfect accuracy, left them too numb.

Young Gustad, who frequently made his first entrance water-beaded as from the shower, with a towel girded chastely around his loins, was nevertheless, in his private life, a modest and slightly bewildered citizen, much given to solitary reading and equipped with a perfect set of the conventional virtues.

These included the cheerful performance of all municipal duties and obligations; like every right-thinking citizen, Gustad held down two jobs in summer and three in winter. At the moment, for example, he was an actor by day and a metals-reclamation supervisor by night.

Chief among his less tangible attributes was that emotion which in some ages has been variously described as civic pride or patriotism. In A.D. 2064, as in B.C. 400, they amounted to the same thing.

Behind the manager's desk, the wall was a single huge slab of black duroplast, with a map of the city picked out in pinpoints of brilliance. As Gustad entered with his manager and his porter, an unseen chorus of basso profundos broke into the strains of "The Slidewalks of New York." After four bars, it segued to "New York, New York, It's a Pip of a Town," and slowly faded out.

The manager himself, the Hon. Boleslaw Wytak, broke the reverent hush by coming forward to take Alvah's hand and lead him toward the desk. "Mr. Gustad—and Mr. Diamond, isn't it? Great pleasure to have you here. I don't know if you've met all these gentlemen. Commissioner Laurence, of the Department of Extramural Relations; Director Ostertag, of the Bureau of Vital Statistics; Chairman Neddo, of the Research and Development Board."

Wytak waited until everyone was comfortably settled in one of the reclining chairs which fitted into slots in the desk, with cigars, cigarettes, liquor capsules, and cold snacks at each man's elbow. "Now, Mr. Gustad—and Mr. Diamond—I'm a plain, blunt man, and I know you're wondering why I asked you to come here today. I'm going to tell you. The City needs a man with great talent and great courage to do a job that, I tell you frankly, I wouldn't undertake myself without great misgivings." He gazed at

Gustad warmly, affectionately but sternly. "You're the man, Alvah."

Little Jack Diamond cleared his throat nervously. "What kind of a job did you have in mind, Mr. Manager? Of course, anything we can do for our City . . ."

Wytak's big face, without perceptibly moving a muscle, somehow achieved a total change of expression. "Alvah, I want you to go to the Sticks."

Gustad blinked and tilted upright in his chair. He looked at Diamond.

The little man suddenly seemed two sizes smaller inside his box-cut, cloth-of-silver tunic. He gestured feebly and wheezed, "*Wake-me-up!*" The porter behind his chair stepped forward alertly, clanking, and flipped open one of the dozens of metal and plastic boxes that clung to him all over like barnacles. He popped a tiny capsule into his palm, rolled it expertly to thumb-and-finger position, broke it under Diamond's nose.

A reeking, sweet green fluid dripped from it and ran stickily down the front of Diamond's tunic.

"Dumbhead!" said Diamond. "Not crème de menthe, a wake-me-up!" He sat up as the abashed servant produced another capsule. "Never mind." Some color was beginning to come back into his face. "*Blotter!*" A wad of absorbent fibers. "*Vacuum!*" A lemon-sized globe with a flaring snout. "*Gon-Stink! Presser!*"

Gustad looked back at the manager. "Your Honor, you mean you want me to go into the Sticks? I mean," he said, groping for words, "you want me to play for the *Muckfeet?*"

"That is just exactly what I want you to do." Wytak nodded toward the commissioner, the director, and the chairman. "These gentlemen are here to tell you why. Suppose you start, Ozzie."

Ostertag, the one with the fringe of yellowish white

hair around his potato-colored pate, shifted heavily and stared at Gustad. "In my bureau, we have records of population and population density, imports and exports, ratio of births to deaths, and so on that go back all the way to the time of the United States. Now this isn't known generally, Mr. Gustad, but although New York has been steadily growing ever since its founding in 1646, our growth in the last thirty years has been entirely due to immigration from other less fortunate Cities.

"In a way, it's fortunate—I mean to say that we can't expand *horizontally*, because it has been found impossible to eradicate the soil organisms—" a delicate shudder ran around the group—"left by our late enemies. And as for continuing to build vertically—well, since Pittsburgh fell, we have been dependent almost entirely on salvaged scrap for our steel. To put it bluntly, unless something is done about this situation, the end is in sight. Not alone of this administration, but of the City as well. Now the *reasons* for this—ah—what shall I say . . ."

With his head back, staring at the ceiling, Wytak began to speak so quietly that Ostertag blundered through another phrase and a half before he realized he had been superseded as interlocutor.

"Thirty years ago, when I first came to this town, an immigrant kid with nothing in the whole world but the tunic on my back and the gleam in my eye, we had just got through with the last of the Muckfeet Wars. According to your history books, we won that war. I'll tell you something—we were licked!"

Alvah squirmed uncomfortably as Wytak raised his head and glanced defiantly around the desk, looking for contradiction. The manager said, "We drove them back to the Ohio, thirty years ago. And where are they now?" He turned to Laurence. "Phil?"

Laurence rubbed his long nose with a bloodless forefinger. "Their closest settlement is twelve miles away. That's to the southwest, of course. In the west and north—"

"Twelve miles," said Wytak reflectively. "But that isn't the reason I say they licked us. They licked us because there are twenty million of us today . . . and about one hundred fifty million of them. Right, Phil?"

Laurence said, "Well, there aren't any accurate figures, you know, Boley. There hasn't been any census of the Muckfeet for almost a century, but—"

"About one hundred fifty million," interrupted Wytak. "Even if we formed a league with every other city on this continent, the odds would be heavily against us—and they breed like flies." He slapped the desk with his open palm. "So do their filthy animals!"

A shudder rippled across the group. Diamond shut his eyes tight.

"There it is," said Wytak. "Rome fell. Babylon fell. The same thing can happen to New York. Those illiterate savages will go on increasing year by year, getting more ignorant and more degraded with every generation . . . and a century from now—or two, or five—*they'll be the human race*. And New York . . ."

Wytak turned to look at the map behind him. His hand touched a button and the myriad of tiny lights went out.

Gustad was not an actor who wept readily, but he felt tears welling over his eyelids. At the same time, the thought crossed his mind that, competition being what it was in the realies, it was a good thing that Wytak had gone into politics instead of acting.

"Sir," he said, "what can we do?"

Wytak's eyes were focused far away. After a moment, his head turned heavily on his massive shoulders, like a gun turret. "Chairman Neddo has the answer to that. I want you to listen carefully to what he's going to tell you, Alvah."

Neddo's crowded small face flickered through a complicated series of twitches, all centripetal and rapidly executed. "Over the past several years," he said jerkily, "under Manager Wytak's direction, we have been developing certain devices, certain articles of commerce, which are designed, especially designed, to have an attraction for the Muckfeet. Trade articles. Most of these, I should say all of—"

"Trade articles," Wytak cut in softly. "Thank you, Ned. That's the phrase that tells the story. Alvah, we're going to go back to the principles that made our ancestors great. Trade—expanding markets—expanding industries. Think about it. From the Arctic Ocean to the Gulf of Mexico, there are some one hundred fifty million people who haven't got a cigarette lighter or a wristphone or a realie set among them. Alvah, we're going to civilize the Muckfeet. We've put together a grab bag of modern science, expressed in ways their primitive minds can understand—and *you're* the man who's going to sell it to them! What do you say to that?"

This was a familiar cue to Gustad—it had turned up for the fiftieth or sixtieth time in his last week's script, when he had played the role of a kill-crazy sewer inspector, trapped by flood waters in the cloacae of Under Brooklyn. "I say—" he began, then realized that his usual response was totally inappropriate. "It sounds wonderful," he finished weakly.

Wytak nodded in a businesslike way. "Now here's the program." He pressed a button, and a relief map of the North American continent appeared on the wall behind him. "Indicator." Wytak's porter put a metal tube with a shaped grip into his hand; a tiny spot on the map fluoresced where he pointed it.

"You'll swing down to the southwest until you cross the Tennessee, then head westward about to here, then up through the Plains, then back north of the Great Lakes and home again. You'll notice that this route keeps you well clear of both Chicago and Toronto. Remember that—it's important. We know that Frisco is working on a project similar to ours, although they're at least a year behind us. If we know that, the chances are that the other cities know it too, but we're pretty sure there's been no leak in our own security. There isn't going to be any."

He handed the indicator back. "You'll be gone about three months . . ."

Diamond was having trouble with his breathing again.

". . . You'll have to rough it pretty much—there'll be room in your floater for you and your equipment, and that's all."

Diamond gurgled despairingly and rolled up his eyes. Gustad himself felt an unpleasant sinking sensation.

"You mean," he asked incredulously, "I'm supposed to go all by myself—without even a *porter?*"

"That's right," said Wytak. "You see, Alvah, you and I are civilized human beings—we know there are so many indispensable time-and-laborsaving devices that nobody could possibly carry them all himself. But could you explain that to a Muckfoot?"

"I guess not."

"That's why only a man with your superb talents can do this job for the City. Those people actually live the kind of sordid, brutal existence you portray so well in the realies. Well, you can be as rough and tough as they are—you can talk their own language, and they'll respect you."

Gustad flexed his muscles slightly, feeling pleased but not altogether certain. Then a new and even more revolting aspect of this problem occurred to him. "Your Honor, suppose I got along *too* well with the Muckfeet? I mean suppose they invited me into one of their houses to—" he gagged slightly—"eat?"

Wytak's face went stony. "I am surprised that you feel it necessary to bring that subject up. All that will be covered very thoroughly in the briefing you will get from

Commissioner Laurence and Chairman Neddo and their staffs. And I want you to understand, Gustad, that no pressure of any kind is being exerted on you to take this assignment. This is a job for a willing, cooperative volunteer, not a draftee. If you feel you're not the man for it, just say so now."

Gustad apologized profusely. Wytak interrupted him, with the warmest and friendliest smile imaginable. "That's all right, son, I understand. I understand perfectly. Well, gentlemen, I think that's all."

As soon as they were alone, Diamond clutched Gustad's sleeve and pulled him over to the side of the corridor. "Listen to me, Al boy. We can still pull you out of this. I know a doctor that will make you so sick you couldn't walk across the street. He wouldn't do it for everybody, but he owes me a couple of—"

"No, wait a minute. I don't—"

"I know, I *know*," said Diamond impatiently. "You'll get your contract busted with Seven Boroughs and you'll lose a couple months, maybe more, and you'll have to start all over again with one of the little studios, but what of it? In a year or two, you'll be as big as—"

"Now wait, Jack. In the first—"

"Al, I'm not just thinking about my twenty percent of you. I don't even *care* about that—it's just money. What I want, I want you should still be alive next year, you understand what I mean?"

"Look," said Gustad, "you don't understand, Jack. I *want* to go. I mean I don't exactly want to, but—" He pointed down the corridor to the window that framed a vista of gigantic columns, fiercely brilliant below, fading to massive darkness above, with a million tiny floater-lights drifting like a river of stardust down the avenue. "Just look at that. It took hundreds of years to build! I mean if I can keep it going just by spending three months. . . . And besides," he added practically, "think of the publicity."

II

The foothill country turned out to be picturesque but not very rewarding. Alvah had bypassed the ancient states of Pennsylvania and Maryland as directed, since the tribes nearest the City were understood to be still somewhat rancorous. By the end of his first day, he was beginning to regard this as a serious understatement.

He had brought his floater down, with flags flying, loudspeakers blaring, colored lights flashing, and streamers flapping gaily behind him, just outside an untidy collection of two-story beehive huts well south of the former Pennsylvania border. He had seen numerous vaguely human shapes from the air, but when he extruded his platform and stepped out, every visible door was shut, the streets were empty, and there was no moving thing in sight, except for a group of singularly unpleasant-looking animals in a field to his right.

After a few moments, Gustad shut off the loudspeakers and listened. He thought he heard a hum of voices from the nearest building. Suppressing a momentary qualm, he lowered himself on the platform stair and walked over to the building. It had a single high window, a crude oval in shape, closed by a discolored pane.

Standing under this window, Alvah called, "Hello in there!" .

The muffled voices died away for a moment, then buzzed as busily as ever.

"Come on out—I want to talk to you!"

Same result.

"You don't have to be afraid! I come in peace!"

The voices died away again, and Alvah thought he saw a dim face momentarily through the pane. A single voice rose on an interrogative note.

"*Peace!*" Alvah shouted.

The window slid abruptly back into the wall and, as Alvah gaped upward, a deluge of slops descended on him, followed by a gale of coarse laughter.

Alvah's immediate reaction, after the first dazed and gasping instant, was a hot-water-and-soap tropism, carrying with it an ardent desire to get out of his drenched clothes and throw them away. His second, as imperious as the first, had the pure flame of artistic inspiration—he wanted to see how many aesthetically satisfying small pieces one explosive charge would make out of that excrescence-shaped building.

Under no conditions, said the handbook he had been required to memorize, *will you commit any act which might be interpreted by the Muckfeet as aggressive, nor will you make use of your weapons at any time, unless such use becomes necessary for the preservation of your own life.*

Alvah wavered, grew chilly, and retired. Restored in body, but shaken in spirit, he headed south.

Then there had been his encounter with the old man and the animal. Somewhere in the triangle of land between the Mississippi and the Big Black, at a point which was not on his itinerary at all, but had the overwhelming attraction of being more than a thousand air-miles from New York, he had set the floater down near another sprawling settlement.

As usual, all signs of activity in and around the village promptly disappeared. With newly acquired caution, Alvah sat tight. Normal human curiosity, he reasoned, would drive the Muckfeet to him sooner or later—and even if that failed, there was his nuisance value. How long could you ignore a strange object, a few hundred yards from your home, that was shouting, waving flags, flashing colored lights, and sending up puffs of pink-and-green smoke?

Nothing happened for a little over an hour. Then, half-dozing in his control chair, Alvah saw two figures coming toward him across the field.

Alvah's ego, which had been taking a beating all day, began to expand. He stepped out onto the platform and waited.

The two figures kept coming, taking their time. The tall one was a skinny loose-jointed oldster with a conical hat on the back of his head. The little one ambling along in front of him was some sort of four-footed animal.

In effect, an audience of one—at any rate, it was Alvah's best showing so far. He mentally rehearsed his opening lines. There was no point, he thought, in bothering with the magic tricks or the comic monologue. He might as well go straight into the sales talk.

The odd pair was now much closer, and Gustad recognized the animal half of it. It was a so-called watchdog, one of the incredibly destructive beasts the Muckfeet trained to do their fighting for them. It had a slender, supple body, a long feline tail and a head that looked something like a terrier's and something like a housecat's. However, it was not half as large or as frightening in appearance as the pictures Alvah had seen. It must, he decided, be a pup.

Two yards from the platform, the oldster came to a halt. The watchdog sat down beside him, tongue lolling wetly. Alvah turned off the loudspeakers and the color displays.

"Friend," he began, "I'm here to show you things that will astound you, marvels that you wouldn't believe unless you saw them with your own—"

"You a Yazoo?"

Thrown off stride, Alvah gaped. "What was that, friend?"

"Ah *said*—you a Yazoo?"

"No," said Alvah, feeling reasonably positive.

"Any kin to a Yazoo?"

"I don't think so."

"Git," said the old man.

Unlikely as it seemed, a Yazoo was apparently a good thing to be. "Wait a second," said Alvah. "Did you say *Yazoo?* I didn't understand you there at first. Am I a *Yazoo!* Why, man, my whole family on both sides has been —" what was the plural of Yazoo?

"Ah'll count to two," said the old man. "*One.*"

"Now wait a minute," said Alvah, feeling his ears getting hot. The watchdog, he noticed, had hoisted its rump a fraction of an inch and was staring at him in a marked manner. He flexed his right forearm slightly and felt the reassuring pressure of the pistol in its pop-out holster. "What makes you Muckfeet think you can—"

"*Two,*" said the oldster, and the watchdog was a spread-eagled blur in midair, seven feet straight up from the ground.

Instinct took over. Instinct had nothing to do with pistols or holsters, or with the probable size of a full-grown Muckfoot watchdog. It launched Alvah's body into a backward standing broad jump through the open floater door, and followed that with an economical underhand punch at the control button inside.

The door slammed shut. It then bulged visibly inward and rang like a gong. Sprawled on the floor, Gustad stared at it incredulously. There were further sounds—a thunderous growling and a series of hackle-raising screeches, as of hard metal being gouged by something even harder. The whole floater shook.

Alvah made the control chair in one leap, slammed on the power switch, and yanked at the steering bar. At an altitude of about a hundred feet, he saw the dark shape of the watchdog leap clear and fall, twisting.

A few seconds later, he put the bar into neutral and looked down. Man and watchdog were moving slowly back across the field toward the settlement. As far as Alvah could tell, the beast was not even limping.

Alvah's orders were reasonably elastic, but he had already stretched them badly in covering the southward leg of his route in one day. Still, there seemed to be nothing else to do. Either there was an area somewhere on the circuit where he could get the Muckfeet to listen to him, or there wasn't. If there was, it would make more sense to hop around until he found it, and then work outward to its limits, than to blunder straight along, collecting bruises and insults.

And if there wasn't—and this did not bear thinking about—then the whole trip was a bust.

Alvah switched on his communicator and tapped out the coded clicks that meant, "proceeding on schedule"—which was a lie—"no results yet"—which was true. Then he headed north.

Nightfall overtook him as he was crossing the Ozark Plateau. He set the floater's controls to hover at a thousand feet, went to bed, and slept badly until just before dawn. With a cup of kaffin in his hand, he watched this phenomenon in surprised disapproval: the scattered lights winking out below, the first colorless hint of radiance, which illuminated nothing, but simply made the universe seem more senselessly vast and formless than before; finally, after an interminable progression of insignificant changes, the rinds of orange and scarlet, and the dim sun bulging up at the rim of the turning earth.

It was lousy theater.

How, Alvah asked himself, could any human being keep himself from dying of sheer irrelevance and boredom against a background like that? He was aware that billions had done so, but his general impression of history was that people who didn't have a city always got busy improving themselves until they could build one or take one away from somebody else. All but the Muckfeet . . .

Once their interest has been engaged, said the handbook at one point, *you will lay principal stress upon the competitive advantages of each product. It will be your aim to create a situation in which ownership of one or more of our products will be not only an economic advantage, but a mark of social distinction. In this way, communities which have accepted the innovations will, in order to preserve and extend the recognition of their own status, be forced to convert members of neighboring communities.*

Well, maybe so.

Alvah ate a Spartan breakfast of protein jelly and citron cakes, called in the coordinates and the time to the operator in New York, and headed the floater northward again.

The landscape unrolled itself. If there were any major differences between this country and the districts he had seen yesterday, Alvah was unable to discern them. In the air, he saw an occasional huge flapping shape, ridden by human figures. He avoided them, and they ignored him. Below, tracts of dark-green forest alternated predictably with the pale green, red, or violet of cultivated fields. Here and there across the whole visible expanse stood isolated buildings. At intervals, these huddled closer and closer together and became a settlement. There were perhaps more roads as he moved northward, dustier ones. That was all.

The dustiness of these roads, it occurred to Alvah, was a matter that required investigation. The day was cloudless and clear; there was no wind at Alvah's level, and nothing in the behavior of the trees or cultivated plants to suggest that there was any farther down.

He slowed the floater and lowered it toward the nearest road. As he approached, the thread of ocher resolved itself into an irregular series of expanding puffs, each preceded by a black dot, the overall effect being that of a line of black-and-tan exclamation points. They seemed to be moving barely perceptibly, but were actually, Alvah guessed, traveling at a fairly respectable clip.

He transferred his attention to another road. It, too, was filled with hurrying dots, as was the next—and all the traffic was heading in approximately the same direction, westward of Alvah's course.

He swung the control bar over. The movement below, he was able to determine after twenty minutes' flying, converged upon a settlement larger than any he had yet seen. It sprawled for ten miles or more along the southern shore of a long and exceedingly narrow lake. Most of it looked normal enough—a haphazard arrangement of cone-roofed buildings—but on the side away from the lake, there was a fairly extensive area filled with what seemed to be long, narrow sheds. This, in turn, was bounded on two sides by a strip of fenced-in plots in which, as nearly as Alvah could make out through the dust, animals of all sizes and shapes were penned. It was this area which appeared to be the goal of every Muckfoot in the central plains.

The din was tremendous as Alvah floated down. There were shouts, cries, animal bellowings, sounds of hammering, occasional blurts of something that might be intended to be music, explosions of laughter. The newcomers, he noted, were being herded with much confusion to one or another of the fenced areas, where they left their mounts. Afterward, they straggled across to join the sluggish river of bodies in the avenues between the sheds.

No one looked up or noticed the dim shadow of the floater. Everyone was preoccupied, shouting, elbowing, blowing an instrument, climbing a pole. Alvah found a clear space at some distance from the sheds—as far as he could conveniently get from the penned animals—and landed.

He had no idea what this gathering was about. For all he knew, it might be a war council or some kind of religious observance, in which case his presence might be distinctly unwelcome. But in any case, there were customers here.

He looked dubiously at the stud that controlled his attention-catchers. If he used them, he would only be following directives, but he had a strong feeling that it would be a faux pas to do so in this situation. At the other extreme, the obvious thing to do was to get out and go look for someone in authority. This would involve abandoning the protection of the floater, however, and he might blunder into some taboo place or ceremony.

Evidently his proper course was to wait unobtrusively until he was discovered. On the other hand, if he stayed inside the floater with the door shut, the Muckfeet might take more alarm than if he showed himself. Still, wasn't it possible that they would be merely puzzled by a floater, whereas they would be angered by a floater with a man on its platform? Or, taking it from another angle . . .

The hell with it.

Alvah ran the platform out, opened the door, and stepped out. He was relieved when, as he was considering the delicate problem of whether or not to lower the stair, a small group of men and urchins came into view around the corner of the nearest shed, a dozen yards away from him.

They stopped when they saw him, and two or three of the smallest children scuttled behind their elders. They exchanged looks and a few words that Alvah couldn't hear. Then a pudgy little man with a fussed expression crowded forward, and the rest followed him at a discreet distance.

"Hello," said Alvah tentatively.

The little man came to a halt a yard or so from the platform. He had a white badge of some kind pinned to his shapeless brown jacket, and carried a sheaf of papers in his hand. "Who might *you* be?" he asked irritably.

"Alvah Gustad is my name. I hope I'm not putting you people out, parking in your area like this, Mr.—"

"Well, I should hope to spit you *is*, though. Supposed to be a tent go up right *there*. *Got* to be one by noon. What did you say your name was, Gus what?"

"Gustad. I don't believe I caught your name, Mr.—"

"Don't signify what *my* name *is*. We talking about *you*. What clan you belong to?"

"Uh—Flatbush," said Alvah at random. "Look, as long as I'm in the way here, you just tell me where to move to and—"

"Some little backwoods clan, I never even *heard* of it," said the pudgy man. "*I'll* tell you where you can *move* to. You can just haul that thing back where you come from. Gustad—Flatbush! *You* ain't on my list, I know *that*."

The other Muckfeet had moved up gradually to surround the little man. One of them, a lanky sad-faced youngster, nudged him with his elbow. "Might just check and see, Jake."

"Well, I ought to know. My *land*, Artie, I got my *work* to do. *I* can't spend all day standing here."

Artie's long face grew more mournful. "You thought them Keokuks wasn't on the list, either."

"Well—all right then, rot it." To Alvah: "What's your marks?"

Alvah blinked. "I don't—"

"Come *down* offa there." Jake turned impatiently to a man behind him. "Give'm a stake." As Alvah came hesitantly down the stair, he found he was being offered a sharpened length of wood by a seamy-faced brown man, who carried a bundle of others like it under his arm.

Alvah took it, without the least idea of what to do next. The brown man watched him alertly. "You c'n make your marks with that," he volunteered, and pointed to the ground between them.

The others closed in a little.

"Marks?" said Alvah worriedly.

The brown man hesitated, then took another stake from his bundle. "Like these here," he said. "These is mine." He drew a shaky circle and put a dot in the center of it. "George." A figure four. "Allister—that's me." A long rectangle with a loop at each end. "Coffin—that's m'clan."

Jake burst out, "Well, crying in a bucket, *he* knows that! You know how to sign your *name*, don't you?"

"Well," said Alvah, "*yes*." He wrote *Alvah Gustad* and, as an afterthought, added *Flatbush*.

There were surprised whistles. "Wrote it just as slick as Doc!" said a ten-year-old tow-headed male, bug-eyed with awe.

Jake stared at Alvah, then spun half around to wave his papers under Artie's nose. "Well, you satisfied now, Artie Brumbacher? I guess *that* ain't on my list, is it?"

"No," Artie admitted, "I guess it ain't—not if you can read the list, that is."

Everybody but Alvah laughed, Jake louder than anyone. "All right," he said, turning back to Alvah, "you just hitch up your brutes and get that thing *out* of here. If you ain't gone by the time I—"

"Jake!" called a businesslike female voice, and a small figure came shouldering through the crowd. "They need you over in the salamander shed—the Quincies is ready to move in, but there's some Sullivans ahead of them." She glanced at Alvah, then at the floater behind him. "You having any trouble here?"

"All settled *now*," Jake told her. "This feller ain't on the list. I just give him his *marching* orders."

"Look, if I can say something—" Alvah began.

The girl interrupted him. "Did you want to exhibit something at the fair?"

"That's right," said Alvah gratefully. "I was just trying to explain—"

"Well, you late, but maybe we can squeeze you in. You won't sell anything, though, if it's what I think it is. Let me see that list, Jake."

"Now *wait* a minute," said Jake indignantly. "You know we ain't got room for nobody that ain't on the *list*. We got enough trouble—"

"The earth-movers won't be here from Butler till tomorrow," said the girl, examining the papers. "We can put him in there and move him out again when they get here. You need any equipment besides what you brought?"

"No," said Alvah. "That would be fine, thanks. All I need is a place—"

"All right. Before you go, Jake, did you tell those Sullivans they could have red, green, and yellow in the salamander shed?"

"Well, *sure* I did. That what it says right there."

She handed him back the papers and pointed to a line. "That's Quincy, see? Dot instead of a cross. Sullivans is supposed to have that corner in the garden truck shed, keep the place warm for the seedlings, but they won't budge till you tell them it was a mistake. Babbishes and Stranahans is fit to be tied. You get over there and straighten them out, will you? And don't worry too much about *him*."

Jake snorted and moved away, still looking ruffled. The girl turned to Alvah. "All right, let's go."

Unhappy but game, Alvah turned and climbed back into the floater with the girl close behind him. The conditioning he'd had just before he left helped when he was in the open air, but in the tiny closed cabin of the floater the girl's triply compounded stench was overpowering.

How did they live with themselves?

She leaned over the control chair, pointing. "Over there," she said. "See that empty space I'm pointing at?"

Alvah saw it and put the floater there as fast as the generator would push it. The space was not quite empty— there were a few very oddly assorted Muckfeet and animals in it, but they straggled out when they saw him hovering, and he set the floater down.

To his immense relief, the girl got out immediately. Alvah followed her as far as the platform.

III

In a tailor shop back in Middle Queens, the proprietors, two brothers named Wynn, whose sole livelihood was the shop, stared glumly at the bedplate where the two-hundred-gallon Klenomatic ought to have been.

"He say anything when he took it away?" Clyde asked.

Morton shrugged and made a sour face.

"Yeah," said Clyde. He looked distastefully at a dead cigar and tossed it at the nearest oubliette. He missed.

"He said a month, two months," Morton told him. "You know what that means."

"Yeah."

"So I'll call up the factory," Morton said violently. "But I know what they're gonna tell me. Give us a deposit and we'll put you on a waiting list. *Waiting* list!"

"Yeah," said Clyde.

In a factory in Under Bronnix, the vice-president in charge of sales shoved a thick folder of coded plastic slips under the nose of the vice-president in charge of production. "Look at those orders," he said.

"Uh-huh," said Production.

"You know how far back they go? *Three years.* You

know how much money this company's lost in unfilled orders? Over two million—"

"I *know*. What do you expect? Every fabricator in this place is too old. We're holding them together with spit and string. Don't bother me, will you, Harry. I got my own—"

"Listen," said Sales. "This can't go on much longer. It's up to us to tell the old man that he's got to try a bigger bribe on the metals people. Mortgage the plant if we have to—it's the only thing to do."

"We have more mortgages now than the plant is worth."

Sales reddened. "Nick, this is serious. Last fall, it looked like we might squeeze through another year, but now. . . . You know what's going to happen in another eight, ten months?" He snapped his fingers. "Right down the drain."

Production blinked at him wearily. "Bribes are no good anymore, Harry. You know that as well as I do. They're out."

"Well, then what are we going to *do?*"

Production shook his head. "I don't know. I swear to God, I don't know."

Over in Metals Reclamation Four, in Under and Middle Jersey, the night shift was just beginning. In the blue-lit cavern of Ferrous, this involved two men, one bald and flabby, the other gray and gnarled. They exchanged a silent look, then each in turn put his face into the time clock's retinascope mask. The clock, which had been emitting a shrill, irritating sound, gurgled its satisfaction and shut up.

"Well, that's it," said the gray one. "I'll be your work gang and you be mine, huh?"

The flabby one spat. "Wonder what happened to Turk."

"Who cares? I never liked him."

"Just wondering. Yesterday he's here, today where is he? Labor pool, army—" he spat again, with care—"repair, maintenance. . . . He was fifteen years in this department. I was just wondering."

"Scooping dreck, probably. That's about his speed." The gray man shambled over to the control bench opposite and looked at the indicators. Then he lit a cigarette.

"Nothing in the hoppers?" the flabby one asked.

"Nah. They ought to put Turk in the hoppers. He had metal in his goddamn *teeth*."

"Turk wasn't old," the flabby one said reproachfully. "No more than sixty."

"I never liked him."

"First it was the kid—you know, Pimples. Then, lessee, the next one was that big guy, the realie actor—"

"Gustad. The hell with him."

"Yeah, Gustad. What I mean is, where do they go to? It's the same thing on my three-to-seven shift, over in Yeasts. Guys I knew for ten, fifteen, twenty years on the same job. All of a sudden, they're gone and you never see them. Must be a hell of a thing, starting all over again somewhere else—guys like that—I mean you get set in your ways, kind of."

His eyes were patient and bewildered in their watery pouches. "Guys like me—no kids, nobody that gives a damn about 'em. Kind of gives you the jumps to think about it. You know what I mean?"

The gray one looked embarrassed, then irritated, then defiant. "Aah," he said, and produced a deck of cards from his kit—the grimy coating on the creaseless, frayless plastic as lovingly built and preserved as the patina in a meerschaum. "Cut for deal. Come on! Let's play."

"I'll have to know what you going to exhibit," the girl said. "For the fair records."

"Laborsaving devices," Alvah told her, "the latest and best products of human ingenuity, designed to—"

"Machines," she said, writing. She added, looking up, "There's a fee for the use of the fairground space. Since you're only going to have it for a day, we'll call it twenty twains."

Alvah hesitated. He had no idea what a twain might be —it had *sounded* like "twain." Evidently it was some sort of crude Muckfoot coinage.

"Afraid I haven't got any of your money," he said, producing a handful of steels from his belt changer-meter. "I don't suppose these would do?"

The girl looked at him steadily. "Gold?" she said. "Precious stones, platinum, anything of that kind?" Alvah shook his head.

"Sure?" Alvah shrugged despairingly.

"Well," she said after a moment, "maybe something can be arranged. I'll let you talk to Doc about it, anyhow. He'll have to decide. Come on."

"Just a minute," Alvah said, and ducked back into the floater. He found what he was looking for and trotted outside again.

"What's that?" asked the girl, looking at the bulky kit at his waist.

"Just a few things I like to have with me."

"Mind showing me?"

"Well—no." He opened the kit. "Cigarette lighter, flashlight, shaver, raincoat, heater, a few medicines over here, jujubes, food concentrates, things like that. Uh, I don't know why I put this in here—it's a distress signal for people who get lost in the subway."

"You never can tell," said the girl, "when a thing like that will come in handy."

"That's true. Uh, this thing that looks like two dumb-bells and a corkscrew . . ."

"Never mind," said the girl. "Come along."

The first shed they passed was occupied by things that looked like turtles with glittery four-foot shells. In the nearest stall a man was peeling off from one of the beasts successive thin layers of this shell-stuff, which turned out to be colorless and transparent. He passed them to a woman, who dipped them into a basin and then laid them on a board to dry. The ones at the far end of the row, Alvah noticed, had flattened into discs.

The girl apparently misread his expression as curiosity. "Glass tortoise," she told him. "For windows and so on. The young ones have more hump to their shells—almost spherical to start with. Those are for bottles and bowls and things."

Alvah blinked noncommittally.

They passed a counter on which metal tools were displayed—knives, axes, and the like. Similar objects, Alvah noted automatically, had only approximately similar outlines. There seemed to be no standardization at all.

"These are local," the girl said. "The metal comes from Iron Pits, just a few miles south of here."

In the next shed was a long row of upright rectangular frames, most of them empty. One near the end, however, was filled with some sort of insubstantial film or fabric. A tiny scarlet creature was crawling rapidly up and down this gossamer substance, working it's way gradually from left to right.

"Squareweb," the girl informed him. "This dress I'm wearing was made that way."

Alvah verified his previous impression that the dress was opaque. Rather a pity, since it was also quite handsomely filled out. Not, he assured himself, that it made any difference—the girl was a Muckfoot, after all.

Next came a large cleared space. In it were half a

dozen animals that resembled nothing in nature or nightmare except each other. They were wide and squat and at least six feet high at the shoulder. They had vaguely reptilian heads, and their scaly hides were patterned in orange and blue, rust and vermilion, yellow and poppy red.

The oddest thing about them, barring the fact that each had three sets of legs, was the extraordinary series of protuberances that sprouted from their backs. First came an upright, slightly hollow shield sort of thing, set crossways behind the first pair of shoulders. Behind that, something that looked preposterously like an armchair—it even had a bright-colored cushion—and then a double row of upright spines with a wide space between them.

"Trucks," said the girl.

Alvah cleared his throat. "Look, Miss—"

"Betty Jane Hofmeyer. Call me B. J. Everybody does."

"All right—uh—B. J. I wonder if you could explain something to me. What's wrong with metal? And plastic, and things like that? I mean why should you people want to go to so much trouble and—and *mess*, when there are easier ways to do things better?"

"Each," she said, "to his own taste. We turn here."

A few yards ahead, the fair ended and the settlement proper began with an unusually large building—large enough, Alvah estimated, to fill almost an entire wing of a third-class hotel in New York. Unlike the hovels he had seen farther south—which looked as if they had been excreted—it was built of some regular, smooth-surfaced material, seamless and fairly well shaped.

Alvah was so engrossed in these and other considerations that it wasn't until the girl turned three steps inside the doorway, impatiently waiting, that he realized a minor crisis was at hand—he was being invited to enter a Muckfoot dwelling.

"Well, come on," said B. J.

Refuse any offers of food, transportation, etc., said the handbook, *firmly, but as diplomatically as possible. Employ whatever subterfuge the situation may suggest, such as, "Thank you, but my doctor has forbidden me to touch fur,"* or, *"Pardon me, but I have a sore throat and am unable to eat."*

Alvah cleared his throat frantically. The situation did not suggest anything at all. Luckily, however, his stomach did.

"Maybe I'd better not come in," he said. "I don't feel very well. Maybe if I just sit down here quietly—"

"You can sit down inside," said the girl briskly. "If there's anything wrong with you, Doc will look you over."

"Well," Alvah asked desperately, "couldn't you bring him out here for a minute? I really don't think—"

"Doc is a busy man. Are you coming or not?"

Alvah hesitated. There were, he told himself, only two possibilities, after all: (a) he would somehow manage to keep his breakfast, and (b) he wouldn't.

The nausea began as a faint, premonitory twinge when he stepped through the doorway. It increased steadily as he followed B. J. past cages filled with things that chirruped, croaked, rumbled, rustled, or simply stared at him. The girl didn't invite comment on any of them, for which Alvah was grateful. He was too busy concentrating on trying not to concentrate on his misery.

For the same reason, he did not notice at what precise point the cages gave way to long rows of potted green plants. Alvah was just beginning to wonder if he would live to see the end of them when, still following B. J., he turned a corner and came upon a cleared space with half a dozen people in it.

One of them was the sad-faced youth, Artie. Another was a stocky man, all chest and paunch and no neck at all, who was talking to Artie while the others stood and listened. B. J. stopped and waited quietly. Alvah, perforce, did the same.

". . . just a few seedlings and a couple of one-year-olds for now—we'll see how they go. If you have more room later on. . . . What else was I going to tell you?" The stocky man rumpled his hair nervously. "Oh, look, Artie, I had a copy of the specifications for you, but the fool bird got into a fight with a mirror and broke his. . . . Wait a second." He turned abruptly. "Hello, Beej. Come along to the library for a second, will you?"

He turned again and strode off, with Artie, B. J., and Alvah in his wake.

The room they entered was, from Alvah's point of view, the worst he had struck yet. It was a hundred feet long by fifty wide, and everywhere—perched on the walls and on multi-leveled racks that ran the length of the room, darting through the air in flutters of brilliance—were tiny raucous birds, feathered in every prismatic shade, green, electric blue, violet, screaming red.

"Mark seven one-oh-three!" the stocky man shouted. The roomful of birds took it up in a hideous echoing chorus. An instant later, a sudden flapping sound turned itself into an explosion of color and alighted on the stocky man's shoulder, preening its feathers with a blunt green beak. "*Rrk*," it said and then, quite clearly, "Mark seven one-oh-three."

The stocky man made a perch of one forefinger and handed the thing across to Artie's shoulder. "I can't give you this one. It's the only copy I got. You'll have to listen to it and remember what you need."

"I'll remember." Artie glanced at the bird on his shoulder and said, "Magnus utility tree."

The stocky man looked around, saw B. J. "Now, Beej, is it important? Because—"

"Magnus utility tree," the bird was saying. "Thrives in all soils, over ninety-one percent resistant to most rusts,

scales, and other infestations. Edible from root to branch.
Young shoots and leaves excellent for salads. Self-
fertilizing. Sap can be drawn in second year for—"

"Doc," said the girl clearly, "this is Alvah Gustad.
From New York. Alvah, meet Doc Bither."

". . . golden orangoes in spring and early summer,
Bither aperries in late summer and fall. Will crossbreed
with—"

"New York, huh?" said Bither. "You a long way from
home, young—Excuse me. Artie?"

". . . series five to one hundred fifteen. Trunks guar-
anteed straight and rectilinear, two-by-four at end of second year, four-by-six at—"

"I all set, Doc."

". . . mealie pods and winterberries—"

"Fine, all right." He took B. J.'s arm. "Let's go someplace we can talk."

". . . absorb fireproofing and stiffening solutions
freely through roots . . ."

Bither led the way into a small, crowded room. "Now," he
said, peering intently at Alvah, "what's the problem?"

B. J. explained briefly. Then they both stared at
Alvah. Sweat was beaded coldly on his brow and his knees
were trembling, but he seemed to have stabilized the nausea
just below the critical point. The idea, he told himself, was
to convince yourself that the whole building was a realie
stage and all the objects in it props. Wasn't there a line to
that effect in one of the classics—*The Manager of Copenhagen*, or perhaps *Have It Your Own Way?*

"What do you think?" Bither asked.

"Might try him out."

"Um. Damn it, I wish we hadn't run out of birds. Can
you take this down for me, Beej? I'll arrange for the fair
rental fee, Alvah, if you just answer a few questions."

It sounded innocuous enough, but Alvah felt a twinge of suspicion. "What kind of questions?"

"Just personal questions, like how old, what you do for a living."

"Twenty-six. I'm an actor."

"Always been an actor?"

"No."

"What else you done?"

"Labor."

"What kind?" B. J. asked.

"Worked with his hands, he means," Bither told her. "Parents laborers, too?"

"Yes."

B. J. and Bither exchanged glances. Alvah shifted uncomfortably. "If that's all . . ."

"One or two more. I want you to tell me, near as you can, when was the first time you remember knowing that our clothes and our animals and us and all the things we make smelled bad?"

It was too much. Alvah turned and lurched blindly out the door. He heard their voices behind him:

". . . minutes."

". . . alley door!"

Then there were hands on him, steering him from behind as he stumbled forward at a half-run. They turned him right, then left, and finally he was out in the cool air, not a moment too soon.

When he straightened, wiping tears away, he was alone, but a moment later the girl appeared in the doorway.

"That's all," she said distantly. "You can start your exhibition whenever you want."

IV

The magic tricks went over fairly well—at least nobody yawned. The comic monologue, however, was a flat failure, even though the piece had been expertly slanted for a rural audience and, by all the laws of psychostatics, should have rated at least half a dozen boffs. ("So the little boy came moseying back up the road, and his grandpa said to him, 'Why didn't you drive them hogs out of the corn like I told you?' And the little fellow piped up, 'Them ain't hogs—them's shoats!' ")

Alvah launched hopefully into his sales talks and demonstrations.

The all-purpose fireless lifetime cooker was received with blank stares. When Alvah fried up a savory batch of protein-paste fritters and offered to hand them out, nobody responded but one small boy, and his mother hauled him down off the platform stair by the slack of his pants.

Smiling doggedly, Alvah brought out the pocket-workshop power tools and accessories. This, it appeared, was more like it. An interested hum went up as he drilled three holes of various sizes in a bar of duroplast, then sawed through it from end to end and finally cut a mortise in one piece, a tenon in the other, and fitted them together. A few more people drifted in.

"And now, friends," said Alvah, "if you'll continue to give me your kind attention . . ."

The next item was the little giant power plant for the home, shop, or office. Blank stares again. Alvah picked out one Muckfoot in the front row—a blear-eyed, open-mouthed fellow, with hair over his forehead and a basket under his arm, who seemed typical—and spoke directly to him. He outdid himself about the safety, economy, efficiency, and unobtrusiveness of a little giant power plant. He explained its operation in words a backward two-year-old could understand.

"A little giant," he concluded, leaning over the platform rail to stare hypnotically into the Muckfoot's eyes, "is the power plant for *you!*"

The fellow blinked, slowly produced a dark brown

lump of something from his pocket, slowly put it into his inattentive mouth, and as slowly began to chew.

Alvah breathed deeply and clutched the rail. "And now," he said, giving the clincher, "the marvel of the age— the superspeed runabout!" He pressed the button that popped open a segment of the floater's hull and lowered the gleaming little two-wheeled car into view.

"Now, friends," he said, "just to demonstrate the amazing qualities of this miracle of modern science—is there any gentleman in the crowd who has an animal he fancies for speed?"

For the first time, the Muckfeet reacted according to the charts. Shouts rocketed up: "Me, by damn!" "Me!" "Right here, mister!" "Yes, sir!"

"Friends, friends!" said Alvah, spreading his hands. "There won't be time to accommodate you all. Choose one of you to represent the rest!"

"*Swifty!*" somebody yelped, and other voices took up the cry. A red-haired young man began working his way back out of the crowd, propelled by gleeful shouts and slaps on the back.

Alvah took an indicator and began pointing out the salient features of the runabout. He had not got more than a quarter of the way through when the redhead reappeared, mounted astride an animal which, to Alvah's revolted gaze, looked to be part horse, part lynx, part camel, and part pure horror.

To the crowd, evidently, it was one of nature's finest efforts. Alvah swallowed bile and raised his voice again. "Clear a space now, friends—all the way around!"

It took time, but eventually self-appointed deputies began to get the crowd moving. Alvah descended, carrying two bright marker poles, and, followed by the inquisitive redhead, set one up at either side of the enclosure, a few yards short of the boundary.

"This will be the course," he told Swifty. "Around

these markers and the floater—that thing I was standing on. We'll do ten laps, starting and finishing here. Is that all right?"

"All right with me," said the redhead, grinning more widely than before.

There were self-appointed timekeepers and starters, too. When Alvah, in the runabout, and the redhead, on his monster, were satisfactorily lined up, one of them bellowed, "On y' marks—Git set . . ." and then cracked a short whip with a noise out of all proportion to its size.

For a moment, Alvah thought Swifty and his horrid mount had simply disappeared. Then he spotted them, diminished by perspective, halfway down the course, and rapidly getting smaller. He slammed the power bar over and took off in pursuit.

Around the first turn, it was Swifty, with Alvah nowhere. In the stretch, Alvah was coming up fast on the outside. Around the far turn, he was two monster lengths behind and, in the stretch again, they were neck and neck. Alvah kept it that way for the next two laps and then gradually pulled ahead. The crowd became a multicolored streak, whirling past him. In the sixth lap, he passed Swifty again—in the eighth, again—in the tenth, still again—and when he skidded to a halt beyond the finish post, fluttering its flags with the wind of his passage, poor old Swifty and his steaming beast were still lumbering halfway down the stretch.

"Now, friends," said Alvah, triumphantly mounting the platform again, "in a moment, I'm going to tell you how you, yourselves, can own this wonderful runabout and many marvels more—but first, are there any questions you'd like to ask?"

Swifty pushed forward, grinless, looking like a man smitten by lightning. "How many to a get?" he called.

Alvah decided he must have misunderstood. "You can

have any number you want," he said. "The price is so reasonable—but I'm going to come to that in a—"

"I don't mean how many will you *sell*. How many to a get?" Alvah looked blank. "How many calves, or colts, or whatever, is what I want to know."

There was a general murmur of agreement. This, it would seem, was what everybody wanted to know.

Appalled, Alvah corrected the misapprehension as quickly and clearly as he could.

"Mean to say," somebody called, "they don't *breed?*"

"Certainly not. If one of them ever breaks down—and, friends, they're built to last—you get it repaired or buy another."

"How much?" somebody in the crowd yelled.

"Friends, I'm not here to take your money," Alvah said. "We just want—"

"Then how we going to pay for your stuff?"

"I'm coming to that. When two people want to trade, friends, there's usually a way. You want our products. We want metals—iron, aluminum, chromium—"

"Suppose a man ain't got any metal?"

"Well, sir, there are a lot of other things we can use besides metal. Natural fruits and vegetables, for instance."

The slack-faced yokel in the first row, the one with the basket under his arm, roused himself for the first time. His mouth closed, then opened again. "*What* kind?"

"Natural products, friend. You know, the kind your great-granddad ate. We use a lot every year for table delicacies, and—"

The yokel came halfway up the platform stair. His gnarled fingers dipped into the basket and came up with a smooth red-gold ovoid. He shoved it toward Alvah. "You mean," he said incredulously, "you wouldn' eat *that?*"

Gulping, Alvah backed away a step. The Muckfoot came after him. "Raise 'em myself," he said plaintively, holding out the red fruit. "I tell you, they're just the juiciest, goodest—Go ahead, try one."

"I'm not hungry," Alvah said desperately. "I'm on a diet. Now if you'll just step down quietly, friend, till after the—"

The Muckfoot stared at him, holding the fruit under Alvah's nose. "You mean you won't *try* it?"

"No," said Alvah, trying not to breathe. "Now go on back down there, friend—don't crowd me."

"Well," said the Muckfoot, "then durn you!" And he shoved the disgusting thing squashily into Alvah's face.

Alvah saw red. Blinking away a glutinous film of juice and pulp, he glimpsed the yokel's face, spread into a hideous grin. Waves of laughter beat about his ears. Retching, he brought up his right fist in an instinctive roundhouse swing that clapped the yokel's grin shut and toppled him over the platform rail, basket, flying fruit, and all.

The laughter rumbled away into expectant silence. Alvah fumbled in his kit for tissues, scrubbed a wad of them across his face and saw them come away daubed with streaky red. He hurled them convulsively into the crowd and, leaning over the rail, shouted thickly, "Lousy, stinking, filthy *Muckfeet!*"

Muckfoot men in the front ranks turned and looked at each other solemnly. Then two of them marched up the platform stair and, behind them, another two.

Still berserk, Alvah met the first couple with two violent kicks in the chest. This cleared the stair, but he turned to find three more candidates swarming over the rail. He swung at the nearest, who ducked. The next one seized Alvah's arm with both hands and toppled over backward. Alvah followed, head foremost, and landed with a jar that shook him to his toes.

The next thing he knew, he was lying on the ground surrounded by upward of twenty thick, seamless boots, choking on dust, and getting the daylights methodically kicked out of him.

Alvah rolled over frantically, climbed the first leg that came to hand, got his back against the platform and, by dint of cracking skulls together, managed in two brisk minutes to clear a momentary space around him. Another dim figure lunged at him. Alvah clouted it under the ear, whirled and vaulted over the rail onto the platform.

His gun popped out into his hand.

For just a moment, he was standing alone, feeling the pistol grip clenched hard in his dirt-caked palm and able to judge exactly how long he had before half a dozen Muckfeet would swarm up the stair and over the rail. The crowd's faces were sharp and clear. He saw Artie, and Doc Bither, and Jake, his mouth open to howl, and he saw the girl, B. J., in a curious posture—leaning forward, her right arm thrust out and down. She had just thrown something at him.

Alvah saw the gray-white blur wobbling toward him. He tried to dodge, but the thing struck his shoulder and exploded with a papery pop. For a bewildering instant, the air was full of dancing bright particles. Then they were gone.

Alvah didn't have time to wonder about it. He thumbed the selector over to *Explosive*, pointed the gun straight up and squeezed the trigger.

Nothing happened.

There were two Muckfeet half over the rail and three more coming up the stair. Incredulous, still aiming at the air, Alvah tried again—and again. The gun didn't work.

Three Muckfeet were on the platform, four more right behind them. Alvah spun through the open door and slapped at the control button. The door stayed open.

The Muckfeet were massed in the doorway, staring in like visitors at an aquarium. Alvah dived at the power bar, shoved it over. The floater didn't lift.

"Holly! Luke!" called a clear voice outside, and the Muckfeet turned. "Leave him alone. He's got enough troubles now."

Alvah was pawing at the control board.

The lights didn't work.

The air conditioner didn't work.

The scent-organ didn't work.

The musivox didn't work.

One of the Muckfeet put his head in at the door. "Reckon he has," he said thoughtfully and went away again. Alvah heard his voice, more faintly. "You do something, B. J.?"

"Yes," said the girl, "I did something."

Moving warily, Alvah went outside. The girl was standing just below the platform, watching as the Muckfoot men filed down the stair.

"You!" he said to her.

She paid him no attention. "Just one of those things, Luke," she said.

Luke nodded solemnly. "Well, the fair don't come but once a year." He and the other men moved past her into the crowd, each one acquiring a train of curiosity-seekers as he went. The crowd began to drift away.

A familiar voice yelped, "Ride'm out on a *razorback* is what I say!"

A chorus of "Now, Jake!" went up. There were murmurs of dissent, of inquiry, of explanation. "Time for the poultry judging!" somebody called, and the crowd moved faster.

Alvah went dazedly down and climbed into the runabout. He waggled its power bar. No response.

He tore open his kit and began frantically hauling out one glittery object after another, holding each for an instant and then throwing it on the ground. The razor, the heater, the vacuum cleaner, the sonotube, the vibromasseur.

Swifty rode by, at ease atop his horse-lynx-camel horror. He was whistling.

The crowd was almost gone. Among the stragglers was Jake, fists on his pudgy hips, his choleric cheeks gleaming with sweat and satisfaction.

"Well, Mister High-and-Mighty," he called, "what you going to do *now?*"

That was just what Alvah was wondering. He was about a thousand miles from home by air—probably more like fifteen hundred across-country. He had no transportation, no shelter, no power tools, no equipment. He had, he realized with horror, been cut off instantly from everything that made a man civilized.

What *was* he going to do?

V

Manager Wytak had his feet on the glossy desktop. So did the comptroller, narrow-faced, old Mr. Creedy; the director of information, plump Mr. Kling; the commissioner of supply, blotched and pimpled Mr. Jackson; and the porcine Mr. McArdle, commissioner of war. With chairs tilted back, they stared through a haze of cigar smoke at each other's stolid faces mirrored on the ceiling.

Wytak's voice was as confident as ever, if a trifle muted, and when the others spoke, he listened. These were not the hired nonentities Alvah had seen; these were the men who had made Wytak, the electorate with whose consent he governed.

"Jack," said Wytak, "I want you to look at it my way and see if you don't think I'm right. It isn't a question of how long we can hold out—when you get right down and look at it, it's a question of *can we do anything.*"

"In time," said Jackson expressionlessly.

"In time. But if we can do anything, there'll be time enough. You say we've got troubles now and you're right, but I tell you we can pull through a situation a thousand times worse than this—*if* we've got an answer. And have we got an answer? We have."

Creedy grunted. "Like to see some results, Boley."

"You'll see them. You can't skim a yeast tank the first day, Will."

"You can see the bubbles, though," said Jackson sourly. "Any report from this Gustad today, while we're talking about it?"

"Not yet. He was getting some response yesterday. He's following it up. I trust that boy—the analyzers picked his card out of five million. Wait and see. He'll deliver."

"If you say so, Boley."

"I say so."

Jackson nodded. "That's good enough. Gentlemen?"

In another soundproof, spyproof office in Over Manhattan, Kling and McArdle met again twenty minutes later.

"What do you think," asked Kling with his meaningless smile.

"Moderately good. I was hoping he would lie about Gustad's report, but of course there was very little chance of that. Wytak is an old hand."

"You admire him," Kling suggested.

"As a specimen of his type. Wytak pulled us out of a very bad spot in thirty-nine."

"Agreed."

"And he has had his uses since then. There are times when brilliant improvisation is better than sound principles —and times when it is not. Wytak is an incurable romantic."

"And you?"

"We," said McArdle grimly, "are realists."

"Oh, yes. But perhaps we are not anything just yet.

Creedy is interested, but not convinced—and until he moves, Jackson will do nothing."

"Wytak's project is a failure. You can't do business with the Muckfeet. But the fool was so confident that he didn't even interfere with Gustad's briefing."

Kling leaned forward with interest. "You didn't? . . ."

"*No*. It wasn't necessary. But it means that Gustad has no instructions to fake successful reports—and that means Wytak can't stall until he gets back. There was no report today. Suppose there's none tomorrow, or the next day, or the next."

"In that case, of course. . . . However, it's always as well to offer something positive. You said you might have something to show me today."

"Yes. Follow me."

In a sealed room at the end of a guarded corridor, five young men were sitting. They leaped to attention when Kling and McArdle entered.

"At ease," said McArdle. "This gentleman is going to ask you some questions. You may answer freely." He turned to Kling. "Go ahead—ask them anything."

Kling's eyebrows went up delicately, but he looked the young men over, selected one and said, "Your name?"

"Walter B. Limler, sir."

Kling looked mildly pained. "Please don't call me sir. Where do you live?"

"CFF Barracks, Tier Three, McCormick."

"CFF?" said Kling with a frown. "McCormick? I don't place the district. Where is it?"

The young man, who was blond and very earnest, allowed himself to show a slight surprise. "In the Loop," he said.

"And where is the Loop?"

The young man looked definitely startled. He glanced at McArdle, moistened his lips, and said, "Well, right here, sir. In Chicago."

Kling's eyebrows went up and then down. He smiled. "I begin to see," he murmured to McArdle. "Very clever."

It cost Alvah two hours' labor, using tools that had never been designed to be operated manually, to get the inspection plate off the motor housing in the floater. He compared the intricate mechanism with the diagrams and photographs in the maintenance handbook. He looked for dust and grime; he checked the moving parts for play; he probed for dislodged wiring plates and corrosion. He did everything the handbook suggested, even spun the flywheel and was positive he felt the floater lift a fraction of an inch beneath him. As far as he could tell, there was absolutely nothing wrong, unless the trouble was in the core of the motor itself—the force-field that rotated the axle that made everything go.

The core casing had an "easily removable" segment, meaning to say that Alvah was able to get it off in three hours more.

Inside, there was no resistance to his cautious finger. The spool-shaped hollow space was empty.

Under *Motor Force-field Inoperative* the manual said simply: *Remove and replace rhodopalladium nodules.*

Alvah looked. He found the tiny sockets where the nodules ought to be, one in the flanged axle-head, the other facing it at the opposite end of the chamber. The nodules were not there at all.

Alvah went into the storage chamber. Ignoring the increasingly forceful protests of his empty stomach, he spent a furious twenty minutes locating the spare nodules. He stripped the seal off the box and lifted the lid with great care.

There were the nodules. And there, appearing out of nowhere, was a whirling cloud of brightness that settled briefly in the box and then went back where it came from. And there the nodules weren't.

Alvah stared at the empty box. He poked his forefinger into the cushioned niches, one after the other. Then he set the box down with care, about-faced, walked outside to the platform and sat down on the top step with his chin on his fists.

"You look peaked," said B. J.'s firm voice.

Alvah looked up at her briefly. "Go away."

"Had anything to eat today?" the girl asked.

Alvah did not reply.

"Don't sulk," she said. "You've got a problem. We feel responsible. Maybe there's something we can do to help."

Alvah stood up slowly. He looked her over carefully, from top to bottom and back again. "There is one thing you could do for me," he said. "Smile."

"Why?" she asked cagily.

"I wanted to see your fangs." He turned wearily and went into the floater.

He puttered around for a few minutes, then got cold rations out of the storage chamber and sat down in the control chair to eat them. But the place was odious to him with its gleaming, useless array of gadgetry, and he went outside again and sat down with his back to the hull near the doorway. The girl was still there, looking up at him.

"Look," she said, "I'm sorry about this."

The nutloaf went down his gullet in one solid lump and hit his stomach like a stone. "Please don't mention it," he said bitterly. "It was really nothing at all."

"I had to do it. You might have killed somebody."

Alvah tried another bite. Chewing the stuff, at any rate, gave him something to do. "What *were* those things?" he demanded.

"Metallophage," she said. "They eat metals in the platinum family. Hard to get them that selective—we weren't exactly sure what would happen."

Alvah put down the remnant of nutloaf slowly. "Who's 'we'? You and Bither?"

"Mostly."

"And you—you bred those things to eat rhodopalladium?"

She nodded.

"Then you must have some to feed them," said Alvah logically. He stood up and gripped the railing. "Give it to me."

She hesitated. "There might be some—"

"*Might* be? There *must* be!"

"You don't understand. They don't actually eat the metal—not for nourishment, that is."

"Then what do they do with it?"

"They build nests," she told him. "But come on over to the lab and we'll see."

At the laboratory door, they were still arguing. "For the last time," said Alvah, "I will not come in. I've just eaten half a nutcake and I haven't got food to waste. Get the stuff and bring it out."

"For the last time," said B. J., "get it out of your head that what you want is all that counts. If you want me to look for the metal, you'll come in, and that's flat."

They glared at each other. Well, he told himself resignedly, he hadn't wanted that nutloaf much in the first place.

They followed the same route, past the things that chirruped, croaked, rumbled, rustled. The main thing, he recalled, was to keep your mind off it.

"Tell me something," he said to her trim back. "If I hadn't gotten myself mixed up with that farmer and his market basket, do you still think I wouldn't have sold anything?"

"That's right."

"Well, why not? Why all this resistance to machinery? Is it a taboo of some kind?"

She said nothing for a moment.

"Is it because you're afraid the Cities will get a hold on you?" Alvah insisted. "Because that's foolish. Our interests are really the same as yours. We don't just want to sell you stuff—we want to help you help yourselves. The more prosperous you get, the better for us."

"It's not that," she said.

"Well, what then? It's been bothering me. You've got all these raw materials, all this land. You wouldn't have to wait for us—you could have built your own factories, made your own machines. But you never have. I can't understand why."

"It's not worth the trouble."

He choked. "*Anything* is worth the trouble, if it helps you do the same work more efficiently, more intel—"

"Wait a minute." She stopped a woman who was passing in the aisle between the cages. "Marge, where's Doc?"

"Down in roundworms, I think."

"Tell him I have to see him, will you? It's urgent. We'll wait in here." She led the way into a windowless room, as small and cluttered as any Alvah had seen.

"Now," she said. "We don't make a fuss about machines because most people simply haven't any need for them."

"That's ridiculous," Alvah argued. "You may think—"

"Be quiet and let me finish. We haven't got centralized industries or power installations. Why do you think the Cities have never beaten us in a war, as often as they've tried? Why do you think we've taken over the whole world, except for twenty-two Cities? You've got to face this sooner or later—in every single respect, *our plants and animals are more efficient than any machine you could build*."

Alvah inspected her closely. Her eyes were intent and brilliant. Her bosom indicated deep and steady breathing. To all appearance, she was perfectly serious.

"Nuts," he replied with dignity.

B. J. shook her head impatiently. "I know you've got a brain. Use it. What's the most expensive item that goes into a machine?"

"Metal. We're a little short of it, to tell the truth."

"Think again. What are all your gadgets supposed to save?"

"Well, labor."

"Human labor. If metal is expensive, it's because it costs a lot of man-hours."

"If you want to look at it that way—"

"It's true, isn't it? Why is a complicated thing more expensive than a simple one? More man-hours to make it. Why is a rare thing more expensive than a common one? More man-hours to find it. Why is a—"

"All right, what's your point?"

"Take your runabout. You saw that was the thing that interested people most, but I'll show you why you never could have sold one. How many man-hours went into manufacturing it?"

Alvah shifted restlessly. "It isn't in production. It's a trade item."

She sniffed. "Suppose it was in production. Make an honest guess. Figure in everything—amortization on the plant and equipment, materials, labor, and so on. You can check your answer against wages and prices in your own money—you'll come pretty close."

Alvah reflected. "Between seven-fifty and a thousand."

"Compare that with Swifty's Morgan Gamma—the thing you raced against. Two man-hours—just two, and I'm being generous."

"Interesting," said Alvah, "if true." He suppressed an uneasy belch.

"Figure it out. An hour for the vet when he was foaled. Call it another hour for amortization on the stable where it happened, but that's too much. It isn't hard to grow a stable and they last a long time."

Alvah, who had been holding his own as long as machines were the topic, wasn't sure he could keep it up—or, more correctly, down. "All right, two hours," he said. "The animals feed themselves and water themselves, no doubt."

"They do, but that comes under upkeep. Our animals forage, most of them—all the big ones. The rest are cheap and easy to feed. Your machines have to be fueled. Our animals repair themselves, like any living organism, only better and faster. Your machines have to be repaired and serviced. More man-hours. Incidentally, if you and Swifty took a ten-hour trip, you in your runabout, him on his Morgan, you'd spend just ten hours steering. Swifty would spend maybe fifteen minutes, all told. And now we come to the payoff—"

"Some other time," said Alvah irritably.

"This is important. When your runabout—"

"I'd rather not talk about it any more," said Alvah, raising his voice. "Do you *mind?*"

"When your runabout breaks down and can't be fixed," she said firmly, "you have to buy another. Swifty's mare drops twins every year. There. Think about it."

The door opened and Bither came in, looking more disheveled than ever. "Hello, Beej, Alvah. Beej, I think we shoulda used annelid stock for this job. These F_3 batches no good at—you two arguing?"

Alvah recovered himself with an effort. "Rhodopalladium," he said thickly. "I need about a gram. Have you got it?"

"Not a scrap," said Bither cheerfully. "Except in the nests, of course."

"I told him I didn't think so," B. J. said.

Alvah closed his eyes for a second. "Where," he asked carefully, "are the nests?"

"Wish I knew," Bither admitted. "It's frustrating as hell. You see, we had to make them awful small and quick, the metallophage. Once you let them out of the sacs, there's no holding them. We did so good a job, we can't check to see how good a job we did." He rubbed his chin thoughtfully. "Of course, that's beside the point. Even if we had the metals, how would you get the alloy you need?"

"Palladium," said the girl, "melts at fifteen fifty-three centigrade. I asked the handbird."

"Best we can get out of a salamander is about six hundred," Bither added. "Isn't good for them, either—they get esophagitis."

"And necrosis," the girl said, watching Alvah intently.

His eyes were watering. It was hard to see. "Are you telling—"

"We're trying to tell you," she said, "that you can't go back. You've got to start getting used to the idea. There isn't a thing you can do except settle down here and learn to live with us."

Alvah could feel his jaw working, but no words were coming out. The bulge of nausea in his middle was squeezing its way inexorably upward.

Somebody grabbed his arm. "In there!" said Bither urgently.

A door opened and closed behind him, and he found himself facing a hideous white-porcelain antique with a pool of water in it. There was a roaring in his ears, but before the first spasm took him, he could hear the girl's and Bither's voices faintly from the other room:

"Eight minutes that time."

"Beej, I don't know."

"We can *do* it!"

"Well, I suppose we can, but can we do it before he starves?"

There was a sink in the room, but Alvah would sooner have drunk poison. He fumbled in his disordered kit until he found a condenser canteen. He rinsed out his mouth, took a tonus capsule and a mint lozenge. He opened the door.

"Feeling better?" asked the girl.

Alvah stared at her, retched feebly and fled back into the washroom.

When he came out again, Bither said, "He's had enough, Beej. Let's take him out in the courtyard till he gets his strength back."

They moved toward him. Alvah said weakly, but with feeling, "Keep your itchy hands off me." He walked unsteadily past them, turned when he reached the doorway. "I hate to urp and run, but I'll never forget your hospitality. If there's ever anything I can do for you—anything at all—please hesitate to call on me."

He heard muttering voices and an odd scraping sound behind him, but he didn't look back. He was halfway down the aisle between the cages when something furry and gray scuttled into view and sat up, grinning at him.

It looked like an ordinary capuchin monkey except for its head, which was grotesquely large. "Go away," said Alvah. He advanced with threatening gestures. The thing chattered at him and stayed where it was.

The aisle behind him was deserted. Very well, there were other exits. Alvah followed his nose back into the plant section and turned right.

There was the monkey-thing again.

At the next intersection of aisles, there were two of them. Alvah turned left.

And right.

And left.

And emerged into a large empty space enclosed by buildings.

"This is the courtyard," said Bither, coming forward with the girl behind him. "Now be reasonable, Alvah. You want to get back to New York, don't you?"

This did not seem to call for comment. Alvah stared at him in silence.

"Well," said Bither, "there's just one way you can do it. It won't be easy—I don't even say you got more than a fighting chance. One thing, though—it's up to you just how hard you make it for yourself."

"Get to the point," Alvah said.

"You got to let us decondition you so you can eat our food, ride on our animals. Now *think* about it, don't just—"

Alvah swung around, looking for the fastest and most direct exit. Before he had time to find it, a dizzying thought stuck him and he turned back.

"Is that what this whole thing has been about?" he said. He glared at Bither, then at B. J. "Is that the reason you were so helpful? *Did you engineer that fight?*"

Bither clucked unhappily. "Would we admit it if we did? Alvah, I'll admit this much—of course we interested in you for our own reasons. This is the first time in thirty years we had a chance to study a Cityman. But what I just told you is true. If you want to get back home, this is your only chance."

"Then I'm a dead man," said Alvah.

"You is if you think you is," Bither told him. "Beej, you try."

She looked at Alvah levelly. "You think what we suggesting isn't possible. Right?"

"Discounting Doc's grammar," Alvah said sourly, "that's exactly what I'm thinking."

She said, "Doc's grammar is all right—yours is sixty years out of date. But I guess you already realize that your people are backward compared to us."

Half-angry, half-curious, Alvah demanded, "Just how do you figure that?"

"Easy. You probably don't know much biology, but you must know this much. What's the one quality that makes human beings the dominant race on this planet?"

Alvah snorted. "Are you trying to tell me I'm not as bright as a Muckfoot?"

"Not intelligence. Try again. Something more general —intelligence is only a special phase of it."

Alvah's patience was narrowing to a thin and brittle thread. "*You* tell *me*."

"All right. We like to think intelligence is important, but you can't argue that way. It's special pleading—the way a whale might argue that size is the measuring stick, or a microbe might say numbers. But—"

"Control of environment," Alvah said.

"Right. Another name for it is adaptability. No other organism is so independent of environment, so adaptable as man. And we could live in New York if we had to, just as we can live in the Arctic Circle or the tropics. And, since you don't dare even try to live here . . ."

"All right," Alvah said bitterly. "When do we start?"

VI

He refused to be hypnotized.

"You promised to help," B. J. said in annoyance. "We can't break the conditioning till we find out how it was done, you big oaf!"

"The whole thing is ridiculous anyhow," Alvah pointed out. "I said I'd let you try and I will—you can prod me around to your heart's content—but not that. I've put in a lot of required-contribution time in restricted laboratories. Military secrets. How do I know you wouldn't ask me about those if you got me under?"

"We're not *interested* in—" B. J. began furiously, but Bither cut her off.

"We is, though, Beej. Might be important for us to know what kind of defenses New York has built up, and I going to ask him if I got the chance." He sighed. "Well, there other ways to skin a glovebeast. Lean back and relax, Alvah."

"No tricks?" Alvah asked suspiciously.

"No, we just going to try to improve your conscious recall. Relax now; close your eyes. Now think of a room, one that's familiar to you, and describe it to me. Take your time. . . . Now we going further back—further back. You three years old and you just dropped something on the floor. What is it?"

Bither seemed to know what he was doing, Alvah had to admit. Day after day they dredged up bits and scraps of memory from his childhood, events he had forgotten so completely that he would almost have sworn they had never happened. At first, all of them seemed trivial and irrelevant, but even so, Alvah found, there was an unexpected fascination in the search through the dusty attics of his mind. Once they hit something that made Bither sit up sharply—a dark figure holding something furry, and an accompanying remembered stench.

Whether or not it had been as important as Bither seemed to think, they never got it back again. But they did get other things—an obscene couplet about the Muckfeet that had been popular in P. S. 9073 when Alvah was ten; a scene from a realie feature called *Nix on the Stix*; a whispered horror story; a frightening stereo picture in a magazine.

"What we have to do," B. J. told him at one point, "is to make you realize that none of this was your own idea. They *made* you feel this way. They did it to you."

"Well, I know that," said Alvah.

She stared at him in astonishment. "You knew it all along—and you don't care?"

"No." Alvah felt puzzled and irritated. "Why should I?"

"Don't you think they should have let you make up your own mind?"

Alvah considered this. "You have to make your children see things the way you do, otherwise there wouldn't be any continuity from one generation to the next. You couldn't keep any kind of civilization going. Where would we be if we let people wander off into the Sticks and become Muckfeet?"

He finished triumphantly, but she didn't react properly. She merely grinned with an exasperating air of satisfaction and said, "Why should they want to—unless we can give them a better life than the Cities can?"

This was absurd, but Alvah couldn't find the one answer that would flatten her, no matter how long and often he mulled it over. Meanwhile, his tolerance of Muckfoot dwellings progressed from ten minutes to thirty, to an hour, to a full day. He didn't like it and nothing, he knew, could ever make him like it, but he could stand it. He was able to ride for short distances on Muckfoot animals, and he was even training himself to wear an animal-hide belt for longer and longer periods each day. But he still couldn't eat Muckfoot food—the bare thought of it still nauseated him—and his own supplies were running short.

Oddly, he didn't feel as anxious about it as he should have. He could sense the resistance within him softening day by day. He was irrationally sure that that last obstacle would go, too, when the time came. Something else was bothering him, something he couldn't even name—but he dreamed of it at night and its symbol was the threatening vast arch of the sky.

After the fair was over, it seemed that B. J. had very little work to do. As far as Alvah could make out, the same was true of everybody. The settlement grew mortuary-still. For an hour or so every morning, lackadaisical trading went on in the central market place. In the evenings, sometimes, there was music of a sort and a species of complicated, ungainly folk dancing. The rest of the time, children raced through the streets and across the pastures, playing incomprehensible games. Their elders, when they were visible, sat—on doorsteps by ones and twos, grouped on porches and lawns—their hands busy, more often than not, with some trifle of carving or needlework, but their faces as blank and sleepy as a frog's in the sun.

"What do you do for excitement around here?" he asked B. J. in a dither of boredom.

She looked at him oddly. "We work. We make things, or watch things grow. But maybe that's not the kind of excitement you mean."

"It isn't, but let it go."

"Our simple pleasures probably wouldn't interest you," she said reflectively. "They're pretty dull. We dance, go riding, swim in the lake . . ."

So they swam.

It wasn't bad. It was unsettling to have no place to swim *to* —you had to head out from the shore, gauging your distance, and then turn around to go back—but the lake, to Alvah's considerable surprise, was clearer and better-tasting than any pool he'd ever been in.

Lying on the grass afterward was a novel sensation, too. It was comfortable—no, it was nothing of the sort; the grass blades prickled and the ground was lumpy. Not comfortable, but—comforting. It was the weight, he thought lazily, the massive mother-weight of the whole Earth cradling you—the endless, slow pendulum-swing you felt when you closed your eyes.

He sat up, feeling cheerfully torpid. B. J. was lying on

her back beside him, eyes shut, one arm flung back behind her head. It was a graceful pose. In a detached way, he admired it, first in general and then in particular—the fine texture of her skin, the firmness of her bosom under the halter that half-covered it, the delicate tint of her closed eyelids—the catalog prolonged itself, and he realized that B. J., when you got a good look at her, was a uniquely lovely girl. He wondered, in passing, how he had missed noticing it before.

She opened her eyes and looked at him. There was a ground-swell of some sort and, without particular surprise, Alvah found himself leaning over and kissing her.

"Beej," he said some time later, "when I go back to New York—I don't suppose you'd want to come with me? I mean—you're different from the others. You're educated, you can read; even your grammar is good."

"I know you mean it as a compliment and I'm doing my best not to sound ungrateful or hurt your feelings, but . . ." She made a frustrated gesture. "Take the reading —that's a hobby of Doc's and I picked it up from him. It's a primitive skill, Alvah, something like manuscript illuminating. We have better ways now. We don't *need* it anymore. Then the grammar—didn't it ever strike you that I might be using your kind just to make things easier for you?"

She frowned. "I guess that was a mistake. As of now, I quit. No, listen a minute! The only difference between your grammar and ours is that yours is sixty years out of date. You still use 'I am, you are, he is' and all that archaic nonsense of tenses, case, and number. What for? If that's good, suppose we hunted up somebody who said 'I am, thou art, he is,' would his grammar be better than yours?"

"Well—" said Alvah.

"And about New York, I appreciate that. But the Cities are done for, Alvah. In ten years there won't be one left. They're *finished*."

Alvah stiffened. "That's the most ridiculous—"

"*Is* it? Then why you here?"

"Well, we're in a crisis period now, but we've come through them before. You can't—"

"This *crisis* of yours started a long while ago. If I remember, it was around 1927 that Muller first changed the genes in fruit flies with X-ray bombardment. That was the first step—over a hundred years before you was even born. Then came colchicine and the electron microscope and microsurgery, all in the next thirty years. But the day biological engineering really grew up—1962, Jenkins's and Scripture's gene charts and techniques—the Cities began to go. Little by little, people drifted out to the land again, raising the new crops, growing the new animals.

"The big Cities cannibalized the little ones, like an insect eating its own body when its food supply runs out. Now that's gone as far as it can, and you think it's just another crisis, but it isn't. It's the end."

Alvah heard a chill echo of Wytak's words: *"Rome fell. Babylon fell. The same thing can happen to New York . . ."*

He said, "What am I supposed to be, the rat that leaves the sinking ship?"

She sighed. "Alvah, you got a better brain than that. You don't *have* to think in metaphors or slogans, like a moron. I'm not asking you to join the wining side. That doesn't *matter*. In a few years there won't be but one side, no matter which way you jump."

"What do you want then?" he asked.

She looked dispirited. "Nothing, I guess. Let's go home."

It was a series of little things after that. There was the time he and Beej, out walking in the cool of the morning, stopped to rest at an isolated house that turned out to be occupied by George Allister of the Coffin clan, the shy little man who'd tried to show Alvah how to make his marks the day he landed.

George, Alvah believed—and questioning of Beej afterward confirmed it—was about as low on the social scale as a Muckfoot could get. But he was his own master. He had a wife and three children and neat fields with his own animals grazing in them. His house was big and cool and clean. He poured them lemonade—which Alvah wistfully had to decline—from a sweating peacock blue pitcher, while sitting at his ease on the broad front porch.

There were no servants among the Muckfeet. Alvah remembered an ancient fear of his, something that had cropped up in the old days every time he got seriously interested in a girl—that his children, if any, might relapse into the labor-pool category from which he had risen, or—it was hard to say which would be worse—into the servants' estate.

He went back from that outing very silent and thoughtful.

There was the time, a few days later, when Beej was working, and Alvah, at loose ends, wandered into a room in the laboratory building where two of Bither's assistants, girls he knew by sight, were sitting with two large, leathery-woody, pod-shaped boxes open on the bench between them.

Being hungry for company and preoccupied with himself at the same time, he didn't notice what should have been obvious, that the girls were busy at something private and personal. Even when they closed the boxes between them, he wasn't warned. "What's this?" he said cheerfully. "Can I see?"

They glanced at each other uncertainly. "These is our bride boxes," said the brunette. "We don't usual show them to singletons—"

They exchanged another glance.

"He's spoke for anyhow," said the redhead, with an enigmatic look at Alvah.

They opened the boxes. Inside each was a multitude of tiny compartments, each with a bit of something wrapped in cloth or paper tissue. The brunette chose one of the largest and unwrapped it with exaggerated care—an amorphous reddish brown lump.

"Houseplant," she said, and wrapped it up again.

The redhead showed him a vial full of minuscule white spheres. "Weaver eggs. Two hundred of them. That's a lot, but I like more curtains and things than most."

"Wait a minute," said Alvah, perplexed. "What does a houseplant do?"

"Grow a house, of course," the brunette said. She held up another vial full of eggs. "Scavengers."

The redhead had a translucent sac with dark specks in it. "Utility trees."

"Garbage converter."

"This grows into a bed and these is chairbushes."

And so on, interminably, while the girls' eyes glittered and their cheeks flushed with enthusiasm.

The boxes, Alvah gathered, contained the germs of everything that would be needed to set up a Muckfoot household—beginning with the house itself. A thought struck him and he asked, "Does Beej have one of these outfits?"

Wide-eyed stares from both girls. "Well, of course!"

Alvah shifted uncomfortably. "Funny, she never mentioned it."

The girls exchanged another of those enigmatic glances and said nothing. Alvah, for some reason, grew more uncomfortable still. He tried once more. "What about the man—doesn't he have to put up anything?"

Yes, the man was expected to supply all the brutes and the seeds for outbuildings and all the crops except the bride's kitchen garden. Everything in and around the home was her province, everything outside was his.

"Oh," said Alvah.

"But if a young fellow don't have all that through no fault of his own, his clan put up for him and let him pay back when he able."

"Ah," said Alvah, and turned to make his escape.

The redhead called after him, "You thought any about what clan you like to get adopted into, Alvah?"

"Uh, no," said Alvah. "I don't think—"

"You talk to Doc Bither. He a elder of the Steins. Mighty good clan!"

Alvah bolted.

Then there was the Shakespeare business. It began in his third week in the Sticks, when he was already carrying a fleshy Muckfoot vegetable around with him—a radnip, B. J. called it. He hadn't had the nerve yet to bite into it, but he knew the time was coming when he would. Beej came to him and said, "Alvah, the Rinaldos' drama group is doing *Hamlet* next Saturday, and they're short a Polonius. Do you think you could study it up by then?"

"What's Hamlet? And who's Polonius?"

She got the bird out of the library for him and he listened to the play, which turned out to be an archaic version of *The Manager of Copenhagen*. The text was nothing like the modernized abridgment he was used to, or the Muckfeet's slovenly speech either. It was full of words like *down-gyved* and *unkennel*. It was three-quarters incomprehensible until he began to get the hang of it, but it had a curious power. *For who would bear the whips and scorns of time, the oppressor's wrong, the proud man's contumely, the pangs of despised love*, and so on and so on. It rumbled, but it rumbled well.

Polonius, however, was the character Alvah knew as Paul Arnson, an inconsequential old man who only existed in the play to foul up the love affair between the principals and got killed in the third act. Alvah ventured to suggest that he might be of more use as Hamlet, but the director, a dry little man with a surprising boom to his voice, stubbornly insisted that all he needed was a Polonius—and seemed to intimate, without actually saying so, that Alvah was a dim prospect even for that.

Alvah, with blood in his eye, accepted the part.

The rehearsals were a nightmare. The lines themselves gave him no trouble—Alvah was a quick study; in the realies, you had to be—and neither, at first, did the rustic crudity of the stage he was asked to perform on. Letter-perfect when the other actors were still stuttering and blowing their lines, he walked through the part with quiet competence and put the director's sour looks down to a witless hayseed hostility—until, three days before the performance, he suddenly awoke to the realization that everyone else in the cast was acting rings around him.

This wasn't the realies. There were no microphones to amplify his voice, no cameras to record every change in his expression. And the audience, what there was of it, was going to be *right—out—there.*

Alvah went to pieces. Trying to emulate the others' wide gestures and declamatory delivery only threw him further off his stride. He had never had stage fright in his life, but by curtain time on Saturday night, he was a pale and quivering wreck.

Dead and dragged off the stage at the end of act three, he got listlessly back into his own clothes and headed for an inconspicuous exit, but the director waylaid him. "Gustad," he said abruptly, "you ever thought of yourself as a professional actor?"

"I had some such idea at one time," Alvah said. "Why?"

"Well, I don't see why you shouldn't. If you work at it. I never see a man pick up so fast."

"*What?*" cried Alvah, thunderstruck.

"You wasn't bad," said the director. "A few rough edges, but a good performance. Now I happen to know some people in a few repertory companies—the Mondrillo Troupe, the Kalfoglou Repertory, one or two more. If you interested, I'll bird them and see if there's an opening. Don't thank me, don't thank me." He moved off a few steps, then turned. "Oh, and, Gustad—get back into your costume, will you?"

"Uh," said Alvah. "But I'm dead. I mean—"

"For the curtain calls," said the director. "You don't want to miss those." He waved and walked back into the wings.

Alvah absently drew out his radnip and crunched off a bite of it. The taste was faintly unpleasant, like that of old protein paste or the wrong variety of culture cheese, but he chewed and swallowed it.

That was when he realized that he had to get out. He didn't put on his costume again. Instead, he rummaged through the property boxes until he found an old pair of moleskin trousers and a stained squareweb shirt. He put them on, left by the rear door and headed south.

South for two reasons. First, because, he hoped, no one would look for him in that direction. Second, because he rememebered what Beej had said that first day when they passed the display of tools: "*The metal comes from Iron Pits, just a few miles south of here.*"

There might be some slender chance still that he could get the metal he needed, delouse the floater and go home in style—without the painful necessity of explaining to Wytak what had happened to the floater and all his goods and equipment. If not, he would simply keep on walking.

He had to do it now. He had almost waited too long as it was.

They had laid out the pattern of a life for him—to marry Beej, settle down in a house that would grow from a seed Beej kept in a pod-shaped box, be a rustic repertory actor, raise little Muckfeet. And the devil of it was, some unreasonable part of him wanted all of that!

A good thing he hadn't stayed for the curtain calls . . .

The sun declined as he went, until he was walking down a ghost-dim road under the stars, with all the cool cricket-shrill world to himself.

He spent the night uncomfortably huddled under a hedge. Birds woke him with a great clamor in the treetops shortly after dawn. He washed himself and drank from a stream that crossed the fields, ate a purplish red fruit he found growing nearby, then moved on.

Two hours later, he topped a ridge and found his way barred by a mile-long shallow depression in the earth. Like the rest of the visible landscape, it was filled with an orderly checker-work of growing plants.

There was nothing for it but to go through if he could. But surely he had gone more than "a few miles" by now?

The road slanted down the embankment to a gate in a high thorn hedge. Behind the gate was a kind of miniature domed kiosk, and in the kiosk a sunburned man was dozing with a green-and-purple bird on his shoulder.

Alvah inspected a signboard that was entangled somehow in the hedge next to the gate. He was familiar enough by now with the Muckfeet's picture writing to be fairly sure of what it said. The first symbol was a nail with an axhead attached to it. That was *iron.* The second was a few stylized things that resembled fruit seeds. *Pits?*

He stared through the gate in mounting perplexity. You might call a place like this "Pits," all right, but imagination boggled at calling it a mine. Still . . .

The kiosk, he noticed now, bore a scrawled symbol in orange pigment. He recognized that one, too; it was one of the common name-signs.

"Jerry!" he called.

"*Rrk*," remarked the bird on the sleeping man's shoulder. "Kerry brogue; but the degradation of speech that occurs in London, Glasgow—"

"Oh, damn!" said Alvah. "You, there. *Jerry!*"

"*Rrk*. Kerry brogue; but the—"

"Jerry!"

"*Kerry brogue!*" shrieked the bird. The sunburned man sat up with a start and seized it by the beak, choking it off in the middle of "*degradation.*"

"Oh, hello," he said. "Don't know what it is about a Shaw bird, but they all alike. Can't shut them up."

"I'd like," said Alvah, "to look through the—uh—Pits. Would that be all right?"

"Sure," the man said cheerfully. He opened the gate and led the way down a long avenue between foot-high rows of plants.

"I Jerry Finch," he said. "Littleton clan. Don't believe you said your name."

"Harris," Alvah said at random. "I visiting from up north."

"Yukes?" the man inquired.

Alvah nodded, hoping for the best, and pointed at the plants they were passing. "What these?"

"Hinge blanks. Let them to forage last month. Won't have another crop here till August, and a poor one then. I tell Angus—he's the Pit boss—I tell him this soil's wore out, but he a pincher—squeeze the last ton out and then go after the pounds and ounces. You should of saw what come off the ringbushes in the east hundred this April. Pitiful. Had to sell them for eyelets."

A cold feeling was running up Alvah's spine. He cleared his throat. "Got any knife blades?" he inquired with careful casualness.

"Mean bowies? Well, sure—right over yonder."

Alvah followed him to the end of the field and down

three steps into the next. The plants here were much taller and darker, with stems thick and gnarled out of all proportion to their height. Here and there among the glossy leaves were incongruous glints of silvery steel.

Alvah stooped and peered into the foliage.

The silvery glints were perfectly formed six-inch chrome-steel knife blades. Each was attached to—*growing* from—the plant by way of a hard brown stem, exactly the right size and shape to serve as a handle.

He straightened carefully. "We do things a little different up north. You mind explaining briefly how the Pits works?"

Jerry looked surprised, but began readily enough. "These like any other ferropositors. They extract the metal from the ores and deposit it in the bowie shape, or whatever it might be. Work from the outside in, of course, so you don't have no wood core to weaken it. We get a year's crops, average, before the ore used up. Then we bring the earth-movers in, deepen the Pit a few feet, reseed and start over. Ain't much more to it."

Alvah stared at the fantastic growths. Well, why not? Plants that grew into knives or doorknobs or . . .

"What about alloys?" he asked.

"We got iron, lead, and zinc. Carbon from the air. Other metals we got to import in granules. Like we get chrome from the Northwest Federation, mostly. They getting too big for their britches, though. Greedy. I think we going to switch over to you Yukes before long. Not that you fellows is any better, if you ask me, but at least—"

"Rhodium," said Alvah. "Palladium. What about them?"

"How that?"

"Platinum group."

"Oh, sure, I know what you mean. We never use them. No call to. We could get you some, I guess—I think the Northwests got them. Take a few months, though."

"Suppose you wanted to make something out of a rhodopalladium alloy. How long would it take after you got the metals?"

"Well, you have to make a bush that would take and put them together, right proportions, right size, right shape. Depends. I guess if you was in a hurry—"

"Never mind," said Alvah wearily. "Thanks for the information." He turned and started back toward the gate.

When he was halfway there, he heard a hullabaloo break out somewhere behind him.

"*Waw!*" the voices seemed to be shouting. "*Waw! Waw!*"

He turned. A dozen paces behind him, Jerry and the bird on his shoulder were in identical neck-straining attitudes. Beyond them, on the near side of a group of low buildings three hundred yards away, three men were waving their arms madly and shouting, "*Waw! Waw!*"

"*Wawnt* to know what it is," the bird squawked. "I wawnt to be a Mahn. Violet, you come along with me, to your own—"

"Shut up," said Jerry, then cupped his hands and yelled, "Angus, what is it?"

"Chicagos," the answer drifted back. "Just got word! They dusting Red Pits! Come *on!*"

Jerry darted a glance over his shoulder. "Come *on!*" he repeated and broke into a loping run toward the buildings.

Alvah hesitated an instant, then followed. With strenuous effort, he managed to catch up to the other man. "Where are we running to?" he panted. "Red Pits?"

"Don't talk foolish," Jerry gasped. "We running to shelter." He glanced back the way they had come. "Red Pits over that way."

Alvah risked a look and then another. The first time, he wasn't sure. The second time, the dusting of tiny particles over the horizon had grown to a cluster of visibly swelling black dots.

Other running figures were converging on the buildings as Angus and Jerry approached. The dots were capsule shapes, perceptibly elongated, the size of a fingernail, a thumbnail, a thumb . . .

And under them on the land was a hurtling streak of golden-dun haze, like dust stirred by a huge invisible finger.

Rounding the corner of the nearest building, Jerry popped through an open doorway. Alvah followed—

And was promptly seized from either side, long enough for something heavy and hard to hit him savagely on the nape of the neck.

VII

Bither was intent over a shallow vessel half-full of a viscous clear liquid, with a great rounded veined-and-patterned glistening lump immersed in it, transparent in the phosphor-light that glowed from the sides of the container—a single living cell in mitosis, so grossly enlarged that every gene of every paired chromosome was visible. B. J. watched from the other side of the table, silent, breathing carefully, as the man's thick fingers dipped a hair-thin probe with minuscule precision, again and again, into the yeasty mass, excising a particle, splitting another, delicately shaving a third.

From time to time, she glanced at a sheet of horn intricately inscribed with numbers and genetic symbols. The chart was there for her benefit, not for Bither's—he never paused or faltered.

Finally, he sat back and covered the pan. "Turn on the lights and put that in the reduction fluid, will you, Beej? I bushed."

She whistled a clear note, and the dark globes fixed to

the ceiling glowed to blue-white life. "You going to grow it right away?"

"Have to, I guess. Dammit, Beej, I hate making weapons."

"Not our choice. When you think it be?"

He shrugged. "War meeting this afternoon over at Council Flats. They let us know when it be."

She was silent until she had transferred the living lump from one container to another and put it away. Then, "Hear anything more?"

"They dusting every ore-bed from here to the Illinois, look like. Crystal, Butler's—"

"*Butler's!* That worked out."

"I know it. We let them land there. They find out." After another pause, Bither said, "No word about Alvah, Beej. I sorry."

She nodded. "Wouldn't be, this early."

He looked at her curiously. "You still thrink he be back?"

"If the dust ain't got him. Lay you odds."

"Well," said Bither, lifting the cover of another pan to peer into it, "I hope you—"

"Ozark Lake nine-one-two-five," said a reedy voice from the corner. "Ozark Lake nine—"

"Get that, will you, Beej?"

B. J. picked up the ocher spheroid from its shelf and said into its tympanum, "Bither Laboratories."

"This Angus Littleton at Iron Pits," the thing said. "Let me talk to Bither."

She passed it over, holding a loop of its rubbery cord —the beginning of a mile-long sheathed bundle of cultivated neurons that linked it, via a "switchboard" oganism, with thousands like it in this area alone, and with millions more across the continent.

"This Doc Bither. What is it, Angus?"

"Something funny for you, Doc. We got a couple prisoners here, one a floater pilot, other a Chicago spy."

"Well, what you want me to—"

"*Wait*, can't you? This spy claim he know you, Doc. Say his name Custard. Alvah Custard."

Alvah stared out through the window, puzzled and angry. He had been in the room for about half an hour, while things were going on outside. He had tried to break the window. The pane had bent slightly. It was neither glass nor plastic, and it wasn't breakable.

Outside, the last of the invading floaters was dipping down toward the horizon, pursued by a small, darting black shape. Golden-dun haze obscured all the foreground except the first few rows of plants, which were drooping on their stems. The squadron had made one grand circle of the mine area, dusting as they went, before the Muckfeet on their incredibly swift flyers—birds or reptiles, Alvah couldn't tell which—had risen to engage them. Since then, a light breeze from the north had carried the stuff dropped over the Pits: radioactive dust with a gravitostatic charge to make it rebound and spread—and then, with its polarity reversed, cling like grim death where it fell.

He turned and looked at the other man, sitting blank-faced and inattentive, wearing a rumpled sky blue uniform, on the bench against the inner wall. Most of the squadron had flown off to the west after that first pass, and had either escaped or been forced down somewhere beyond the Pits. This fellow had crash-landed in the fields not five hundred yards from Alvah's window. Alvah had seen the Muckfeet walking out to the wreck—strolling fantastically through the deadly haze—and turkey trotting their prisoner back again. A little later, someone had opened the door and shoved the man in, and there he had sat ever since.

His skin color was all right. He was breathing evenly

and seemed in no discomfort. As far as Alvah could see, there was not a speck of the death-dust anywhere on his skin, hair, or clothing. But mad as it was, this was not the most incongruous thing about him.

His uniform was of a cut and pattern that Alvah had seen only in pictures. There was a "C" on each gleaming button and, on the bar of the epaulette, CHICAGO-LAND. In short, he was evidently a Floater Force officer from Chicago. The only trouble was that Alvah recognized him. He was a grip by day at the Seven Boroughs Studios, famous for his dirty jokes, which he acquired at his night job in the Under Queens Power Station. He was a lieutenant j.g. in the N. Y. F. F. Reserve, and his name was Joe "Dimples" Mundry.

Alvah went over and sat down beside him again. Mundry's normally jovial face was set in wooden lines. His eyes focused on Alvah, but without recognition.

"Joe—"

"My name," said Mundry obstinately, "is Bertram Palmer, Float Lieutenant, Windy City Regulars. My serial number is 79016935."

That was the only tune he knew. Alvah hadn't been able to get another word out of him. Name, rank, and serial number—that was normal. Members of the armed services were naturally conditioned to say nothing else if captured. But why throw in the name of his outfit?

One, that was the way they did things in Chicago, and there just happened to be a Chicago soldier who looked and talked exactly like Joe Mundry, who had the same scars on his knuckles from brawls with the generator monkeys. Two, Alvah's mind had snapped. Three, this was a ringer foisted on Alvah for some incomprehensible purpose by the Muckfeet. And four—a wild and terrible suspicion . . .

Alvah tried again. "Listen, Joe, I'm your friend. We're on the same side. *I'm not a Muckfoot.*"

"My name is Bertram Palmer, Float Lieutenant—"

"Joe, I'm leveling with you. Listen—remember the Music Hall story, the one about the man who could . . ." Alvah explained in detail what the man could do. It was obscenely improbable and very funny, if you liked that sort of thing, and it was a story Joe had told him two days before he left New York.

A gleam of intelligence came into Joe's eyes. "What's the punchline?" he demanded.

" 'What the hell did you change the key on me for?' " Alvah replied promptly.

Joe looked at him speculatively. "That might be an old joke. Maybe they even know it in the Sticks. And my name isn't Joe."

He really believed he was Bertram Palmer of the Windy City Regulars, that much seemed clear. Also, if it was possible that the Muckfeet knew that story, it was likelier still that the Chicagolanders knew it.

"All right," said Alvah, "ask me a question—something I couldn't know if I were a Muckfoot. Go ahead, anything. A place, or something that happened recently, or whatever you want."

A visible struggle was going on behind Joe's face. "Can't think of anything," he said at last. "Funny."

Alvah had been watching him closely. "Let's try this. Did you see *Manhattan Morons?*"

Joe looked blank. "What?"

"The realie. You mean you missed it? *Manhattan Morons?* Till I saw that, I never really knew what a comical bunch of weak-minded, slobber-mouthed, monkey-faced, drooling idiots those New Yorkers—"

Joe's expression had not changed, but a dull red flush had crept up over his collar. He made an inarticulate sound and lunged for Alvah's throat.

When Angus Littleton opened the door, with Jerry and B. J. behind him, the two men were rolling on the floor.

"What made you think he was a spy?" B. J. demanded. They were a tight self-conscious group in the corridor. Alvah was nursing a split lip.

"Said he a Yuke," Jerry offered, "but didn't seem too sure, so I said the Yukes greedy. He never turned a hair. And he act like he never see a mine before. Things like that."

B. J. nodded. "It was a natural mistake, I guess. Well, thanks for calling us, Angus."

"Easy," said Angus, looking glum. "We ain't out of the rough yet, Beej."

"What do you mean? He didn't have anything to do with this attack—he's from New York."

"He *say* he is, but how you know? What make you think he ain't from Chicago?"

Alvah said, "While you're asking that, you might ask another question about him." He jerked a thumb toward the closed door. "What makes you think he *is?*"

The other three stared at him thoughtfully. "Alvah," Beej began, "what are you aiming at? Do you think—"

"I'm not sure," Alvah interrupted. "I mean I'm sure, but I'm not sure I want to tell you. Look," he said, turning to Angus, "let me talk to her alone for a few minutes, will you?"

Angus hesitated, then walked away down the hall, followed by Jerry.

"You've got to explain some things to me about this raid," said Alvah when they were out of hearing. "I *saw* those floaters dusting and it was the real thing. I can tell by the way the plants withered. But your people were walking around out there. Him, too—the prisoner. How come?"

"Antirads," said the girl. "Little para-insects, like the metallophage—the metallophage was developed from them. When you've been exposed, the antirads pick the dust particles off you and deposit them in radproof pots. They die in the pots, too, and we bury the whole—"

"All right," Alvah said. "How long have you had those things? Is there any chance the Cities knew about it?"

"The antirads were developed toward the end of the last City war. That was what ended it. At first we stopped the bombing, and then when they used dust—You never heard of any of this?"

"No," Alvah told her. "Third question, what are you going to do about Chicago now, on account of this raid?"

"Pull it down around their ears," B. J. said gravely. "We never did before, partly because it wasn't necessary. We knew for the last thirty years that the Cities could never be more than a nuisance to us again. But this isn't just a raid. They've attacked us all over this district—ruined the crops in every mine. We must put an end to it now—not that it makes much difference, this year or ten years from now. And it isn't as if we couldn't save the people . . ."

"Never mind that," said Alvah abstractedly. Then her last words penetrated. "No, go ahead—what?"

"I started to say, we think we'll be able to save the people, or most of them—partly thanks to what we learned from you. It's just Chicago we're going to destroy, not the—"

"Learned from *me?*" Alvah repeated. "What do you mean?"

"We learned that, when it's a question of survival, a Cityman can overcome his conditioning. You proved that. Did you eat the radnip?"

"Yes."

"There, you see? And you'll eat another and, sooner or later, you'll realize they taste good. A human being can learn to like anything that's needful to him. We're adaptable—you can't condition that out of us without breaking us."

Alvah stared at her. "But you spent over two weeks on me. How are you going to do that with fifteen or twenty million people all at once?"

"We can do it. You were the pilot model—two weeks for you. But now that we know how, we're pretty sure we can do it in three days—the important part, getting them to eat the food. And it's a good thing the storehouses are full, all over this continent."

They looked at each other silently for a moment. "But the Cities have to go," B. J. said.

"Fourth and last question," he said. "If a City knew about your radiation defenses all along, what would be their reason for attacking you this way?"

"Our first idea was that it was just plain desperation—they had to do something and there wasn't anything they could do that would work, so they just did something that wouldn't. Or maybe they hoped they'd be able to hold the mines long enough to get some metal out, even though they knew it was foolish to hope."

"That was your first idea. What was your second?"

She hesitated. "You remember what I told you, that the Cities cannibalized each other for a while, the big ones draining population away from the little ones and re-claiming their metals—and you remember I said that had gone as far as it could?"

"Yes."

"Well, when the big fish have eaten up all the little fish, they can eat each other till there's just one big fish left."

"And?" asked Alvah tensely.

"And maybe one City might think that, if they got us to make war on another, they could step in when the fighting was over and get all the metals they'd need to keep them going for years. So they might send raiding parties out in the other City's uniforms, and condition them to think they really were from that City. Was that what happened, Alvah?"

Alvah nodded reluctantly. "I don't understand it. They must have started planning this as soon as I stopped communicating. It doesn't make sense. They couldn't be that desperate—or maybe they could. Anyway, it's a dirty stunt. It isn't like New York."

She said nothing—too polite to contradict him, Alvah supposed.

Down at the end of the hall, Angus was beginning to look impatient. Alvah said, "So now you'll pull New York down?"

"Alvah, it may sound funny, but I think you know this, really—you're doing your people a favor."

"If that's so," he said wryly, "then New York was 'really' trying to do one for Chicago."

"I was hoping you'd see that it doesn't matter. It might have been Chicago that went first, or Denver, or any of the others, but that isn't important—they all have to go. What's important is the people. This may be another thing that's hard for you to accept, but they're going to be happier, most of them."

And maybe she was right, Alvah thought, if you counted in everybody, labor pool, porters and all. Why shouldn't you count them, he asked himself defiantly—they were people, weren't they? Maybe the index of civilization was not only how much you had, but how hard you had to work for it—incessantly, like the New Yorkers, holding down two or three jobs at once, because the City's demands were endless—or, like the Muckfeet, judiciously and with honest pleasure.

"Alvah?" said the girl. She put her question no more explicitly than that, but he knew what she meant.

"Yes, Beej," replied Alvah Gustad, Muckfoot.

VIII

On the Jersey flats, hidden by a forest of traveler trees, a sprawling settlement took form—mile after mile of forced-growth dwellings, stables, administration buildings, instruction centers. It was one of five. There was another farther north in Jersey, two in the Poconos, and one in the vestigial state of Connecticut.

They lay empty, waiting, their roofs sprouting foliage that perfectly counterfeited the surrounding forests. Roads had been cleared, converging toward the City, ending just short of the half-mile strip of wasteland that girdled New York, and it was there that Alvah stood.

He found it strange to feel himself ready to walk unprotected across that stretch of country, knowing it to be acrawl with tiny organisms that had been developed not to tolerate man's artificial buildings, whether of stone, metal, cement, or plastics, but crumbled them all to the ground. Stranger still, to be able to visualize the crawling organisms without horror or disgust.

But the strangest of all was to be looking at the City from this viewpoint. The towers stared back at him across the surrounding wall, tall and shining and proud, the proudest human creation—a century ago. Pitifully outdated today, the gleaming Cities fought back, unaware that they had lost long ago, that their bright spires and elaborate gadgets were as antiquated as polished armor would have been against a dun-painted motorized army.

"I wish I could go with you," said Beej from the breathing forest at his back.

"You can't," Alvah said without turning. "They wouldn't let you through the gate alive. They know me, but even so, I'm not sure they'll let me in after all this time. Have to wait and see."

"You know you don't have to go. I mean—"

"I know what you mean," said Alvah unhappily, "and you're right. But all the same, I do have to go. Look, Beej, you've got that map I drew. It's a ten-to-one chance that, if I don't make the grade, they'll put me in the quarantine cells right inside the wall. So you're not to worry. Okay?"

"Okay," she promised, worried.

He kissed her and watched her fade back into the forest where the others were—Bither and Artie Brumbacher and a few others from home, the rest Jerseys and other clansmen from the Seaboard Federation—cheerful, matter-of-fact people who were going to bear most of the burdens of what was coming, and never tired of reminding the inlanders of the fact.

He turned and walked out across the wasteland, crunching the dry weeds under his feet.

There was a flaming moat around the City and, beyond the moat, high in the wall, a closed gateway—corroded tight, probably; it was a very long time since the City had had any traffic except by air. But there was a spy tower above the gate. Alvah walked up directly opposite its bulbous idiot eyes, waved, and then waited.

After a long time, an inconspicuous port in the tower squealed open and a fist-sized dark ovoid darted out across the flames. It came to rest in midair, two yards from Alvah, clicked and said crisply, "State your name and business."

"Alvah Gustad. I just got back from a confidential mission for the city manager. Floater broke down, communicator, everything. I had to walk back. Tell him I'm here."

The ovoid hovered exactly where it was, as if pinned against the air. Alvah waited. When he got tired of standing, he dropped his improvised knapsack on the ground and sat on it. Finally the ovoid said harshly, in another voice, "Who are you and what do you want?"

Alvah patiently gave the same answer.

"What do you mean, broke down?"

"Broke *down*," said Alvah. "Wouldn't run anymore."

Silence. He settled himself for another long wait, but it was only five minutes or thereabouts before the ovoid said, "Strip."

When he had done so, the gate opposite broke open with a scream of tortured metal and ground itself back into a recess in the wall. The drawbridge, a long rust-pitted tongue of metal, thrust out and down to span the moat, a wall of flame on either side of it.

Alvah walked across nimbly, the metal already hot against his naked soles, and the drawbridge whipped back into its socket. The gate screamed shut.

The room was the same, the anthems were the same. Alvah, disinfected, shaved all over, and clad in an airtight glassine coverall with its own air supply, stopped short two paces inside the door. The man behind the manager's desk was not Wytak. It was jowly, red-faced Ellery McArdle, commissioner of the department of war.

One of the guards prodded Alvah and he kept going up to the desk. "Now I think I get it," he said, staring at McArdle. "When—"

McArdle's cold gaze flickered toward the guards. Then his heavy head dropped forward a trifle, and he said, "Finish what you were saying, Gustad."

"I was about to remark," Alvah said, "that when Wytak's pet project flopped, he lost enough support to let you impeach him. Is that right?"

McArdle nodded and seemed to lose interest. "Your feet are not swollen or blistered, Gustad. You didn't walk back from the Plains. How did you get here?"

Alvah took a deep breath. "We flew—on a passenger roc—as far as the Adirondacks. We didn't want to alarm you by too much air traffic so near the City, so we joined a freight caravan there."

McArdle's stony face did not alter, but all the meaning went suddenly out of it. It was as if the man himself had stepped back and shut a door. The porter behind his chair swayed and looked as if he were about to faint. Alvah heard one of the guards draw in his breath sharply.

"*Fthub!*" said McArdle abruptly, his face contorting. "Let's get this over. What do you know about the military plans of the Muckfeet? Answer me fully. If I'm not satisfied that you do, I'll have you worked over till I am satisfied."

Alvah, who had been feeling something like St. George and something like a plucked chicken, discovered that anger could be a very comforting thing. "That's what I came here to do," he said tightly. "The Muckfeet's military plans are about what you might have expected, after that lousy trick of yours. They know it wasn't Chicago that raided them."

McArdle started and made as if to rise. Then he sank back, staring fixedly at Alvah.

"They've had a gutful. They're going to finish New York."

"When?" said McArdle, biting the word off short.

"That depends on you. If you're willing to be reasonable, they'll wait long enough for you to dicker with them. Otherwise, if I'm not back in about an hour, the fun starts."

McArdle touched a stud, said "Green alert," pressed the stud again and laced his fingers together on the desk. "Hurry it up," he said to Alvah. "Let's have the rest."

"I'm going to ask you to do something difficult," said Alvah. "It's this—think about what I'm telling you. You're not thinking now, you're just reacting—"

He heard a slight movement behind him, saw McArdle's eyes flicker and his hand make a *Not now* gesture.

"You're in the same room with a man who's turned Muckfoot and it disgusts you. You'll be cured of that eventually—you can be, I'm the proof—but all I want you to do now is put it aside and use your brains. Here are the facts. Your raiding parties got the shorts beat off them. I saw one of the fights—it lasted about twenty minutes. The

Muckfeet could have polished off the Cities any time in the last thirty years. They haven't done it till now, because—"

McArdle was beating time with his fingertips on the polished ebonite. He wasn't really listening, Alvah saw, but there was nothing for it except to go ahead.

". . . they had the problem of deconditioning and reeducating more than twenty million innocent people, or else letting them starve to death. Now they have the knowledge they need. They can—"

"The terms," said McArdle.

"They're going to close down this—this reservation," Alvah said. "They'll satisfy you in any way you like that they can do it by force. If you help, it can be an orderly process in which nobody gets hurt and everybody gets the best possible break. And they'll keep the City intact as a museum. I talked them into that. Or, if they have to, they'll take the place apart slab by slab."

McArdle's mouth was working violently. "Take him out and kill him, for City's sake! And, Morgan!" he called when Alvah and his guards were halfway to the door.

"Yes, Mr. Manager."

"When you're through, paint him green and dump him out the gate he came in."

It was a pity about Wytak, Alvah's brain was telling him frozenly. Wytak was a scoundrel or he could never have got where he was—had been—but he wasn't afraid of a new idea. It might have been possible to deal with Wytak.

"Where we going to do it?" the younger one asked nervously. He had been pale and sweating in the floater all the way across Middle Jersey.

"In the disinfecting chamber," Morgan said, gesturing with his pistol. "Then we paint him and haul him straight out. In there, you."

"Well, let's get it over with," the younger one said. "I'm sick."

"You think *I'm* not sick?" said Morgan in a strained voice. He gave Alvah a final shove into the middle of the room and stood back, adjusting his gun.

Alvah found himself saying calmly, "Not that way, Morgan, unless you want to turn black and shrivel up a second after."

"What's he talking about?" the boy whispered shakily.

"Nothing," said Morgan. The hand with the gun moved indecisively.

"To puncture me," Alvah warned, "you've got to puncture the suit. And I've been eating Muckfoot food for the last month and a half. I'm full of microorganisms—swarming with them. They'll bloop out of me straight at *you*, Morgan."

Both men jerked back as if they had been stung. "I'm getting outa here!" said the boy, grabbing for the door stud.

Morgan blocked him. "Stay here!"

"What're you going to do?" the younger one asked.

He swore briefly. "We'll tell the O. D. Come on."

The door closed and locked solidly behind them. Alvah looked to see if there was a way to double-lock it from his side, but there wasn't. He tried the opposite door to make sure it was locked, which it was. Then he examined the disinfectant nozzles, wondering if they could be used to squirt corrosive in on him. He decided they probably couldn't and, anyhow, he had no way to spike the nozzles. Then there was nothing to do but sit in the middle of the bare room and wait, which he did.

The next thing that happened was that he heard a faint far-off continuous noise through the almost soundproof door. He stood up and went over and put his ear against the door, and decided it was his imagination.

Then there *was* a noise, and he jumped back, his skin

tingling all over, just before the door slid open. The sudden maniacal clangor of a bell swept Morgan into the room with it, wild-eyed, his cap missing, drooling from a corner of his mouth, his gun high in one white-knuckled fist.

"*Glab!*" said Morgan and pulled the trigger.

Alvah's heart went *bonk* hard against his ribs, and the room blurred. Then he realized that there hadn't been any hiss of an ejected pellet. And he was still on his feet. And Morgan, with his mouth stretched open all the way back to the uvula, was standing there a yard away, staring at him and pulling the trigger repeatedly.

Alvah stepped forward half a pace and put a straight left squarely on the point of Morgan's jaw. As the man fell, there were shrieks and running footsteps in the outer room. Somebody in guard uniform plunged past the doorway, shouting incoherently, caromed off a wall, dwindled down a corridor. Then the room was full of leaping men in motley.

The first of them was Artie Brumbacher, almost unrecognizable because he was grinning from ear to ear. He handed Alvah a four-foot knobkerrie and a bulging skin bag and said, "Le's go!"

The streets were full of grounded floaters and stalled surface cars. The bells had fallen silent, and so had the faint omnipresent vibration that was like silence itself until it was gone. Not a motor was turning in the borough of Jersey. Occasional chittering sounds floated on the air, and muffled buzzings and other odd sounds, all against the background chorus of faraway shrieks that rose and fell, rose and fell.

At the corner of Middle Orange and Weehawken, opposite the Superior Court Building, they came upon a squad of Regulars who had thrown away their useless guns and picked up an odd lot of assorted bludgeons—lengths of pipe, tripods, and the like.

"Now you'll see," said Artie.

The Regulars set up a ragged yell and came running

forward. The two Muckfeet on either side of Alvah, Artie and the buck-toothed one called Lafe, dipped heaping dark-brown handfuls out of the bags they carried slung from their shoulders. Alvah followed suit, and recognized the stuff at last—bran meal, soaked in some fragrant syrup until it was mucilaginous and heavy.

Artie swung first, then Lafe, and Alvah last—and the soggy lumps smacked the foremost faces. The squad broke, wiping frenziedly. But you couldn't wipe the stuff off. It clung coldly and grainily to the hair on the backs of your hands and your eyelashes and the nap of your clothing. All you could do was move it around.

One berserker with a smeared face didn't stop, and Lafe dropped him with a knobkerrie between the eyes. One more, a white-faced youth, stood miraculously untouched, still hefting his club. He took a stride forward menacingly.

Grinning, Artie raised another glob of the mash and ate it, smacking his lips. The youth spun around, walked drunkenly to the nearest wall and was rackingly sick.

An hour later, Knickerbocker Circle in Over Manhattan was littered with amoeba-shaped puddles of clear plastic. Overhead, the stuff was hanging in festoons from the reticulated framework of the roof and, for the first time in a century, an unfiltered wind was blowing into New York. Halfway up the sheer façade of the Old Movie House, the roc that had brought Alvah from Jersey was flapping along, a wingtip almost brushing the louvers, while its rider sprinkled pale dust from a sack. Farther down the street, a sickly green growth was already visible on cornices and window frames.

The antique neon sign of the Old Movie House dipped suddenly, its supports softening visibly. It swung, nodded and crashed to the pavement.

Three hours later, a little group of whey-faced men in

official dress was being loaded aboard a freight roc opposite the underpass to the Cauldwell Floatway in Over Bronnix. Alvah thought he saw McArdle among them, but he couldn't be sure.

Twilight—all the streets that radiated from the heart of the City were afloat with long, slowly surging tides of humanity, dim in the weak glow from the lumen globes plastered haphazardly to the flanks of the buildings. At the end of every street, the wall was crumbled down and the moat filled, its fire long gone out. And down the new railed walkways from all three levels came the men, women and children, stumbling out into the alien lumen-lit night and the strange scents and the wide world.

Watching from the hilltop, with his arm around his wife's waist, Alvah saw them being herded into groups and led away, unprotesting—saw them in the wains, rolling off toward the temporary shelters where, likely as not, they would sleep the night through, too numbed to be afraid of the morrow.

In the morning, their teaching would begin.

Babylon, Alvah thought, *Thebes, Angkor, Lagash, Agade, Tyre, Luxor and now New York.*

A City grew out and then in—it was always the way, whether or not it had a wall around it. Growing, it crippled itself and its people—and died. The weeds overleaped its felled stones.

"Like an egg," B. J. said, although he had not spoken. "*Omne ex ovo*—but the eggshell has to break."

"I know," said Alvah, discovering that the empty ache in his belly was not sentiment but hunger. "Speaking of eggs—"

B. J. gave his arm a reassuring squeeze. "Anything you want, dear. Radnip, orangoe, pearots, fleetmeat—*you* pick the menu."

Alvah's mouth began to water.

Probably the most frequent complaint about city life is that it is too crowded, too rigidly controlled, too oppressive. Yet here we have a city where life becomes too soft and debilitating. Who would choose the hardships of a primitive life if it meant depriving one's family of comforts and perhaps life-saving technology?

Plenitude

by Will Worthington

"Why can't we go home now, daddy?" asked Mike, the youngest. And the small tanned face I saw there in the skimpy shade of the olive tree was mostly a matter of eyes —all else, hair, cheeks, thumb-sized mouth, jelly-bean body, and usually flailing arms and legs, were mere accessories to the round, blue, endlessly wondering *eyes*. (*"The Wells of 'Why'"* . . . It would make a poem, I thought, if a poem were needed, and if I wasn't so damned tired. And I also thought, Oh, God! It begins. Five years old. No, not quite. Four.)

"Because daddy has to finish weeding this row of beans," I said. "We'll go back to the house in a little while."

I would go back to the house and then I would follow the path around the rocks to the hot springs, and there I would peel off what was left of my clothes, and I would soak myself in the clear but pungent water that came bubbling—perfect—from a cleft in the rocks to form a pool in the hollow of a pothole—also perfect. And while I steeped in the mineral water I could think about the fish that was soon to be broiling on the fire, and I could think of Sue turning it, poking at it, and sprinkling herbs over it as though it was the first or perhaps the last fish that would ever be broiled and eaten by human creatures. She would perform that office with the same total and unreserved dedication with which, since sunup, she had scraped deer-skin, picked worms from new cabbage leaves, gathered firewood, caulked the walls of the cabin where the old chinking had fallen away or been chewed or knocked away by other hungry or merely curious creatures, and other-wise filled in the numberless gaps in the world—trivial things mostly, which would not be noticed and could not become great things in a man's eyes unless she were to go away or cease to be. I don't think of this because, for all immediate purposes—there are no others—she is the first woman in the world and quite possibly—the last.

"Why don't we live in the Old House in the valley, daddy?"

It is All-Eyes again. Make no mistake about it; there is a kind of connectedness between the seemingly random questions of very small kids. These are the problems posed by an *Ur*-logic which is much closer to the pulse of reality than are any of the pretentious, involuted systems and the mincing nihilations and category juggling of adults. It is we who are confused and half-blinded with the varieties of special knowledge. But how explain? What good is my ex-perience to him?

"There are too many old things in the Old House which don't work," I say, even as I know that I merely open the floodgates of further questions.

"Don't the funny men work, daddy? I want to see the funny men! Daddy, I want . . ."

The boy means the robots. I took him down to see the Old House in the valley once before. He rode on top of my haversack and hung on to my hair with his small fingers. It was all a lark for him. I had gone to fetch some books—gambling that there might be a bagful of worthwhile ones

that had not been completely eaten by bugs and mice; and
if the jaunt turned out depressing for me, it was my fault,
which is to say the fault of memory and the habit of com-
paring what has been with what is—natural, inevitable, un-
avoidable, but oh, God, just the same. . . . The robots
which still stood on their size-thirty metal feet looked like
grinning Mexican mummies. They gave me a bad turn even
though I knew what they were, and should have known
what changes to expect after a long, long absence from that
house, but to the kid they were a delight. Never mind trans-
phenomenality of rusted surfaces and uselessly dangling
wires; never mind the history of a senile generation. They
were the funny men. I wish I could leave it at that, but of
course I can't. I hide my hoe in the twigs of the olive tree
and pick Mike up. This stops the questions for a while.

"Let's go home to mummy," I say; and also, hoping to
hold back the questions about the Old House long enough
to think of some real answers, "Now aren't you glad we
live up here where we can see the ocean and eagles and hot
springs?"

"Yeth," says Mike firmly by way of making a queru-
lous and ineffectual old man feel better about his decision.
What a comfort to me the little one is!

I see smoke coming from the chimney, and when we
round the last turn in the path we see the cabin. Sue waves
from the door. She has worked like a squaw since dawn,
and she smiles and waves. I can remember when women
would exhaust themselves talking over the phone and eating bonbons all day, and then fear to smile when their beat
husbands came home from their respective nothing-
foundries lest they crack the layers of phony "youthful
glow" on their faces. Not like Sue. Here is Sue with
smudges of charcoal on her face and fish scales on her
leather pants. Her scent is of woodsmoke and of sweat.
There is no artificial scent like this—none more endearing
nor more completely "correct." There was a time when

the odor of perspiration would have been more of a social disaster for a woman than the gummata of tertiary pox. Even men were touched by this strange phobia.

Sue sees the question on my face and she knows why my smile is a little perfunctory and strained.

"Chris? . . ." I start to ask finally.

"No. He took his bow and his sleeping bag. Muttered something about an eight-point buck."

We do not *need* the venison. If anything has been made exhaustively and exhaustingly clear to the boy it is that our blessings consist in large part of what we do not need. But this is not the point, and I know it is not the point.

"Do you think he'll ever talk to me again, Sue?"

"Of course he will." She pulls off my sweaty shirt and hands me a towel. "You know how twelve is. Everything in Technicolor and with the most throbbing background music possible. Everything drags or jumps or swings, or everything is Endsville or something else which it actually isn't. If it can't be turned into a drama it doesn't exist. He'll get over it."

I can think of no apt comment. Sue starts to busy herself with the fire, then turns back to me.

"You did the best thing. You did what you had to do, that's all. Go take your bath. I'm getting hungry."

I make my way up the path to the hot springs and I am wearing only the towel and the soles of an ancient pair of sneakers held on with thongs. I am thinking that the hot water will somehow dissolve the layers of sickly thought that obscure all the colors of the world from my mind, just as it will rid me of the day's accretion of grime, but at once I know that I am yielding to a vain and superstitious hope. I can take no real pleasure in the anticipation of my bath.

When I emerge from the underbrush and come in sight of the outcroppings of rock where the springs are, I can see Sato, our nearest neighbor and my oldest friend, making his way along the path from his valley on the other side of the mountain. I wave to him, but he does not wave back. I tell myself that he is concentrating on his feet and simply does not see me, but myself answers back in much harsher terms. Sato knows what happened when I took my older son to the City, and he knows why my son has not spoken more than a dozen coherent words since returning. He knows what I have done, and while it is not in the man's nature to rebuke another, or set himself above another, or mouth moral platitudes, there are limits.

Sato is some kind of a Buddhist. Only vaguely and imperfectly do I understand what this implies; not being unnecessarily explicit about itself is certainly a part of that doctrine. But there is also the injunction against killing. And I am—notwithstanding every meretricious attempt of my own mind to convert that fact into something more comfortable—a killer. And so . . . I may now contemplate what it will mean not merely to have lost my older son, but also the priceless, undemanding and yet immeasurably rewarding friendship of the family in the next valley.

"It was not intentional," I tell myself as I lower my griminess and weariness into the hot water. "It was necessary. How else explain why we chose? . . ." But it isn't worth a damn. I might as well mumble Tantric formulae. The water feels lukewarm—*used*.

I go on flaying myself in this manner. I return to the house and sit down to supper. The food I had looked forward to so eagerly tastes like raw fungus or my old sneakers. Nothing Sue says helps, and I even find myself wishing she would go to hell with her vitamin-enriched cheerfulness.

On our slope of the mountain the darkness comes as it must come to a lizard that is suddenly immured in a cigar box. Still no sign of Chris and so, of course, the pumas are more vocal than they have been all year. I itemize and savor every disaster that roars, rumbles, creeps, slithers,

stings, crushes, or bites: everything from rattlers to ava-
lanches, and I am sure that one or all of these dire things
will befall Chris before the night is over. I go outside every
time I hear a sound—which is often—and I squint at the
top of the ridge and into the valley below. No Chris.

Sue, from her bunk, says, "If you don't stop torturing
yourself, you'll be in no condition to *do* anything if it *does*
become necessary." She is right, of course, which makes me
mad as hell on top of everything else. I lie on my bunk and
for the ten-millionth time reconstruct the whole experience.

We had been hacking at elder bushes, Chris and I. It had
been a wet winter and clearing even enough land for garden truck out of the encroaching vegetation began to seem
like trying to hold back the sea with trowels. This problem
and the gloomy knowledge that we had about one hatful of
beans left in the cabin had conspired to produce a mood in
which nothing but hemlock could grow. And I'd about had
it with the questions. Chris had started the "why" routine
at about the same age as little Mike, but the questions, instead of leveling off as the boy began to exercise his own
powers of observation and deduction, merely became more
involved and challenging.

The worst thing about this was that I could not abdi-
cate: other parents in other times could fluff off the questions of their kids with such hopeless and worthless
judgments as "Well, that's how things *are*," thereby imply-
ing that both the questioner and the questioned are standing
passively at the dead end of a chain of historical cause, or
are existentially trapped in the eye of a storm of supernal
origin, or are at the nexus of a flock of processes arising out
of the choices of too many other agencies to pinpoint and
blame definitively . . . *our* life, on the other hand, was
clearly and in every significant particular our own baby. It

did not merely proceed out of one particular historical choice, complete with foreseeable contingencies, but was an entire fabric of choices—*ours*. Here was total responsibility, complete with crowding elder bushes, cold rain, chiggers, rattlers, bone-weariness, and mud. I had elected to live it—even to impose it upon my progeny—and I was prepared for its hardships, but what galled me was having to justify it.

"The people in the City don't have to do *this*, do they?" ("This" is grubbing out elder bushes, and he is right. The people in the City do not have to do *this*. They do not have to hunt, fish, gather, or raise their own food. They do not have to build their own cabins, carry their own water from springs, or fashion their own clothes from the skins of beautiful, murdered—by me—animals. They do not have to perspire. One of these days I will have to explain that they do not even have to sleep with their own wives. *That* of itself should be the answer of answers, but twelve is not yet ready; twelve cares about things with wheels, things which spin, roar, roll, fly, explode, exude noise and stench. Would that twelve were fourteen!)

In the meantime it is *dig—hack—heave; dig—hack—heave!* "Come on, Chris! It isn't sundown yet."

"Why couldn't we bring an old tractor up here in pieces and put it together and fix it up and find oil and . . ." (I try to explain for the fifty-millionth time that you do not simply "fix up" something which is the outgrowth of an enormous organization of interdependent organizations, the fruit of a dead tree, as it were. The wheel will not be turned back. The kid distrusts abstractions and generalities, and I don't blame him, but God I'm tired!) "Let's just clear off this corner by the olive tree, Chris, and then we'll knock off for the day."

"Are we *better* than the City-People?"

(This one hit a nerve. "Better" is a judgment made by people after the fact of their own decisions. Or there isn't any "better." As for the Recalcitrants, of which vague class of living creatures we are members, they were and are certainly both more and less *something* than the others were—the City-People—the ones who elected to go along with the organization. Of all the original Recalcitrant families, I would guess that not ten percent are now alive. I would if I had any use for statistics. If these people had something in common, you would have to go light-years away to find a name for it. I think it was a common lack of something—a disease perhaps. Future generations will take credit for it and refer to their origins as fine old stock. I think most of them were crazy. I am glad they were, but most of them were just weird. Southern California. I have told Chris about the Peters family. They were going to make it on nothing but papaya juice and stewed grass augmented by East Indian breathing exercises. Poor squittered-out souls! Their corpses were like balsa wood. Better? What is better? Grandfather was going to live on stellar emanations and devote his energies to whittling statues out of fallen redwoods. Thank nature his stomach had other ideas! And God I'm tired and fed up!)

"Dammit, boy! Tomorrow I'll *take* you to the City and let you answer your own questions!"

And I did. Sue protested and old Sato just gave me that look which said "I'm not saying anything," but I *did*.

The journey to the City is necessarily one that goes from bad to worse. As a deer and a man in the wilderness look for downward paths and lush places if they would find a river, the signs which lead to the centers of human civilization are equally recognizable.

You look for ugliness and senselessness. It is that simple. Look for places which have been overlaid with mortar so that nothing can grow or change at its will. Look for things which have been fashioned at great expense of time and energy, and then discarded. Look for tin and peeling paint, for rusted metal, broken neon tubing, drifts and drifts of discarded containers—cans, bottles, papers. Look for flies and let your nose lead you where it would rather not go.

What is the difference between the burrow of a fox and a huge sheet-metal hand that bears the legend, in peeling, garish paint: THIS WAY TO PERPETUAL PARMENIDEAN PALACES . . . ? I do not know why one is better than the other, or *if* it is. I know that present purposes—purposes of intellect—lead one way, and intuition leads the other. So we resist intuition, and the path of greatest resistance leads us from one vast, crumbling, frequently stinking artifact or monument to another.

Chris is alternately nauseated and thrilled. He wants to stay in the palatial abandoned houses in the outskirts, but I say "no." For one thing the rats look like Doberman pinschers, and for another . . . well, never mind what it is that repels me.

Much of the City looks grand until we come close enough to see where cement and plaster, paint and plastic have sloughed away to reveal ruptured tubes and wires, which gleam where their insulation has rotted away, and which are connected to nothing with any life in it. We follow a monorail track, which is a silver thread from a distance, but which has a continuous ridge of rust and bird droppings along its upper surface as far as the eye can see. We see more of the signs that point to the PERPETUAL PARMENIDEAN PALACES, and we follow them, giving our tormented intuition a rest even while for our eyes and our spirits there is no relief.

When we first encounter life we are not sure that it *is* life.

"They look like huge grapes!" exclaims Chris when we find them, clustered about a central tower in a huge sunken place like a stadium. The P. P. Palaces are indeed like huge grapes—reddish, semitransparent, about fifteen feet in diameter, or perhaps twenty. I am not used to meas-

uring spaces in such terms anymore. The globes are connected to the central tower, or stem, by means of thick
cables . . . their umbilicals. A high, wire-mesh fence sur-
rounds the area, but here and there the rust has done its
work in spite of zinc coating on the wire. With the corn
knife I have brought to defend us from the rats and God
knows what, I open a place in the fence. We are trespass-
ing, and we know this, but we have come this far.

"Where are the people?" asks Chris, and I see that he
looks pale. He has asked the question reluctantly, as though
preferring no answer. I give none. We come close to one of
the spheres, feeling that we are doing the wrong thing and
doing it anyway. I see our objective, and I point. It is a
family of them, dimly visible like floating plants in an un-
cleaned aquarium. It is their frightened eyes we first see.

I do not know very much about the spheres except
from hearsay and dim memory. The contents, including the
occupants, are seen only dimly, I know, because the outer
skins of the thing are filled with a self-replenishing liquid
nutrient that requires the action of the sun and is augmented by the waste-products of the occupants. We look
closer, moving so that the sun is directly behind the sphere,
revealing its contents in sharper outline.

"Those are not real people," says Chris. Now he looks
a little sick. "What are all those tubes and wires for if
they're real people? Are they robots or dolls or what?"

I do not know the purpose of all the tubes and wires
myself. I do know that some are connected with veins in
their arms and legs, others are nutrient enemata and for
collection of body wastes, still others are only mechanical
tentacles that support and endlessly fondle and caress. I
know that the wires leading to the metal caps on their
heads are part of an invention more voracious and terrible
than the ancient television—direct stimulation of certain
areas of the brain, a constant running up and down the di-

apason of pleasurable sensation, controlled by a sort of electronic kaleidoscope.

My imagination stops about here. It would be the ultimate artificiality, with nothing of reality about it save endless variation. Of senselessness I will not think. I do not know if they see constantly shifting masses or motes of color, or smell exotic perfumes, or hear unending and constantly swelling music. I think not. I doubt that they even experience anything so immediate and yet so amorphous as the surge and recession of orgasm or the gratification of thirst being quenched. It would be stimulation without real stimulus; ultimate removal from reality. I decide not to speak of this to Chris. He has had enough. He has seen the wires and the tubes.

I have never sprung such abstractions as "dignity" upon the boy. What good are such absolutes on a mountainside? If there is dignity in grubbing out weeds and planting beans, those pursuits must be more dignified *than* something, because, like all words, it is a meaningless wisp of lint once removed from its relativistic fabric. The word does not exist until he invents it himself. The hoe and the rocky soil or the nutrient enema and the electronic ecstasy; he must judge for himself. That is why I have brought him here.

"Let's get away from here," he says. "Let's go home!"

"Good," I say, but even as I say it I can see that the largest of the pallid creatures inside the "grape" is doing something—I cannot tell what—and to my surprise it seems capable of enough awareness of us to become alarmed. What frightening creatures we must be—dirty, leather clothes with patches of dried animal blood on them, my beard, and the small-boy grime of Chris! Removed as I am from these helpless aquarium creatures, I cannot blame them. But my compassion was a short-lived thing. Chris screamed.

I turned in time to see what can only be described as a huge metal scorpion rushing at Chris with its tail lashing, its fore-claws snapping like pruning shears and red lights flashing angrily where its eyes should have been. A guard robot, of course. Why I had not foreseen such a thing I will never know. I supposed at the time that the creature inside the sphere had alerted it.

The tin scorpion may have been a match for the reactions and the muscles of less primitive, more "civilized" men than ourselves, or the creators of the Perpetual Parmenidean Palaces had simply not foreseen barbarians with heavy corn knives. I knocked Chris out of the way and dispatched the tin bug, snipping off its tail-stinger with a lucky slash of the corn knife and jumping up and down on its thorax until all its appendages were still.

When the reaction set in, I had to attack something else. I offer no other justification for what I did. We were the intruders—the invading barbarians. All the creatures in the spheres wanted was their security. The man in the sphere set the scorpion on us, but he was protecting his family. I can see it that way now. I wish I couldn't. I wish I was one of those people who can always contrive to have been right.

I saw the frightened eyes of the things inside the sphere, and I reacted to it as a predatory animal reacts to the scent of urea in the sweat of a lesser animal. And they had menaced my son with a hideous machine in order to be absolutely *secure!* If I reasoned at all, it was along this line.

The corn knife was not very sharp, but the skin of the sphere parted with disgusting ease. I heard Chris scream, "No! Dad! No! . . ." but I kept hacking. We were nearly engulfed in the pinkish, albuminous nutritive which gushed from the ruptured sac. I can still smell it.

The creatures inside were more terrible to see in the open air than they had been behind their protective layers of plastic material. They were dead white and they looked to be soft, although they must have had normal human skeletons. Their struggles were blind, pointless, and feeble, like those of some kind of larvae found under dead wood, and the largest made a barely audible mewing sound as it groped in search of what, I cannot imagine.

I heard Chris retching violently, but could not tear my attention away from the spectacle. The sphere now looked like some huge coelenterate, which had been halved for study in the laboratory, and the hoselike tentacles still moved like groping cilia.

The agony of the creatures in the "grape" (I cannot think of them as people) when they were first exposed to unfiltered, unprocessed air and sunlight, when the wires and tubes were torn from them, and, especially, when the metal caps on their heads fell off in their panicky struggles and the whole universe of chilly external reality rushed in upon them at once, is beyond my imagining; and perhaps this is merciful. This and the fact that they lay in the stillness of death after only a very few minutes in the open air.

Memory is merciful too in its imperfection. All I remember of our homeward journey is the silence of it.

"Wake up! We have company, old man!"

It is Sue shaking me. Somehow I did sleep—in spite of Chris and in spite of the persistent memory. It must be mid-morning. I swing my feet down and scrub at my gritty eyes. Voices outside. Cheerful. How cheerful?

It is Sato and he has his old horse hitched to a crude travois of willow poles. It is Sato and his wife and three kids and my son Chris. There trussed up on the travois is the biggest buck I have seen in ten years, its neck transfixed with an arrow. A perfect shot and one that could not have been scored without the most careful and skillful stalking.

I remember teaching him that only a bad hunter . . . a heedless and cruel one . . . would risk a distant shot with a bow.

Chris is grinning and looking sheepish. Sato's daughter is there, which accounts for the look of benign idiocy. I was wondering when he would notice. Then he sees me standing in the doorway of the cabin and his face takes on about ten years of gravity and thought, but this is not for the benefit of the teen-age female. Little Mike is clawing at Chris and asking *why* he went away like that and *why* he went hunting without daddy, and several other *whys* which Chris ignores. His answer is for his old man.

"I'm sorry, dad. I wasn't mad at you . . . just sort of crazy. Had to do . . . this. . . ." He points at the deer. "Anyhow, I'm back."

"And I'm glad," I managed.

"Dad, those elder bushes . . ."

"To hell with them," say I. "Wednesday is soon enough."

Sato moves in grinning, and just in time to relieve the awkwardness. "Dressed out this buck and carried it down the mountain by himself." I think of mountain lions. "He was about pooped when I found him in a pasture."

Sue holds open the cabin door and the Satos file in. Himself first, carrying a jug of wine, then Mrs. Sato, grinning greetings. She has never mastered English. It has not been necessary.

I drag up what pass for chairs. Made them myself. We began talking about weeds and beans, and weather, bugs and the condition of fruit trees. It is Sato who has steered the conversation into these familiar ways, bless his knowing heart. He uncorks the wine. Sue and Mrs. Sato, meanwhile, are carrying on one of their lively conversations. Someday I will listen to them, but I doubt that I will ever learn how they communicate . . . or what. Women.

I can hear Chris outside talking to Yuki, Sato's

daughter. He is not boasting about the deer; he is telling her about the fight with the tin scorpion and the grape-people.

"Are they blind . . . the grape-people?" the girl asks.

"Heck no," says Chris. "At least one of them wasn't. One of them sicced the robot bug on us. They were going to kill us. And so, dad did what he had to do. . . ."

I don't hear the details over the interjections of Yuki and little Mike, but I can imagine they are as pungent as the teen-age powers of physiological description allow. I hear Yuki exclaim, "Oh how utterly *germy!*" and another language problem occurs to me. How can kids who have never hung around a drugstore still manage to evolve languages of their own . . . characteristically adolescent dialects? It is one more mystery that I shall never solve. I hear little Mike asking for reasons and causes with his favorite word. "*Why*, Chris?"

"I'll explain it when you get older," says Chris, and oddly it doesn't sound ridiculous.

Sato pours a giant-size dollop of wine in each tumbler.

"What's the occasion?" I ask.

Sato studies the wine critically, holding the glass so the light from the door shines through.

"It's Tuesday," he says.

About the Editor

Georgess McHargue is the author of ten books for young people, among them: *The Beasts of Never*, a compendium of mythological animals; *The Best of Both Worlds*, an anthology of short stories for all ages; *The Impossible People*, A History Natural and Unnatural of Beings Terrible and Wonderful; and *The Mermaid and the Whale*, a retelling of an old sailor's yarn.

As for this present volume, Ms. McHargue says she feels eminently qualified to compile a book on cities, having survived cheerfully for thirty years in New York City. "It may not be a record, but it's at least the equivalent of an advanced degree."

Ms. McHargue now lives in Massachusetts, where she devotes much of her time to research in folklore, mythology, and archaeology.

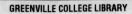